LOST HILL

Lost Hill

Dorothy Evelyn Smith

PEOPLES BOOK CLUB

Chicago

This is a special edition published exclusively for the members of THE PEOPLES BOOK CLUB, P. O. Box 6570A, Chicago 80, Illinois, and 228 Bloor Street West, Toronto 5, Ontario, Canada. It was originally published by E. P. Dutton & Company, Inc.

LIBRARY OF CONGRESS CATALOG CARD NUMBER: 52-7786

FOR

MY HUSBAND

LOST HILL

CHAPTER ONE

THE land lay parched and silent under the noonday sun; the only sound the creaking of the cart's wheels; the driver's scarlet scarf the only splash of colour.

There had been no rain for many weeks. Moor and rough stony track and drooping tree were all coated with a fine fawnish dust. The dust lay on the shafts and the wheel spokes of the cart; on the man's clothes and his black, upspringing curls; on the rough brown coat of the pony. It lay on the child curled in the bottom of the cart staring listlessly at nothing.

He was a young child, pinched, malodorous and ragged. He lay on a heap of clothing, an old blanket thrown over him to keep off the flies. One hand rested on the blanket, the thin, grimy fingers half curled, as if undecided whether to grasp at life or not.

From time to time the man glanced over his shoulder at the child, then turned away, pursing up his lips in a soundless whistling. He flicked his whip across the pony's back, but he neither received nor appeared to expect any response. The pony plodded on patiently, silently, hoofs muffled in dust. Its rough sides heaved and constantly it shifted the bit in its parched mouth.

There was no sound but the creaking of the wheels. No bird called. No water trickled amongst stones. No wind stirred the dry, twisted heather.

The sky arched brassily above the barren silence; cloudless, pitiless.

The man glanced behind him.

"Djink," said the child softly.

The man nodded.

"Soon now."

He stared ahead over the faded gorse and heather. Away to the left—five miles; maybe more—a handful of grey cottages huddled beneath the spire of a church. On his right sheep grazed sluggishly: some farm was probably not far off. But he kept straight on, flicking the pony's back and whistling his soundless whistle.

He must be nearly there now. It would be a fool's trick to give up within a stone's throw of the end. There was nothing much wrong with the child; nothing that rest and shade and a handful of herbs could not cure, he thought. If only he could get the herbs. . . .

He thought of misty green valleys running between Welsh mountains; of cool Irish bogs and Devon hedgerows filled with healing. He had known them all; would know them again. This wind-bitten, sun-scorched, forsaken Yorkshire moorland held few charms for him.

He never stayed long in any place. His life was fluid as a mountain stream, bound by no rules of man, no ties of blood or heritage. He lived from day to day, from hand to mouth; cunning and arrogant, subservient with tongue in cheek; his body's boldness balanced by a sly knowledge of men and women and animals, and an innate respect for the laws of nature.

The pony's head glistened with flies. He flicked at them. They rose in a buzzing cloud and settled back again. The moor trembled in the heat.

The child set up a fretful wailing. The man halted the pony and jumped down.

"Shut up," he said, not unkindly.

The small head burned beneath his hand. He shifted the bed further back under the tattered tarpaulin cover. From the back of the cart he unearthed a beer bottle, squinted at it against the light. There was just a drain left. Dipping his fingers into the beer dregs he moistened the child's lips and forehead. Then he poured the remainder into a cupped palm and held it to the pony's mouth. The pony muzzled it greedily.

Flies settled instantly round its mouth, swollen and glistening.

Licking dry lips the man climbed back on to the cart and jerked the reins.

"Not long now it will be," he said aloud.

Rounding a hillock, he came suddenly upon a girl sitting in the heather, a basket half filled with bilberries beside her. She glanced up, startled, at the sound of wheels. Her hands and mouth were stained with purple juice. Strands of ginger hair clung to fat cheeks damp and pasty with heat. She was heavy-limbed, scowling and sluttish, but she had a full red mouth, and the unbuttoned neck of her print frock showed a fine white skin lightly powdered with freckles.

She smiled, showing strong, uneven teeth.

"Hot enough for you?"

Because she was a woman and young the man smiled back. "Am I right for Shaws?"

She nodded, preening her thick body up at him.

"Straight on. Foller yer nose."

"How far?"

"A goodish way. Three miles, happen. What's the hurry?"

"Business," he said laconically.

She undid another button of her frock.

"It'll have to wait then. There'll be nobody there, only the hands, and Miss Ellen at the lodge."

He stared down at the girl, chagrined at her news. Shaw not there? . . . Somehow he had never thought of that. He felt a momentary impulse to turn the pony's head and go back the way he had come.

But that, of course, was silly. There was the child to think of. Shaw didn't matter all that much. He would keep. But the child needed attention, the pony needed rest and water. He himself was ravenously hungry.

"Who's in charge there?"

"Mester Sanderson. He's run t'farm all t'while the Major's been in the Army. But he'll be at the market today, like all of 'em." Her eyes rested on him in frank desire. The black, wiry curls, the brown skin, the eyes dark and unfathomable as the Tarn, the grace of his thin, supple body. . . . The afternoon might be passed in a pleasanter fashion than picking filthy bilberries. "He's a tough nut, is Sanderson," she added. "You'll not get much outen *him*."

The implied invitation left him cold. This was no time for women.

"Is there a house nearer? Somewhere I could put the tent for a night or two, and get food an' that? Pay for it I can."

"There's Lost Hill, where I work," she said slowly. "I dunno if She'd let you stop there. Maybe She would if you was willin' to lend a hand with the apple picking, and a bit of diggin', like."

"I could do that."

"Well. . . . I dunno if She will, mind; She's not easy. Still, you could try. It's nobbut about a half-mile. First house you come to. Off on the right you'll see a white gate an' a sort of drive. You keep left till you skirt the orchard. There's a hilly field with some goats tethered in it. Mek a good place to stop the night. . . . On'y don't say nowt about seeing me. Her an' me had a bit of a set-to this mornin', and I'm not exactly Missus's little pet just now." She grinned derisively. Then her face altered. "What's yon noise? What you got in t' cart—a kid?"

He nodded. Lumbering up, the girl stepped on the wheel and hauled herself to the cart's edge.

"Lawks! Do with a wash, wouldn't he? What's up with 'im?"

"Sick he is with the great heat."

"Well, he don't look too good to me! Hope it's nothin' catching. . . ." She snapped her fingers at the child, clucking good-naturedly. "Hullo, there! Hullo, luv! What they doin' traipsing you all over t'place in this heat, then? . . . Poor little sod, he don't feel like grinning, I reckon. Tek my tip, brother, you'll put yer tent up first, an' ask afterwards." She jumped heavily to the ground. "Well, be seein' yer, I shouldn't wonder. I got to fill this flamin' basket before I go back, or I'd ask you for a

lift. I'll try an' slip you summat out at supper. Apple pie an'
cheese, or summat o' that. So long."

He lifted his whip in thanks.

"My name's Iris," she said. "What's yours?"

"Gethin."

"Go on with you!"

He flashed a sudden white smile at her and turned away.
The cart's wheels began to creak again. The pony tossed his
head and the flies rose, buzzing, and settled back, obscene
and insatiable.

The girl watched the cart out of sight and returned, sighing, to her bilberry picking. The sun beat down on her head
and sweat trickled between her heavy breasts, but she worked
diligently; for now there was some point in hurrying home.
He was a handsome chap, if he *was* only a gyppo. They could
have a bit of fun if she played her cards right. . . .

The cart creaked onwards and the man whistled his soundless whistle. He gave no thought to the girl. He flicked her
from his mind as he flicked the flies from the pony's head.

The path rose suddenly and he saw the house away on the
right: a solid, well-built house of weathered grey stone standing back from a cobbled yard with stables and long, timbered
barns. A stark, unfriendly house—he sensed that instantly—
even with the sun beating down on it so that the walls trembled
and the cobbles danced blindingly. A house that stared inimically; that said: *"Go away. Pass on and let me alone."* Trees
branched behind it, standing like guards, their shadow-hands
laid across the roof in warning. He was sensitive to atmosphere, as animals and some children are.

But he heard the distant clatter of pails that meant water,
the bleating of goats that meant milk; the smell of woodsmoke
came faintly on the hot, still air, speaking to his empty stomach of roasting meat, succulent pastry, mugs of hot, sweet
tea. . . .

He sniffed the air like a starving dog.

"Get up," he said to the pony. "Get along there."

****

CHAPTER TWO

JENNY had awakened late.

The house was brisk and clamorous with morning. Brooms banged and pots clattered; the smell of frying bacon floated up the stairs; sun poured through open windows and starched white curtains of spotted muslin stirred crisply in the breeze.

Iris was singing out in the yard—where she certainly should not be this time of the day, Jenny thought austerely—and Bailey could clearly be heard grooming old Posy on the cobbles. "Coom up. Coom up, will t'a! . . . Ovver then . . ." *hiss, hiss, hiss. . . .* "Nah then! . . ." *hiss, hiss, hiss. . . .*

There was the stamping of Posy's ancient hoofs, the flurry of greedy fowls, the bang of a door and a girl's loud, meaningless laugh.

Wheels on the cobbles: Posy was being backed into the trap. Soon Bailey would be gone to the market over at Huffley, leaving his wife and Iris to drink a last cup of tea before setting her breakfast tray. Iris would come rattling and banging up the stairs. Her great moon-face would come round the door and her little eyes go darting about the room. The red, sullen mouth hanging open. The untidy swathes of ginger hair. The heavy breasts straining the print blouse almost to bursting point. The twisted cotton stockings. . . .

I don't think I can stand Iris much longer, Jenny thought, wrinkling her nose in distaste. I'll go over to Huffley some time and see the Registry Office.

The thought flickered in her mind without much conviction.

She might go to Huffley or she might not. It was only seven miles, and a grand drive over the moor. Indeed, she had walked it, there and back, many a time, and been thankful to do it. In all the seven years she had been married to George there had been no escape, no real happiness save in those walks, most blessedly alone.

In all weathers she had walked. With rain slashing in her face, soaking through her clothes, trickling down between her shoulder blades and squelching in her heavy shoes. With sun scorching her arms, her neck, beating relentlessly down on her like molten hammers. With head down to the northeasters that swept off the sea and leapt roaring across the moor in winter. In the green, flowered tenderness of April mornings; and in the splendour of September sunsets, when one edge of the moor was flame and the other a pale, translucent green on which a paler moon was lightly etched, and all between was such unearthly loveliness as stilled the breath in your body. . . .

'I wish George wanted to come, too,' she had thought at first. And then, as the years slid by: 'I wish I could get away oftener.' And finally: 'I wish George were dead.'

And now George was dead. . . .

Abruptly Jenny sat up in bed, smoothing the long, dark hair back from her face.

She was too thin, much too thin. Her shoulder blades ridged the worn flannelette of her nightgown. The line of her jaw was too sharp and shadows hollowed the base of her throat. Her eyes were dark grey and enormous. Her long, beautifully made hands looked worn and fleshless. She was only twenty-seven, but in this searching light of early morning she looked older.

'I didn't really wish it,' she thought half fearfully. And then, because above all things she was ruthlessly honest: 'Yes I did. I did want him to die . . . because that was the only way we'd ever have any peace, either one of us. . . .'

Now came the clump of feet upon the stairs, the rattle of

crockery, the thump of Iris' foot against the door. Jenny lay down, pulling the bedclothes up to her neck.

She was not used to having the servants in her bedroom. She hated Iris' seeing her in bed. It made her feel defenceless, even faintly improper. She did not want to be in bed at all. But Doctor Waller had insisted, and this strange feeling of lassitude that had fallen upon her since George's death had rendered her incapable of defiance.

"Thank you, Iris. Just put the tray on the table and I can manage."

Breathing heavily, Iris obeyed, thumping the tray down so that the teapot spurted and stained the heavy linen cloth, beautifully embroidered and edged with drawn-thread work, as was all the linen in the house. George's mother had been a famous needlewoman.

"Oh, Iris, how clumsy!"

Iris's heavy red underlip shot out.

"I'm not used to folks layin' abed for their meals."

"You don't try."

'I'd have summat better than flannelette if I was her,' Iris thought, eyeing the collar of Jenny's nightdress with contempt. 'Still, what's the odds when you look like her. Summat the cat brought home, that's what she looks like.' "Do you more good if you was to get up an' do a hand's stir, if you ask me," she said.

"I haven't asked you."

"Mrs. Bailey was only sayin' this mornin' that Owd Missus 'ud turn in her grave if she could see the way things was goin'. 'Nobody laid in their beds,' she says, 'not when Owd Missus was alive. You mark my words,' she says, 'when folks start layin' abed, that's the beginnin' of the end. Work it off,' she says, 'that's best road when you're feelin' out o' sorts.' I've heard Ma say t'same many a time."

Jenny reached out and poured a cup of tea.

"I'm not interested in what you and Mrs. Bailey gossip about in the kitchen, Iris. Has Bailey gone yet?"

"No."

"Tell him to call at the doctor's and pick up the medicine. And don't forget to give him the empty bottles to take back."

"Okeydoke. Anything else you want?" Iris was incapable of uttering without sounding insolent.

"Yes. Tell Mrs. Bailey I shall want a hot bath presently. And don't say Okeydoke. I'm always telling you."

The kitchen was square and dark and very clean. Geraniums in pots crowded the window sills. An old-fashioned range took up most of one wall, shining like black satin. Two cats, a black and a tabby, were washing themselves on the hearthrug and a canary leapt, chirping shrilly, in a hanging cage. It was very hot. The windows were never opened though the door was seldom shut.

Mrs. Bailey was kneading dough in a huge red earthenware pancheon. Her skinny, wrinkled arms worked violently; and as she swung the creaking, floury mass over from left to middle, over from right to middle, her lips worked over her nearly toothless gums and the tip of her long nose twitched.

"What She want a bath for?" she demanded. "She had one nobbut last Sat'dy."

"Search me!" said Iris.

"She goin' to get up to her dinner?"

"She never said."

Mrs. Bailey made a clicking noise with her tongue and bent over the dough again. "Get yon pots washed up," she said briefly. "Stand an' gawp an' gossip all day you would, given half a chance. Nine o'clock, an' not a thing done yet! Owd Missus 'ud turn in her grave. . . . An' give over grinnin'," she added fiercely.

"That's what I told her," Iris said, still grinning. " 'Do you good,' I says, 'to get up an' do a hand's stir.' I told her straight."

"Then you'd no business," Mrs. Bailey said sharply. "It's none your place to tell anybody what to do an' what not to do in this house. You're here to do as you're telled: And

I'm telling you to get yon pots sided, an' quick about it."

Iris sauntered into the scullery. Water splashed and gurgled in the sink.

"You'd think she'd get hersen summat decent to wear," she shouted above the noise of running water. "Proper sight she looks in them owd-fashioned flannelettes. She hasn't got a dress anybody'd be seen dead in. Them owd slacks, day in, day out, or yon tweed costume 'at come out of the Ark. . . . It's not as if she was old. My word, I'd have some clothes if I was in her shoes—I would that!"

"Mucky trash they'd be, an' all."

The dough creaked and smacked in the earthenware bowl as the brown, stick-like arms worked powerfully. The old woman thought poorly of Mrs. George, as she had of George himself when he was alive. She did not approve of the living. The dead were different. Virtue emanated from them with their latest breath; hung mistily in the memory for evermore. Even Owd Missus, with whom she had waged bitter warfare from the moment she entered her service, forty years back, had now become a saint in her mind.

"If she'd only got hersen some decent blacks," Iris' voice continued above the clatter of crockery. "I felt downright queer at t' funeril, an' her following the poor Mester in her tweeds, bare head an' all! I dunno what folks must have thought. And nobody coming back to the house for a feed, nor nothing. . . . I never heard tell of such a thing in all my born days! An' then for her to flop into bed an' stop there all this while—nay, it beats all. Though I will say she looks downright queer. Let hersen go, that's what she's done, if you ask me. I told her straight. 'Do you more good to get up an' do a hand's stir,' I says. And I thought to meself: 'If you don't, my girl, we're goin' to have another funeril in this house.' But of course I never said nothing of that." There was the sharp tinkle of breaking china and a yelp from Iris. "That's the handle of the blue cup," she called. "Must 'ave bin cracked, because I never give it a knock. Cut me finger it has, deep." She appeared in the kitchen and began rummaging in a drawer for linen to bind the wound.

The old woman pursed her lips, covered the bowl with a clean cloth and set the dough down in the hearth.

"Happen you'll stop yer clatter now, an' get on with yer work," she remarked grimly. "I want the bilberries picked this afternoon. They'll be just right for jamming."

"I'm not picking no bilberries in this heat," Iris stated. It was her usual fighting approach to any command. She made it automatically, without any real expectation of victory.

Aware of this, Mrs. Bailey made no comment, but stumped out of the kitchen and across the yard to the barn. The two cats, with the curiosity common to their kind, and the ability to dissemble it, languidly accompanied her.

She stood in the doorway of the barn gazing dispassionately at her husband who was leaning against a decayed cart, slowly stuffing tobacco into a filthy pipe. He was a lean, stooping man with an unregenerate eye and a fondness for practical jokes of the cruder sort. He was some years younger than his wife, a fact which had greatly influenced her choice of him as husband. For though she was an indefatigable worker, there would come a time, she told herself, when her kidneys finally caught up with her and she could work no more.

With a husband as old as, or even older than herself, this would inevitably have involved the disbursing of the secret hoard of money which she had acquired by fair means and foul during the years of her servitude; a circumstance which she was prepared to combat with every force at her command.

But Bailey, when the time came for her to pack up, would still be hale and hearty, with ten good years' work in him yet. And work he should or she would know the reason why. She relished with a sour pleasure the thought of sitting in a wheel chair in a cottage of her own (she never visualised herself as bedridden) watching Bailey toil and slave; cooking her meals and setting them before her on a cloth he had washed himself; tending her favourite flowers in a sheltered patch of garden;

sweeping and beating and dusting as she had swept and beaten and dusted, washed and baked and toiled for others all her life. And the money, her beautiful money, quite intact and known to nobody but herself, still resting safely at the bottom of the ornamental biscuit tin that always stood beside her bed. She was partial to a biscuit if she woke up in the night.

Whenever Mrs. Bailey thought of the biscuit tin she allowed herself the peculiar sound and contortion that passed with her for mirth.

Bailey did not like biscuits. That was the cream of it. That was the joke that convulsed her when she reached for the tin in the night, pulling the clothes away from his shoulders. "Allus thinkin' of yer belly!" he would grumble, twitching at the blankets. And she would grin to herself, munching her toothless jaws and thinking of what lay below the Oval Maries and the Ginger nuts that smelled and tasted so sweet in the stuffy darkness of their attic room.

Aye, she'd not starve when that time came. There was the brass Owd Missus had left her, and the bit from Mester George, too. But that was all tied up in these War Savings and gave her no personal pleasure. It was nice to know she'd got it; but there was nowt like brass you could handle and count and see the colour of now and again. . . . What lay in the biscuit tin was her own savings over forty years' service, together with what she had bullied out of Jos. It meant more to her than a bank full of gold.

She faced her husband now, one glazed brown hand smoothing the other on the curve of her stomach.

"You goin' to market today or tomorrer?"

He did not answer this purely rhetorical question, but continued to ram tobacco down his pipe with a thumb of the same colour. One of the cats leapt up beside him with a cry, rubbing against his arm. He elbowed it away and it leapt lightly down again and began to wash the place he had touched.

"Wheer's them bottles She wants tekken back?" he asked.

"In t'scullery. You're to bring the new lot, think on. And I want a half of biscuits. Digestive if they've got 'em, but bring what they've got."

"Allus thinkin' of yer belly."

"I works for it, anyroad." She turned away, hesitated, and then turned back, facing him grimly, her glazed hands still smoothing each other, her lips sucked in. Her small blue eyes were hard as bits of rock. "Keep off that Iris," she said. "I've told you afore and now I'm warnin' you. Any more hanky-panky an' I'll see as Missus George gets to know of it."

He grinned, showing buck teeth, discoloured and strong. "What good'll that do?"

"She's Missus now."

He made a scornful noise with his lips.

"She'll send the girl packin'."

"And who else will she get, god-forsaken place like Lost Hill? Girls goes into factories now; eight-hour day, five-day week, an' summat doin' every night. They know when they're well off."

"Then *you'll* have to shift yer stumps a bit more if Iris goes. You know the remedy. Keep off her—an' I'm not tellin' you again, that's all."

She ran a possessive eye over him; noting that he wore the clean shirt she had laid out for him, had blacked his boots, put on a tie and run a wet comb through his unruly thicket of hair. He was a man who got dirty very easily—already there was a brown stain on the collar of his shirt—but he didn't look too bad. She liked him to set off to market decently dressed, whatever state he came home in.

He was not a bad figure of a chap, her Jos, if only he'd hold himself up. Strong in the legs and chest, anyroad. A good ten years' work in him after she was done for. . . .

She left him and went back to the kitchen.

The two cats watched her go. Their tails twitched and they licked themselves furtively. Then feigning indifference, they sauntered after her.

When Jenny set her feet to the floor it rocked slightly beneath her, so that she was tempted to get back into bed.

She felt horribly weak. There was a woolly feeling in her head. Her hands and legs trembled.

'What's the matter with me,' she thought, impatient but dismayed. 'I can't spend all my life in bed. I've got to get going somehow. It's time I began seeing to things.'

But what things? . . .

However tortuous his approach to life, George's death had been a tidy affair leaving no frayed ends for others to unravel. The house was hers and the thirty-odd acres surrounding it. There had been bequests to the Baileys and various societies, but still enough was left—more than enough. By her standards she was a rich woman.

Was it possible that after all George had really loved her in some queer, twisted fashion? Was his will a final gesture of regret for the seven years of bickering and frustration and fear that their marriage had been? Had it indicated merely a loss of interest in earthly matters; a sick reaction from a surfeit of the meanness, the spying, nagging, jeering that had been the whole sum of his relations with her? Or was it simply that the law compelled him? She did not know.

She did not know and never would know. Nor did she care. George was dead. Already her body had half forgotten him and his image blurred upon her memory.

How could that happen so quickly? It was incredible.

Was it because George had been so warped a personality that he had verged on the unreal? Or was she herself unreal? . . .

She ran her hands over her body and shivered slightly. She leaned forwards to peer at herself in the mirror.

A pale slice of a face. Dark grey eyes, hollowed and enormous. Dark hair, very long and straight: difficult hair to cope with. . . . 'I'm so colourless,' she thought, frowning. 'Darkness and paleness and thinness—that's all I am. Just a black-and-white sketch, a silhouette.' She pinched her cheek. Red flowered briefly and faded again. Sighing, she pulled on an old dressing gown and went into the bathroom.

She bathed quickly and austerely; soaping with carbolic, scrubbing herself with a small, coarse towel. She cleaned her teeth with a brush dipped in salt.

The bathroom at Lost Hill, orginally a bedroom, was large and airy; bitterly cold in winter but pleasantly cool on such a day as this. It contained no luxuries, no hot towel rails or glass shelves of bathsalts and talcum powders, no gaily coloured bathmat or revealing mirror or gleam of chromium. The bath was large, coffin-like and scabrous, the floor bare save for a small cork mat. The only mirror was the small round one George had used for shaving and which, she suddenly thought, could now be disposed of. The walls were still hung with the original shiny yellow paper of indeterminate pattern down which steam rolled like tears.

But the view from the bathroom window was magnificent. Vast undulating miles of moor rolled beneath an unbroken sky. The purple was dimmed by the unrelenting heat, the gold scorched and faded. But the moor was beautiful as a lovely woman is beautiful in old age, because her bones are right.

The window was wide open. The air flowed in, hot and balmy, and her body relished it, drew strength from it. She breathed deeply, flexed the muscles of back and arms and legs. 'I must do something with my life,' she thought. 'My life is my own now. I'm free. . . .'

George's toothbrush still hung beside hers in the porcelain rack. Suddenly the intimacy seemed obscene, an outrage. She flung the toothbrush out of the window with all her force and wiped her fingers on the towel.

She felt better for that. But it reminded her that George's room upstairs was full of his belongings. The suits and ties and shoes he was always brushing and airing, but had never worn. The piles of underwear beautifully darned and patched by Owd Missus. The masses of correspondence, all arranged in taped bundles. The cardboard boxes, neatly graded for size and packed inside each other like a Chinese puzzle. The various collections he had started and abandoned at one time or another, and refused to dispose of: stamps, birds' eggs, old coins, old etchings mottled with damp and dirt, old, musty books with microscopic print. . . . They were all piled up there in George's room, dusty and mouldering. They would all have to be dealt with.

There was so much to be done, she felt guilty thinking of the time she had wasted in bed.

And then again realisation came flooding.

She was free, she was free! She was answerable to nobody for what she did or did not do. She was absolute mistress of the house; of all things within the house and the land that belonged to it and the people who served it. Bailey and his wife and the girl, Iris; she could pay them a month's wages and send them packing tomorrow. She could sell the house and the land. She could burn cardboard boxes and the old pictures and the musty books; give away the carbon-smelling clothes, the tree'd footwear, the butterflies and the coins. . . .

The whole truth flooded over her, so that she must sit, trembling, on the edge of the bath, frightened by her freedom as a bird is frightened when the door of its cage is first thrown open.

How could she sell Lost Hill? It was the only home she had. It was the servants' home, too: how could she send them away! Mrs. Bailey had lived here for over forty years. The Baileys were too old to start afresh. Iris could go—and good riddance!—but then, whom could she get in her place?

'I could shut up some of the rooms,' she thought. 'I could let most of the land. Just have a flower garden and vegetables and a few fowls. . . .'

The thought of all there was to do pressed down on her with an almost tangible weight. But then again, she was not bound to do any of it. 'I'm free,' she thought. 'I can do what I like!'

But that, of course, was the point: she had no idea what she wanted to do.

Out in the yard the heat came at her like a tidal wave, broke over her, submerged her, left her stranded on the burning cobbles, trembling and exhausted. 'I ought to have a hat,' she thought vaguely. But she never wore a hat. Only a scarf sometimes in the wettest of winter weather. A scarf would be too hot today. She went back into the dim hall and took an old panama of George's from a peg. She looked at it distastefully, banged dust from its brim. It would have to do.

The cobbles dazzled and shivered in heat. She had to force herself out into it. Fowls came hurrying at her step. She went across to the barn and dipped into a sack, threw them a slithering handful of grain. Her hand explored the dimness of a nest, discovered the warm smoothness of eggs.

Before George's illness the fowls had been her job. She had enjoyed looking after them. They had made no demands on her affections, neither had they rejected her. She had given them food, they had repaid her with eggs, and there the matter had ended. If one had to go for the pot she had not cared particularly. Fowls were not like dogs, who gave and demanded love, or horses, so swift and beautiful in dignity, or jewel-eyed Jerseys dreaming in meadows. Or people. . . .

She threw the fowls another handful of grain and went out into the yard again.

Iris was banging mats against a wall. She grinned when she saw Jenny and said, "Hot enough for yer?" Dust rose round her in a little cloud.

Hearing voices, Mrs. Bailey came to the kitchen door. She eyed Jenny sharply. "How're you feeling today?"

"I'm all right," Jenny replied, as she would have replied on her deathbed.

"You don't look too grand. You don't want to go traipsing about, getting yersen done up."

"I thought you were complaining just now that I was lying in bed," Jenny said dryly.

"Layin' abed's one thing. Mailicking and larkin' about t'moor in this 'eat's another. You want to tek it slow."

"I'm all right," Jenny said shortly. Then, on an impulse

she added: "I think I'll take my dinner out on the moor. Make me some sandwiches, will you? And put a thermos of coffee in the haversack, and some fruit. You can give my room a good clean out while I'm away."

Mrs. Bailey pinched in her lips.

"It's bread day."

"Iris doesn't make the bread, does she?"

"Iris has got to pick bilberries, or they'll be past jamming."

"Who says she's got to?"

"I do."

The two women eyed each other warily. Sooner or later the battle for supremacy was inevitable and they both knew it; but neither really wanted it so soon. At present they were inter-dependent, and each wanted to see which way the wind would blow. When, therefore, Mrs Bailey tempered her truculence by a grudging: " You know you're right set on bilberry jam, an' now's the time, if ever," Jenny met her half-way with: "Let her do the room this morning and the picking this afternoon."

"Don't mind me!" Iris remarked audibly. She shook an ancient piece of matting so that the dust followed Jenny's retreating form.

"Stir yer stumps," Mrs. Bailey said curtly. "It's high time yon room had a good do, an' sooner you start, sooner you'll be finished."

"Nowt but a slave, that's what I am," the girl said sulkily. "On t'go from mornin' to night. Come 'ere, go theer, do this, do that. . . . I dunno why I stop."

"You stop because yer ma would flay the hide off you if you gev up a good place like Lost Hill, an' went back eatin' 'em out of house an' home—that's why," Mrs. Bailey said dryly. "You're none that hard done by. Owd Missus'd turn in her grave if she could see t'way you mailick about, gettin' nowt done, an' bletherin' fit to mek folks giddy. Come on, now, look sharp with them mats an' get room done."

It was always so, Jenny thought; the further she got from the house the more at home she felt.

The moor was her home. On the rare occasions when she had gone away, and the thought had come to her 'tomorrow I shall be home again,' it had always been the moor she had visualised, not the square, stone house frowning amongst its cobbles and barns.

It was a good house, strongly built, dry and well-tended. The land about it, though neglected of late, was still in reasonably good heart. But it was not her house. It still belonged to George and Old Missus. No signing of deeds, no last bequests could make it hers. It had never accepted her and never would do so. Any more than Old Missus had accepted her, or the Baileys, or even George. . . .

Jenny walked slowly, for she was weak and the heat was terrific. The breeze of early morning had died, and heat struck up from the parched surface of the moor like the blast from a furnace. The heather was brown and brittle beneath her feet, the gorse burnt-out and faded; the hills quivered dizzily in the distance. Leaves were fallen untimely from the small, thirsty trees. The calamitous hands of drought lay heavily on the moor.

It was better up by the Tarn. Here was shade of trees and the very sight of water brought coolness, though its level was lower than she had ever known it and the touch of it was lukewarm.

Jenny lay down under the trees, and the arms of the moor held her with kindness. Moss was soft and dry beneath her cheek. She touched it lovingly, running fingers lightly through minute green miracles of stars and shell-like fronds and delicate feathers. A tiny beetle climbed and slipped its way amongst the miniature forest, its iridescent back gleaming bravely in the sun. A lizard appeared from nowhere; stood for a moment watching her with jewelled eyes, its throat going in and out, in and out; vanished as suddenly as it had come. Unaware of her, an adder slid past like a dream and poured itself into a clump of bracken.

The air was so still that the clock on Staving church, all of five miles across the valley, sounded clearly.

Two o'clock. . . . Could it really be so late? Had she been sleeping? Up here by the Tarn time seemed to have no meaning. 'I wish I could stay here for ever,' she thought. 'Just lie here alone, not aware I was alive, not knowing when I died. Perhaps I am dead now,' she thought dreamily. 'Perhaps I have never really been alive. Maybe I'm just a part of somebody else's dream. . . . And so I am not bound to make an effort to get rid of all those pictures and cardboard boxes and old coins, and all that clothing. . . . I need not worry about what to do, make any decisions, come to terms with life. I can just lie here with the sun hot on my body, and the feel of the moss, and the little beetle burning and shining in the quietness, until the dream is done and I am done with it.'

But in that moment, undreamlike and fierce, hunger seized her and with a wry smile she sat up and foraged in the knapsack.

The sandwiches were good, the coffee hot and strong, the golden globes of pear delicate-skinned, sweet, dripping with juice. 'I've eaten it all!' she thought, amazed. 'Every single bit of it. I haven't felt hungry for weeks. . . . I feel strong,' she thought, torn between pleasure and reluctance. 'I have to live whether I want to or not. There are years and years of life waiting for me. I am young and strong, I've got to live. . . . But I'll stay alone. I don't want people or possessions, or things happening to me. I just want to be me, and alone. . . .'

Skirting the edge of the Tarn she came to where the land plunged downwards to a valley and soared up again in a vast, majestic wave of bracken patched with heather and gorse, crowned by an outcrop of limestone forming a natural terrace. Clough's Gill. She had not been there for years. George had not liked her going so far afield. 'Come with me,' she had begged. But he never would. He had been busy, or out-of-sorts, or she had been in disgrace for some fault, unspecified but punishable. . . . And there was Setton Gill, where a stream meandered through fine green grass and then plunged suddenly down a rocky gorge into a black, foam-flecked pool.

And lovely little Staving, whose church spire thrust upwards through a clump of elms: she had loved to ride to Staving in those early days. Every time she heard the clock on Staving church, far-off and dreamlike, she thought, 'I must go back there some time.' Now she could go. . . .

And there were other places she had heard of but never seen. Scartop and Buckham and Close Caulton, all lying over that beckoning wave of bracken. And on this side of the valley, beyond Huffley, lay Beck Mills and Gatling Common, Hawks Hill, Manifold and Greeth. Lovely names. Lovely places. Waterfalls and dark, sombre ravines and small, secret woods; bright hills where Roman legions had marched—still marched, maybe, when night folded them in mist. Rounded valleys cupped grey stone villages holding inns and churches steeped in history; broad, windswept uplands were striped in green and gold and chocolate, rippled by cloud shadows, loud with lark song. . . .

She would get another horse. A dappled grey like the one George had given her when they were first married, and which he had afterwards sold because he had said she was getting too fond of it.

Grey Boy. . . . The smooth, firm sides, the gentle eyes, the delicate nostrils quivering against the palm of her hand, the eager whinny at sound of her footsteps on the cobbles. The lovely feeling of oneness with the great gentle creature as he obeyed her lightest touch of knee or rein. . . . Yes, George was right, she had been too fond of Grey Boy.

It didn't do to get fond of animals or people or things. Animals died. People disappointed you. Things became mill-stones round your neck. You were better alone. . . .

Her eye was caught by a scarlet speck moving along the moor track towards Lost Hill. She screwed up her eyes against the glare, and presently she made out a hooded cart moving slowly. A tinker's cart probably: they came over the moor from time to time, begging, whining ill-luck, stealing anything they could lay hands on. That red speck was probably the driver's scarf.

Moving back to the shade of the trees Jenny lay down again; and this time she really did fall asleep.

When she woke it was past six.

The heat was as great as ever, but the brightness of the day was done. A hot wind stirred the heather and the harsh branches above her head. It came in sudden fitful gusts over the moor from the east; in the west, massing brassy ranks to meet it, storm clouds moved in majesty.

'This is the end of the drought,' she thought.

She set out for home walking as quickly as possible. She had no personal fear of storms but to be caught so far from shelter would be no joke. She must not be ill again. The whole business of illness and doctors, of medicine glasses and special food on trays, of thermometers and nightlights and the empty-ing of slops sickened her. First Old Missus, then George, and then herself: she had been caught up in it for months, and she meant to be done with it now. Now she was beginning to live. Now the drought was breaking, the world would soon be green and vital again. . . .

The first hot, slow drops fell as she came within sight of the house. She forced herself to run. Squeezing through the gap in the hedge she remembered, half guiltily, how George had scolded her for doing just this. He had put wire netting across the hole but it had soon disappeared again. Jenny surmised that Bailey, and possibly Iris also, had found it a short and convenient cut to freedom.

Three white goats bawled at her, straining at their tethers, absurdly posturing. She knew they were restless, aware of the coming storm, and she loosed them as she passed. They made for their shed, lamenting loudly, jostling each other, heavy udders swinging, beards outthrust, yellow eyes inimi-cal. Busby and Witch and the outsize, bad-tempered Fatima. George had read an article in some magazine, had talked of nothing but goats for days. Their milk, he announced, was free from the T.B. germ, whereas cows' milk was little less

than a deathtrap. Goats were easier to house than cows, easier
to milk, cheaper to feed and more intelligent. He had come
home one day with Fatima, loudly complaining and all too
handy with her horns; and soon afterwards the lovely little
Jerseys had been sold.

The field sloped upwards, then sharply down again to the
orchard flanking the south wall of the house. As she reached
the hill's crest Jenny paused, then stood motionless, staring.

There below her on the rough turf a tent had been erected.
A cart rested on its shafts, a thin brown pony cropped steadily
at the coarse grass: the sound of the tearing teeth came loudly
on the silence. A pot hung steaming from a tripod over a fire
and above this a man bent, whistling in a thin, flutelike tone.

The man stood up and stretched, lifting his arms widely
and yawning with a flash of white teeth. Even from here she
could see he was a magnificent creature, broad-shouldered
and narrow-hipped, his whole body instinct with an animal
grace. He wore nothing but khaki slacks belted about his
waist. His torso was brown and strong-looking. His feet were
bare.

Glancing upwards as he yawned and stretched, the man
caught sight of Jenny standing motionless on the crest of the
hill. And for one instant he stood as motionless as herself,
head thrown back, body taut, upstretched—almost, she
thought with a sudden, shrinking distaste, as though reaching
for her.

Then he was gone. Amongst the trees—into the tent— somewhere. . . .

He was gone. And the rain was falling in good earnest now.

She began to run down the steep slope; stumbling a little
because of her weakness, frightened a little, though she could
not tell why.

Lightning flickered among the hills and presently thunder
stuttered and slowly died. The rain stopped for a moment,
as if taking a deep breath; then it came in a sudden hissing
downpour that wet her to the skin long before she reached
the house.

CHAPTER THREE

THE next morning windows were blank with mist. The house was hazy with it. Polished surfaces were bloomed over, curtains hung dank and limp, discarded clothing was clammy to the touch.

Jenny dressed hurriedly. Iris had lit a fire in the living room and its cheer was surprisingly welcome. Jenny stood beside it, one foot on the fender, gazing down at the small, licking flames. She was glad she had gone up on the moor yesterday. There would probably be a lot of rain now. There would be days and days of this mist; then, as the furnace-heat of the moor cooled down, it would become clearer, colder. Green would come thrusting everywhere. Low Meadow would be flooded, the yard would be puddled with water reflecting moving clouds. Then the winds would come roaring over the moor, and then the frosts, the ice, the deep isolation of snow. . . . It might be a long time before she could lie by the Tarn again.

Iris came in and began to bang the breakfast on to the table. She seemed less aggressive than usual, more anxious to please, so Jenny thanked her for the fire. "We're in for a wet spell," she said amicably.

Iris agreed, sidling towards the door as if pressed for time. She wore a cleaner apron than usual and her hair had evidently been crimped overnight. She smelt strongly of scent. Her mouth was generously supplied with lipstick. Jenny decided to ignore the lipstick and scent, but not the down-at-heel shoes thickly plastered with mud that was still wet.

"You should change your shoes, Iris."

"How can I, when I'm in an' out all the time?"

"Those shoes never got as bad as that in the yard. You must have been through some pretty deep mud. Better change them right away."

"Okeydoke." Iris stood banging the empty tray against her knees. "Is that all?"

"Don't say okeydoke, Iris."

"It's what I allus say," the girl said mulishly.

"I know. And shut the door when you go out."

"Okeydoke."

The door banged and immediately clicked open again. Jenny got up and shut it properly.

Iris was hopeless, of course, not worth bothering about. She irritated Jenny almost beyond endurance. . . . And that was not quite honest, either. She was more irritated by her own inability to command obedience and respect.

She was nothing in this house, never would be anything that mattered. Nevertheless she was Missus now. She must make an effort.

She finished her breakfast and went out to the kitchen. Mrs. Bailey was washing potatoes at the sink.

"Where's Bailey?"

The old woman did not look up.

"How should I know?"

"Did you give him my message last night?"

"Aye, I told him."

"Did he get rid of that man?"

"I know nowt about it."

Jenny hesitated. She knew by the closed look on Mrs. Bailey's face, and by long experience, that Bailey was sleeping off the effects of market day. This was one of the things George had known how to deal with. . . .

"Did he bring the medicine?"

"It's on t'dresser."

Jenny took the bottle and went back to the living room. 'It's not doing me a pennyworth of good,' she thought. She put the bottle on the sideboard and stared out of the window, trying to make up her mind how to cope with the situation. She felt young, forlorn and inadequate.

Presently she put on a sou'wester coat and hat, slipped her feet into tall rubber boots and went out, hunching shoulders against the pelting rain.

The cobbled yard was clean, shining with water, but the orchard had a treacherous patina of thin, greasy mud. Strong though it was, the downpour could not yet penetrate the iron surface of the earth. She picked her way across fallen apples and the leafy, brittle ends of branches. The smell of rotting fruit rose all about her, thick and steamy.

When she reached the far end of the orchard she stood in the shelter of a tree.

It was all there: the tilted cart, the tethered pony, the tent, the tripod with its pot hanging above grey ashes. Only the fire was out and the man was not there. The little encampment was lifeless, incredibly forlorn, with rain drumming on the taut surface of the tent and darkening the rough sides of the pony who stood with lowered head, passively accepting his fate.

"Hi, there!" she called suddenly. But nobody appeared. Even the pony gave no sign of awareness.

Jenny stood frowning and disconcerted. There was nothing to do but go back, wait until Bailey had slept off his hangover.

She turned to go. But in that moment something familiar caught her eye: a splash of blue lying at the door of the tent. One of the Willow-pattern dinner plates that stood in splendid isolation round the high shelf in the drawing room. One of Old Missus' plates.

And at once the whole thing connected up. Iris' clean apron; the crimped hair and the lipstick; the muddy shoes ... Iris again. Any man would do. Any chance caller at the house, loaded hiker or stranded motorist asking for help. Even old

Bailey, if no one else were available. Even George's cold indifference to women had not daunted her. . . .

Jenny moved forward and picked up the blue-and-white plate. It had not been washed: food was crusted on the surface. Moreover it was cracked right across. Old Missus' Willow-pattern plate.

Once again Jenny felt a spasm of anger at her own incompetence. If Old Missus had been alive Iris would never have dreamed of touching one of the Willow-pattern plates.

Holding the soiled plate gingerly she tapped the taut wet surface of the tent.

"Will you come out, please?" she called.

There was no reply, no sound at all. Yet she knew very certainly that someone was within the tent. No voice, no definite movement; but somebody was there; some living creature listening, waiting for her next move.

"I want to speak to you, please," she called again.

She was frightened, but it was no use being frightened. Silly, because she was in the right and he in the wrong. This was her land and he had camped without permission. He had accepted food from an unauthorised person. He had built a fire, allowed his pony to graze. He had stared insolently at her, offering no apology for the trespass.

She stooped and entered the tent.

It was small and dim; the drumming of rain on the canvas was loud. A sourish smell offended her. It seemed to come from a bundle of blankets lying on one of the two mattresses which were placed side by side on the ground. In one corner of the tent crockery and cooking utensils and a primus stove were heaped together. In another stood a pail of water, a jug of milk and a cardboard box containing groceries of some sort. There was nothing else in the tent at all, as far as she could see.

Jenny turned to go. A movement among the blankets arrested her. The pale, tousled head of a child appeared above them, stared at her with fever-bright eyes.

"Djink," it said softly; and then, as she stood staring back at it, unmoving, the word came again, louder and more imperative. "Djink!"

She had not the slightest idea what it meant.

She knew nothing about children. It did not even astonish her that so young a child should have been left alone in the tent without supervision. It was just another irritation superimposed on the mounting irritations of the day.

"I don't know what you mean," she said absurdly.

The over-bright eyes stared thirstily. Then, as if sensing the futility of appeal, the child began to cry quietly, in a hopeless, unchildlike fashion which Jenny found peculiarly disturbing. She wanted to leave the tent, but it seemed quite impossible to turn her back on such small loneliness. 'I ought to be able to do something,' she thought irritably. 'I'm a woman; why don't I know what to do?'

Experimentally she straightened the blankets, handling them with shrinking disgust as she saw that the child had been sick quite recently. It occurred to her that the man might have abandoned the child. He could easily have slipped away last night; by now he might be many miles on the road, irretrievably lost. Then she remembered that the cart was still there, and the pony. It was unlikely that he would leave those.

The child continued to cry. Its forehead felt very hot. Taking a clean handkerchief from her pocket, Jenny dipped it in the pail of water and began to bathe the tiny forehead. Instantly the child grabbed at the handkerchief and began to suck avidly at the soaked fabric.

"So that's what you meant," Jenny murmured. "The point is, I don't know if you ought to drink much. I shouldn't think a little drop would hurt."

She held a cup of water to the child's lips. It drank thirstily, grabbing at the cup when Jenny pulled it away. "No more," she said, expecting a gale of tears. But it accepted the refusal with a stoicism that touched her more than tears could have done. "You've learned young," she muttered. "Here, let's see if I can't make you a bit more comfortable."

Lifting the child on to the other mattress she steeled herself to refolding the blankets and the man's shirt which had been, used as a pillow. Both were soiled and malodorous. The child's clothing was even worse, but there was nothing she could do about that. With a soaked handkerchief she washed the small, streaked face, the hot hands and feet, and was rewarded by a flickering smile.

"Gessin," it said.

She lifted the child in her arms and held it a moment, feeling a sort of kinship with the small, helpless creature. She held it awkwardly, insecurely, so that instinctively it gripped at her coat, its eyes widening in apprehension. They stared appraisingly at each other; lonely woman and lonely child; each occupied with alien and rather terrifying sensations. Jenny had never held a child in her arms before. The child had never, within its short memory, been held by a woman.

The rain drummed on the tent with increasing violence. The pony neighed loudly outside and the child's head twisted on Jenny's arm. "Gessin!" it chirped hoarsely.

Still holding the child, Jenny swung round to face the man.

He was standing just inside the tent, watching her. Water dripped from his long black oilskin, making a puddle on the floor. Water dripped from his hair, from the bundle he carried. His shoes squelched with water, his brown face glistened with it.

With a quick movement of the shoulders he slid the oilskin to the ground. He stepped forward and took the child from her arms.

"Gessin!"

"Okay." He wrapped the child in its blankets, laid it on the bed again. "You don't know how to hold a child," he said to Jenny; an amused contempt in his voice brought her anger flooding back.

"This child is ill," she accused him.

"That is why I camped here."

"Without permission."

He did not speak. She felt her face go hot.

"I said you camped here without permission."

"The child and the pony needed rest," he said softly.

"But you could have asked my permission."

The dark eyes were expressionless.

"Would you have let me stop?"

"That's not the point."

"My point it is." A smile lifted a corner of his mouth and was gone.

"I told Bailey—my yard-man—to tell you I would not allow campers."

"Nobody came to tell me."

"Somebody gave you food!" She glanced meaningly at the cracked Willow-pattern plate.

"That was kind. Thanks for the food."

"I did not tell anyone to give you food!" she cried furiously.

"Pay for it I can. For the plate, too. There's a pity it broke. A good plate. How much will I give you for my supper and the broken plate?" He was holding a purse in his hand. His eyes still regarded her with that dark, unfathomable stare.

"Put it away," she said curtly. "I don't want your money. All I ask is that you pack up and go as quickly as possible." She turned away, longing to get out of the tent; away from the drumming rain, from the sick child, from that dark, disturbing stare.

"Lady, the child is ill!" For the first time the hint of a professional whine underlaid the words.

"Why don't you look after it better, then? Those blankets are absolutely filthy, and so are its clothes."

"A young child gets dirty very quick. Few clothes he needed all the summer, so hot it's been, and he's grown out of them. Into the village I've been now to buy him some more, and some medicine for him, and another blanket." He indicated the bundle on the ground. "That is why I had to leave him. Soon as I get some water boiling I'll fix him up okay."

"Haven't you got a wife or—or some woman to look after him?"

"Only me he has. I can look after him okay."

Jenny glanced round the damp, steamy tent with its jumble of pots and pans, the filthy blankets, the worn mattresses. "This place is quite impossible for a sick child. You'd better get him cleaned up a bit while I try to get an ambulance or a car to take him into Huffley. There's a good hospital there. Doctors and nurses who'll look after him properly."

The man moved between her and the child; like an animal guarding its young, she thought.

"No hospital or doctor I need. I can nurse him myself. I got some herbs in the village and I know what to do. Nothing much wrong with him there is, only a chill. If the weather hadn't changed so sudden he'd be okay."

She shrugged and turned away.

"Go to a hospital or not, just as you please," she said coldly, "but I expect you to be off my land before noon."

Back at the house the atmosphere was electrical. Mrs. Bailey had discovered the loss of the Willow-pattern plate, and Iris was in tears; tears of rage rather than remorse, Jenny judged, noticing the angry red marks of fingers across the girl's plump white cheek. Bailey was, apparently, still sleeping it off. Further questioning brought to light the news that he was in great pain, having slipped in his wavering climb upstairs last night and injured his ankle. He could not, Mrs. Bailey declared, put foot to the ground. And serve him right.

"No doubt," Jenny agreed. "But who's going to milk the goats and groom Posy, and all the late apples to be picked, and the hedging and ditching, and all the rest of it?"

"It's a judgement on 'im," Mrs. Bailey declared with sour enjoyment. "Many's the time I've warned 'im. 'You'll fall an' break yer neck on them stairs one o' these nights,' I've told

'im, time an' again. If only he'd keep off the drink, there's
not a better worker anywhere. Strong in the arms, he is, an'
spry enough on 'is feet when he's not got a bellyful o' beer.
Years of work in 'im yet," she insisted, shooting a shrewd
glance at Jenny's frowning face.

"We shall just have to manage. I'll milk the goats—Iris never
strips them dry. Tell her to go down to the Post Office and
get Mrs. Emmett to ring up the doctor to come and look at
Bailey's ankle. I hoped we'd finished with doctors in this
house, but it's no use taking chances."

"I can put a poultice on 'im," Mrs. Bailey objected.

"Please do as I say, Mrs. Bailey."

The old woman pinched in her mouth, but she went out
of the kitchen without further argument, to Jenny's secret
relief.

Jenny milked the goats. They were restive, resenting enforced confinement. Busy and Witch bounced and bellowed.
Fatima waited sullenly until she was stripped, then neatly
kicked the pan across the shed. Jenny fed and watered them,
removed the soiled bedding and supplied them with new.
Their yellow eyes watched her inimically. The rain drummed
ceaselessly on the corrugated iron roof.

She thought of Iris's blubbered countenance, Mrs. Bailey's
pinched-in mouth, the strange man's black, enigmatic eyes.
The goats had no affection for her. Iris and the Baileys despised her. The man openly disobeyed her orders. 'I can't
cope,' she thought, angry and frustrated. 'I can't cope with
any of them. Even that baby was frightened I should drop it.'

It had clutched at her with an astonishing strength. Small
hot fingers clutching at her coat; frightened of being
dropped.... But not frightened of *her*. Its eyes had been wide
and interested. It hadn't cried while she held it in her arms.
The fine, pale hair had stuck up in comical tufts. Not a pretty
child, even when she had washed some of the grime from
its face. "Djink!" it had said, and had sucked the water from
the handkerchief. And what was the other word? Gessin.

What did Gessin mean? . . . At what age did children talk?
She knew nothing about children. It had known that instinctively. The man had known it, too. "You don't know how to
hold a child," he had said, and his voice had pitied her. He
had thought her a poor thing.

'I am a poor thing,' she thought. 'I can't cope with people—
not even with a child.'

She shut the door of the goat's shed, leaving the upper half
open for light and air, and trudged back to the house.

As she skirted the orchard she saw that the tent was still
there, and the tilted cart, and the pony. A line had been
strung between two apple trees and a blanket, torn, but quite
clean, hung dripping in the pouring rain.

She heard the man whistling. He came out of the tent,
stripped to the waist, his arms filled with small, wet, steaming
garments which he proceeded to peg on the line. She wondered impatiently how he expected to get them dry, much
less aired. His own trousers were soaking wet. It seemed
improbable that he owned another pair. His brown, naked
torso glistened in the rain. He shook himself like a dog before
he entered the tent. 'Used to it, I suppose,' she thought.

She wondered if he had made the child clean and comfortable and suppressed a strong desire to find out for herself.
The child was none of her business and the sooner it was
taken away the better.

What should she do if he were not gone by noon?

There was always the police, of course; but she did not like
the idea of calling in the police. After all, what harm was he
actually doing down there beyond the orchard? And if he did
snare a rabbit or two, or steal a few apples and turnips, would
she miss them?

No, definitely not the police. Quite likely he did not want
them nosing too deeply into his affairs. 'I'm only just begin-
ing to realise what it's like to be free myself,' she thought.
'Why should I spoil anyone else's freedom?'

Doctor Waller, she learned from Iris, was even now up in Bailey's room. Iris had chanced to meet his car on the road and had been given a lift back. Which circumstance had obviously dispersed for her the dolours of early morning. She looked like a cat who had sighted cream. 'Even poor old Sam Waller!' Jenny thought with an inward spasm of amusement. Was no man safe from Iris?

When the doctor came downstairs he informed her that Bailey's ankle was badly sprained, and he would be out of commission for some time. "I'm a bit worried about him," he confessed. "He's a bad colour and I think there might be something else. I've been questioning him but of course he lied like a trooper—his sort always do. I may have to get him down to the hospital for a look-over, but keep mum about that, or you'll scare the daylights out of him."

This was serious news.

"The late apples will rot on the trees," she worried. "I suppose I can manage the livestock myself, but there's a lot of heavy work that needs a man. It would happen just as the weather broke, of course."

The doctor eyed her speculatively as he sipped a glass of the elderberry wine for which Mrs. Bailey was justly famed. He had known Mrs. George ever since she was married. She had been bonnier then; there had been curves where curves should be, and a confiding, childish charm about her that he had found endearing. She had had colour then and a certain spirit. Old Missus had dealt with that long before she died, the old buzzard. The colour, the endearing charm had soon frozen and died under George Rowland's chilly touch.

He had been sorry for the girl, stuck away in this bleak, lonely place with an old tyrant of a mother-in-law and a husband like George Rowland. Doctor Waller had disliked George increasingly from the night he had brought him into the world to that bleak dawn some forty years later when he had ushered him out of it.

He hadn't pretended to know what was the matter with

George. He left all that to these newfangled psychiatrist chaps. He was a blunt, overworked, county G.P., with neither the time nor the patience to meddle with what was beyond him. But what he had forgotten of his textbooks he made up for in common sense and a large and varied experience, and it was his considered opinion that George Rowland had been as near certifiable as no matter. A good thing for everybody when his duodenal had finally carried him off. . . .

"Why worry your head?" he said gruffly. "Let the apples rot. Shut the house up. Let it—sell it! Get out of it and take a long holiday. Go abroad—you can afford it now. Ever been out of England?"

"Only to school."

"Neither have I. Never had the time or the money. You've got both. Do you more good than all those bottles of medicine." He sipped at the wine, enjoying it. "First-rate stuff, this! A good excuse for visiting at Lost Hill." His kind little eyes twinkled at her above the glass. "You're looking better, m'dear. How's the pulse?" He took her wrist in his fingers. "And the tongue, eh? . . . . H'm, you'll do. A nice long holiday in the south of France, and you'll be a new woman. We don't want to lose you, as they used to tell us in the First War, but we think you ought to go."

"I don't know what I should do about the servants," Jenny confessed.

"Leave 'em put for the time being. Shut up most of the house. Mrs. Bailey's quite capable of carrying on yet. As for yon fat ginger wench, she'd be better at home where her mother could deal with her. A good ducking in the Tarn is what she needs! Well, I must be off. . . . You get away, me dear. You've had a rough time, but it's over. That's what you've got to remember—it's over. And you're still young, think on. And bonny," he added gallantly, though her shadowed eyes and the fine-drawn features of her face filled him with pity. "By the way," he added, slapping his leather gloves against the palm of his hand, "Tod's coming back."

"Tod?" she said blankly.

"Tod Shaw. Good heavens, you know Tod Shaw, don't you? Neighbour of yours."

"Oh, you mean Major Shaw over at Backshaws? No, I never spoke to him. George didn't like him I think."

The old doctor shot out his lips and nodded.

"Well, that's nothing to do with you. Tod's a good chap. He'll be a good neighbour if you let him. Very reliable sort of bloke. If you need any help, Tod's the chap, and don't you forget it. I'll tell him to keep an eye on you."

She turned away, frowning.

"I don't want anyone to look after me. I don't want people. It's time I learned to look after myself."

'Time she called her soul her own is what she means,' the doctor thought. 'Poor child, I can understand that. Better leave her alone.' And he glanced at his watch, remembering the young husband dying slowly and painfully, the worn-out woman whose unwanted child he must deliver within the next few hours. He couldn't carry everyone's burdens. . . .

It was not until his ancient Morris had gone snorting and exploding out of sight that Jenny remembered the encampment down by the orchard.

It would have been so easy to say: 'There's a man with a sick child down in the field. Please do something about them.'

There would have been no question of yea or nay. Once Doctor Waller had poked his nose inside that tent things would have moved quickly, and she need never have set eyes on man or child again.

But she had not said it. They were still down there by the orchard. Maybe the child's condition was more serious than the man realised. It might die. . . . She might be blamed for not notifying the doctor or the police or somebody. . . .

She began to walk restlessly about the house; in and out of the large, square rooms filled with massive, ornate furniture, gilt-framed pictures, hangings of heavy, expensive, remarkably ugly materials. There were calf-bound, gilt-edged volumes, all arranged in strict order of size behind locked glass doors. On sideboard and cupboards stood heavy china ornaments: piping shepherds and reclining maidens, old men with beer mugs, groups of obese, half-naked children. The mantelpieces bore massive glass-domed clocks supported by Corinthian pillars of black marble, flanked by bronze statues of horses wildly rearing, on whose bridles naked, muscular men dragged desperately. Dark, floral wallpapers were covered with oil paintings of Highland cattle, dogs with bleeding birds gripped in their jaws and steel engravings of Biblical stories of the grimmer sort.

Upstairs, beds were enormous, with brass rails and knobs, feather mattresses and heavy white honeycomb quilts. The floors were covered in polished linoleum on which mats treacherously slid. Old Missus had disapproved of carpets in bedrooms. The blue carpet that Jenny had bought cheaply at a sale for her own comfort had been the object of a long and bitter wrangle which had convinced her, once and for all, that defiance was not worth the candle.

Old Missus had been almost savagely proud of this house. Every corner of it had been kept in shining, spotless perfection. She and Mrs. Bailey and Iris had slaved for it morning, noon and night. Only Jenny, the wife George had so unexpectedly, so disastrously foisted on to them following a London visit, had never been admitted to its service. She had not even been allowed to keep her own room clean. "I want none o' your lah-di-dah London ways in my house!" Old Missus had stated vigorously. "But I kept house for my father," Jenny had protested. And Old Missus had given the loud, derisive snort that passed with her for mirth. "Ah, I'll be bound you did," she had said contemptuously, with the shattering scorn of the north for all aliens. "Over a mucky shop in a mucky street. What sort of a place were that to live in!"

Fingering the bobble fringe of a dark chenille curtain, Jenny remembered Soho. The narrow, noisy streets; the colour and the smells. The gay little foreign restaurants. The dark, animated faces and varied, fluent tongues. The spicy foods you could buy ready-cooked. The easy, slipshod life in the four rooms above her father's shop. . . . It was like a dream, a tale that is told. It had nothing to do with Jenny Rowland. Nothing to do with George's widow, the spineless thing she had become in the bleak seven years that were past.

Yet Old Missus had been kind, too, in a contemptuous, overbearing way. She had been human, at least. She had urged food upon her, nursed her in illness, given her presents of hideous, sensible clothes, allowed her to make a flower garden for herself. She had given George the edge of her tongue when he had sold Grey Boy. At the same time she had had no patience with Jenny's tears. "Thing's over and done with," she had said impatiently. "You want to pull yourself together. Pity you haven't got a pack of bairns to give you summat to cry *for*."

Sometimes Jenny thought Old Missus had been sorry for her. Once or twice she had made a sort of apology for George's behaviour. "He's too old and set in his ways for marriage," she had said gruffly. And:"Tek no notice on him. He's got a queer streak, like all the Rowlands."

When she lay dying she had sent for Jenny. Her mouth, unfamiliar without the ill-fitting artificial teeth, had worked up and down, and the old eyes, less sharp now, had rested first on the girl's hand with its long, delicate fingers, then on the dark hair, the dark eyes, the adolescent thinness of her body. "Don't let 'im get you down," she had said, her harsh voice strangely weak and subdued. "It'll none be for so long. The Rowland men never mek old bones."

Dust. Dust everywhere. It was enough to make Old Missus turn in her grave. Mrs. Bailey could not cope with it, and Iris would not. Jenny had had her hands full with George's illness and, when he was not ill, with George himself; his tantrums and fears and sudden, devilish cruelties; his whining self-pity; his tortuous hobbies; the unpleasant personal habits that became ever more pronounced as his health deteriorated.

She went into George's room now; shut the door and stood

staring at the heavy honeycomb quilt, so flat and white over the empty bed.

George was not there. He was dead. Gone. He could never frighten her again, never sicken her by his habits, weary her with his endless, futile hobbies, infuriate her with his petty economies, his sudden, outlandish prodigality.

This was the room where George had died. It was swept bare and clean. The chill of death still seemed to hang in the air.

But in the adjoining dressing room chaos met her eyes.

Here were the fantastic collections of cardboard boxes, of letters and circulars, of free samples of patent foods, hair restorers, shaving creams, pills and a dozen other quack remedies. Here were the broken butterflies, the muddled heaps of stamps, the mildewed pictures, the coins. . . .

Here was George: still alive, still to be feared, pitied, hated. Here was the death in life that now became the even greater menace of life in death. . . .

Suddenly Jenny knew what she must do.

Opening a linen press on the landing, she took out a sheet and spread it on the floor of the room. Into the sheet she bundled them: letters and circulars, pills and butterflies and foreign stamps, boxes and coins and tattered books, musty, mildewed pictures cut from magazines long years ago. She staggered downstairs with her burden, tipped them all out on the floor of the nearest shed, and went upstairs for more.

Up and down she went, up and down. She saw Iris' moon-face staring, Mrs. Bailey's taut, disapproving figure watching from the kitchen door. The rain beat on her as she ran from house to shed and back again, but she only shook herself and kept on.

As the room emptied her heart lightened.

This was something she was doing for herself; something she had decided on and carried out without asking help or permission from anyone. And she thought: 'I mustn't let the house beat me. The house belongs to me now. I can do as I like with it. Doctor Waller was wrong. I mustn't go away or

I shall never be free. The house will have beaten me if I go away. I must stay here until I find myself.'

When the floor was quite clear Jenny attacked the chest of drawers, the tallboy, the heavy, carved wardrobe. All these were filled with the clothes George had acquired over a period of at least twenty years. There were piles of woollen undergarments, some new, some patched and darned beyond belief; scores of ties and collars and at least two dozen handkerchiefs of the finest Irish linen that had never been used. There were suits of tweed and worsted and flannel, some in good condition, some bad, and all outmoded. There was a dress suit, she saw with faint astonishment, and an ancient morning suit upon whose striped trousers moths had been busy. There were piles of shirts of every type, pullovers and fancy vests, silk scarves with George's initials on them, two dressing gowns of elaborate pattern, at least a dozen pairs of shoes and a number of hats, including a yachting cap. There was also an opera cloak sumptuously lined with quilted satin.

Jenny had never seen George in any of these clothes.

On his rare visits to the shop in Soho he had been an unremarkable figure in shabby trench coat and Homburg hat. These had been his wedding garments. They were what he had worn when he drove into Huffley. They still hung on a peg in the passage downstairs. About the house he had always worn a tweed sports' coat over stained flannel trousers. Pottering about fields or yard, a sack laid across the shoulders had been his answer to inclement weather.

What sort of life had George led in the years before she had known him? Social contacts were indicated by the dress suit, a streak of foppishness by the elaborate dressing gowns and scarves. And what did the opera cloak and the yachting cap mean?

She tried to imagine George as a dashing young blade escorting pretty women to dances, attending first nights, supping uproariously at night clubs, being elegantly nautical at Henley. . . . Her imagination boggled. From being shabby and silent George had merely become more shabby, more silent; from being irritable and aloof he had become increasingly suspicious, savage-tempered, morose; inimical to youth, gaiety, affection, all the more colourful evidences of life.

If George had a past she had never guessed it, and would never know it now.

It was not important, anyway. What was important was her own future.

She pulled out the underwear, the suits, hats, shoes, everything, staggering downstairs with load after load. They lay on the floor of the shed with all the other junk.

Mrs. Bailey came and stood beside her, smoothing clawlike hands over her apron.

"What might you be reckonin' to do with all t'Mester's things?" she demanded sourly.

"I haven't decided yet."

"You'll none throw all them good clothes out?"

"I told you I hadn't decided yet."

"It'd be a cryin' shame."

The old voice was shrill with consternation. Change was in the air, and she feared change. Mrs. George was acting queer. That was the worst of them quiet ones, you never knew what they'd be up to. "He thought a deal of his butter-flies an' pictures, did Mester. It fair gev me a turn seein' 'em all thrown out in yon shed before he's cold in his grave, poor chap."

Jenny threw open the window and the rain came spattering in. She pushed her hair out of her eyes and glanced at her watch. It was noon.

Had the man and the child gone? Or were they still there, defying her?

"I shall be ready for dinner soon," she said. "Afterwards, this room is going to be thoroughly swept and scrubbed, and most of the furniture turned out."

Mrs. Bailey's nose came down over her chin.

"Iris has got to go into Huffley and I've got me hands full enough, what with Bailey upstairs an' all."

"I shall do it myself," Jenny said curtly.

CHAPTER FOUR

Mrs. Bailey dumped a tray of food upon her husband's prostrate body and regarded him sombrely.

"Sooner you come downstairs an' give a hand, the better."

"Give a hand?" he exclaimed indignantly. "How can I do owt, state I'm in!"

"You can peel taters, can't yer? You don't do them with yer feet! You can clean silver an' brass, can't yer? An' slice beans, an' that? I'll find plenty you can do, nivver fear. I can't be climbin' these stairs fifty times a day."

"You can send Iris," he leered.

"Aye, happen I can. And have to climb 'em again to get 'er down!" She punched a pillow into the small of his back. "Mind how you sup yon stew, I don't want it all over t'bedclothes. I'm goin' to mek a bed up for you in t'kitchen."

"She won't like that."

"Then She can lump it."

"How am I goin' to git down them stairs?"

"On yer behind," she said shortly.

He applied himself to the basin of stew, shovelling the food into his mouth with a spoon and masticating noisily. "You're rare an' late with me dinner," he grumbled.

"Thank yer lucky stars you've got any, state the house is in. She's turned Mester's room inside out. All his clothes an' his bits of things chucked in a heap on t'floor of the little shed—every blessed thing out of the room bar the heavy furniture—an' somebody's got to heave that out, an' all, she says. She's goin' at yon floor with a scrubbin' brush like a mad thing. Got a fire blazin' in t'grate an' all. Curtains down. Iris must wash 'em, if you please—nivver heed how thronged we are! Scarce gev hersen time to swally her food afore she were at it again. I tell you, I don't like it. I don't like it at all."

"What's she reckon to do wi' yon clothes?"

"That's what I asked her, but all she says is, she hasn't decided. And out she throws 'em all in t'shed—good suits an' woollens an' hats, an' I don't know what!"

"I'll have some o' them," he said, licking his spoon clean and drawing the back of his hand across his mouth.

His wife picked up the tray and stumped to the door.

"Sooner you come downstairs the better, then. There's summat up, an' I don't know what it is. But it's no time to be laying' abed up top o' t'house. And keep a civil tongue in yer head, mind. There's a tinker chap campin' in t'orchard field, an' you was supposed to get rid on him last night, on'y you was in such a state you couldn't have turned a rabbit away, let alone a man. She's not best pleased about that, for a start. Chap's getten a sick bairn with him, Iris says."

"What's Iris got to do wi' him?" Bailey said jealously.

"Same as she's got to do wi' any man as comes within a mile of 'er. Took 'im some food down last night in one of the Willow-pattern plates, an' got it broke. I gev 'er Willow-pattern!" the old woman said with sour satisfaction. "I'll get yer bed made up in t'kitchen now."

"Ain't I gettin' no pudden?" he enquired in an aggrieved voice.

"Pudden?" his wife repeated shrilly. "You've got a cheek lyin' there talkin' about pudden! An' me fair run off me feet, not knowin' which way to turn!"

She slammed the door behind her. He listened to the slow, flat sound of her descending feet.

He lay still in the bed sucking his teeth and thinking about the pain in his ankle, and the questions the doctor had fired at him that morning. Prodding a chap about, wanting to know this, that and the other. . . . He hadn't got much change out of him, anyroad. It wasn't likely he'd let on how queer he had been feeling for the past week or two. Give them doctors an inch and they take a mile! Hurting his ankle had been a bit

of luck, really. It would probably keep him cosily indoors for
a few days, and that would put him right all over.

But in the meantime he fancied something sweet, and it
didn't look as if he was going to get it.

He eyed the biscuit tin that stood on the table on his wife's
side of the bed. That tin had stood there more years than he
could remember. It had roses painted on the lid. Every night
Em was sucking and smacking away at her biscuits, and
always buying more. He couldn't make out what she saw in
them. Still, it was something sweet. . . .

He reached out for the tin, opened it, poked a finger amongst
the Oval Maries and the ginger nuts, to see if there was anything more to his liking.

Suddenly his eyes narrowed. He tipped the tin upside down
and the biscuits came tumbling out on the counterpane.

And after the biscuits came the money. Silver coins in a
tuneful slither. Six golden sovereigns spilling out of a cardboard pill box. And then the thump of paper; green notes and
brown tightly packed together and secured with an elastic
band.

He swore softly and repeatedly. He gaped at the money;
fingered the shining golden coins, admiring the half-forgotten
things; slid his fingers through the silver; flicked a blackened
thumbnail against the tightly packed edges of the notes. Why,
there must be hundreds of notes!

The owd buzzard! . . . She must have been saving it for
donkeys' years—all her life since she came to Lost Hill, he
did not doubt. And most of his money, too. . . .

He'd never known anybody spend less than Em spent.
Never a jaunt into Huffley to get herself a new dress or a fal-
lal. Owd Missus's castoffs had fitted her near enough, and
she'd still got a cupboard full of them. Never a visit to the
pictures or a bus ride to the sea in summer, or even a sixpenny
seat at the church concert.

The only brass he'd ever known her to part with had been
for these biscuits. She'd put them away in this tin week after

week. For years the tin had stood there, right under his nose. . . .

He swore again; a soft, fluent stream of invective, not un-mixed with a reluctant admiration.

"The owd buzzard—ee, the perishin' owd buzzard! Her and her ginger nuts! Who'd 'a thowt she'd got it in 'er!" He lay back grinning at the ceiling, showing his brownish buck teeth, running his dirty fingers over the money.

He'd always guessed she was saving, had wondered where she kept her post office book and how much stood to her credit. All over the house he had searched. In drawers and cupboards. Behind wardrobes. In the linen press. Amongst the books in the drawing room and behind pictures. And all the time, right under his nose . . . in a daft bit of a biscuit tin that he'd helped to keep filled. . . . Last place anybody would have thought of, the cunning owd vixen. Nay!. . . .

Bailey replaced the money with great care. There was no time to count it: that could be done at any time. As far as he could tell there must be all of four hundred pounds there—very likely more. It wasn't going to be easy to pinch, either. He hadn't a doubt she counted it over and over again.

It wanted thinking about.

He piled the biscuits over the money and replaced the tin on the bedside table. He had a bit of bother with that. Had it been set straight with the table edge, or caty-cornered? The little mat it had rested upon had slipped on the polished surface. He straightened it and decided to put the tin back caty-cornered, like she always stood the big Bible and the family album in the drawing room. If it wasn't right he could always say he had knocked the table. It would be a bit of a laugh to watch her. . . .

With enormous care he picked up every single crumb from the counterpane and stretched himself out in the bed. His ankle throbbed but he scarcely noticed it. He no longer de-sired something sweet.

He lay grinning in the frowsy bed, comfortably conscious

of the rain beating on the window, and the vague sounds of people hard at work downstairs, and the money in the tin beside him.

He seldom remembered spending a pleasanter afternoon.

The rain had stopped.

As she squelched through the orchard mud Jenny could hear the thin, hard sound of the child's coughing.

The man stood outside the tent smoking a cigarette. He still wore nothing but the khaki trousers belted about his flat waist. As soon as he saw Jenny he opened the flap of the tent and stood aside, as if he had been waiting for her to come. His white teeth showed in a smile.

"I told you to be off my land by midday," she said valiantly.

It was not what she had meant to say, but the man was really intolerable smiling like that.

"I can't travel with the child yet."

His eyes ran over her. She was conscious of her thinness, of the tired hollow under her eyes, the limp intractability of her hair. She scowled at him.

"You must take the child to the hospital at once."

"If you put people like us in hospitals," he said, "we die."

"Gessin!" the child called, and he answered "Okay" without turning his head. He drew deeply on his shapeless cigarette.

"What does Gessin mean?" Jenny asked.

"That's me—Gethin." He smiled at her again.

"Gessin!" the child repeated, and coughed loudly. Its tufty head appeared over the edge of the blanket. It smiled flickeringly and Jenny smiled back. She had nothing against the child.

"Why does he call you that?" she asked.

The man flicked ash from the cigarette.

"He picked it up. I kind of like him to call me that."

She walked over to the child's bed.

It was wrapped in the new, clean blanket. Its face and hands were clean too, and the fluff of hair had been combed.

A kettle ejected tiny puffs of aromatic steam close by the bed.

Beneath it an oil-stove glowed with a scarlet eye. You couldn't say he hadn't tried. . . . Nevertheless, it was no place for a sick child.

"I could compel you to go to the hospital," she said.

He threw the cigarette down and rubbed it out with his foot.

"But you're not going to. Or you would have set that old doctor on to me. There's glad I am you didn't," he said softly.

She moved a little further away from him. There was a short silence.

"If I let you stay, would you be willing to work?"

"Anything," he assured her eagerly.

"The man who works for me had an accident last night."

"Drunk as a dillop he was," he agreed.

She wondered how he knew, and then remembered. Iris, of course. . . . All that must be stopped.

"It will be hard work," she warned.

"Oh, I am strong. Look you." He flexed the muscles of his arms, smiling with pride. Jenny glanced at him quickly, and away again. She found the hard, brown torso, the rippling muscles, rather overwhelming.

"What is a dillop?" she found herself saying.

"That's just something my mam used to say."

"Are you Welsh?"

He shrugged, grinning.

"Bits of me, perhaps."

"You speak rather like a Welshman."

"Ah, but I can speak Irish, too, and Scotch, and this lingo of yours. And you should hear me talk Devonshire!" He rumbled out a string of soft, burring words, surprising a laugh out of her. The man laughed, too, pleased with the small success. The child's laugh joined in: a hoarse, chirping that was merged into a spasm of coughing.

'It's a long time since I laughed,' Jenny thought.

Then she remembered that it was no laughing matter she

had come about. Her face straightened into the severe mask she judged proper to the occasion.

"There's the mare to be seen to," she told him. "You understand horses—grooming and so on?"

"Yes indeed," he replied with a gravity matching her own.

"And goats. Can you milk?"

"I can."

"And all the late apples to be picked. It's unfortunate about the rain, but it can't be helped. We must save as many as possible."

"Get on to it I will, right away."

"There'll be plenty of other jobs. The water has to be pumped up into the tank and the yard kept clean. Mrs. Bailey is getting old. She can't lift and carry as she used to. And the girl who helps her. . . ." Jenny hesitated; then, pulling courage about her, she plunged on, conscious that she was blushing and despising herself for it. "The girl, Iris, is lazy and incompetent. If you give her the slightest encouragement she will . . . waste your time. I am offering you this job on the understanding that you earn your money honestly. You do understand what I mean?"

"I do." He was standing to attention, she noticed. As if he were a raw recruit and she barking orders at him. Well, let him listen to her orders, then, and obey them. It was something, she thought, to be giving orders instead of taking them.

"I shall pay you the usual rates."

"There's no usual rates for casual labour."

"Well . . . I'll find out about that. I'll give you what is customary."

"I'm not wanting money."

"That's silly," she said impatiently. "Of course you want money. How will you live otherwise?"

"I've got the tent and I shall get my food. When I need money, there's the time to think about getting it."

"How?"

He shrugged, glancing over her head.

She regarded him uncertainly.

"Well, we'll talk about that later. Have you had any dinner?"

"Oh, sure."

"Very well then. You'd better come up to the yard with me." She stood still, however, and he waited expectantly. And presently she said: "What about the child? You can't leave him here alone."

He said nothing but waited for her to continue.

And presently she said in an offhand manner: "It just happens that I've got an empty room. There's a fire there, and I dare say I could manage beds. It would be far better for him than this tent. . . ."

"There's kind," he said softly.

She did not look at him.

"What is the child's name?"

"Clem."

Clem. . . .

The child turned towards her smiling. It wrinkled its absurd nose when it smiled. The tufty head bobbed above the blanket.

"How old is he?"

"Just on two."

"Two! Oughtn't he to talk better than that?"

"No hurry." He gave his quick smile. "Once they start talking no stopping them there is."

"Very well, Gethin, you and Clem had better move in as soon as possible, while the rain keeps off. I want some heavy furniture moved out of the room. I'll see you presently. . . . By the way, I'd rather you wore a coat when you're working near the house."

She would not look at him as she stalked from the tent.

What was he doing with those black eyes of his? Weighing her up? Scorning her for being soft? Laughing at her?

What did it matter!

Let him laugh so long as he worked for his bread. He was nothing but a dark-eyed tinker chap with a slick tongue in his head. What did it matter so long as the child was cared for?

'And who's to care for him?' she thought angrily. 'I've had enough of illness, and I know nothing about children. Why am I cluttering up my life with people, just when I'm free?' . . . And she thought: 'He likes me a bit. He smiled when I held him. I love the way his little nose wrinkles up when he smiles. . . .'

Mrs. Bailey would be furious. Iris was going to be a nuisance—might as well face it, there would be trouble with Iris.

She strode on, half dismayed, half charmed by the thought of the child lying asleep in the bare, firelit room. There was a cot up in one of the attics. A camp bed, too. And there'd be clothes to buy for him. Toys, too. A cuddly bear. She would go into Huffley and buy him a cuddly bear . . . Clem. Clem. . . . What a dear little name.

During the night the rain stopped and a wind sprang up. A straggle of clouds drifted past the window and a young moon dodged flirtatiously between them.

Jenny lay sleepless in the bed. She felt worn out, physically and mentally, by the day's doings. Her body ached from the unaccustomed exercise of scrubbing, lifting, carrying. Her mind felt bruised by the decisions she had made and the doubts and fears that now assailed her.

'I've started something,' she thought bleakly.

She saw it as a snowball such as children push along the ground until it assumes gigantic proportions; breaks away from control on a declivity, gathering size and momentum as it goes.

What had she done? Merely given shelter to two fellow creatures for a few nights in return for help that was urgently needed.

Yet if she had hurled a bomb into the kitchen of Lost Hill she could scarcely have caused more consternation. Bailey scowling from his improvised bed in the corner. Mrs. Bailey's shrill defiance and sullen, thwarting silence. Iris' gratified gigglings and squirmings, her small eyes darting from face to face with the crude enjoyment of her kind; and always coming back to the dark, smiling face that watched as if it were utterly detached from, instead of being the focal point of the whole scene.

It had taken courage to lead him into the kitchen and face them all.

"This is Gethin, Mrs. Bailey. He's going to do Bailey's work for a few days. I've given him Mr. George's room. He'll be needing something to eat, and some milk for his little boy, please."

There had been a brief, breathless pause; then the storm had broken.

"I'll have no gypsy trash at my table," the old woman had shrilled, anger mottling her shrunken cheeks, shaking the glazed brown hands that clutched each other at her waist.

Bailey's buck teeth had showed at that. Iris had squawked and giggled. Gethin had continued to smile.

They had all looked at Jenny, waiting to see what she would do next. They had known—they must have known—how helpless she had felt, how inadequate.

It was to Iris that she had turned.

"Will you please get Gethin his supper, and whatever he needs for the child?"

"She'll do nowt o' t'sort!" The old woman had taken a step forward, fixing Iris with a baleful eye. "Iris, you'll do as I say, or I'll fetch you a crack you'll not forget in a hurry."

Iris had begun to blubber. Bailey's laugh had grated across the kitchen.

Remembering, Jenny marvelled at what she had said then.

"Very well, Mrs. Bailey. If that is your attitude, you'd better take a month's notice."

With the words the whole kitchen had seemed struck into immobility: the old woman bunched defiantly on the hearth-rug; Bailey's half-filled pipe suspended in midair; Iris' blubbered countenance gaping; Gethin's dark smile. . . . It was as if a spell had fallen upon the kitchen, and she the witch who had laid it.

It had been an effort to force her limbs into action. In complete silence she had walked to and from the pantry, piling cheese and bread and beer upon a tray, heating milk, finding plates, knives, cups. They had watched her silently, all four of them, each thinking his own secret thoughts.

She had given the tray to Gethin. Her face had been a flame.

"I must apologise for my servants," she had said stiffly. "I expect you would rather eat in your room."

Incredible. Quite incredible in retrospect.

Yet it had all happened.

Would Mrs. Bailey go? If so, her husband must go with her, and Iris would surely follow.

And all because a tinker fellow had come driving over the moor, bringing a child with a tufty head and a nose that wrinkled ridiculously when it smiled. . . .

'I'm mad,' she thought.

The moon leapt behind a cloud, and the room was drowned in blackness.

Her room was at the far end of the corridor from George's room. She had moved there less than a year after her marriage. It had been George's idea, so Old Missus had not been able to blame her. Had she known how thankfully she had gone?

Here she had gathered her small treasures about her. Her beloved books. Cheap little frames containing faded snapshots of school friends. Two carved wooden horses her father had given her out of the shop when she had been recovering from measles, years and years ago. A small picture of trees and water, all delicate blues and greens and pearly-greys, which her father had said was a genuine Corot. She had tried to recreate a small island of the past in the chill, illimitable ocean of the present. But it had been no good. The room had remained a room in Old Missus' house—and always within sound of George's voice. . . .

Jenny slept and waked and slept again.

Each time she waked she listened for the child; but there were only the night noises and the rushing sound of the wind.

Once she wondered if a distant door shut softly. Once she could have sworn that footsteps padded past her room. "We shall all be murdered in our beds" Mrs. Bailey had promised her. Ridiculous old creature: Gethin was no killer, whatever else he might be.

But what else was he? Thief? Seducer? A fugitive from the law? . . .

She moved restlessly in the bed, thinking again: 'I'm mad, quite mad!' And suddenly she slipped out of bed and turned the key in the door.

It was then that she heard the child cry.

It was a startling, almost a shocking sound in that house so long given over to age and silence. But it was a reassuring sound, it restored Jenny's morale. She unlocked the door and got back into bed.

The child continued to cry. From a fretful, spasmodic wailing the sound swelled to anger and finally settled to a steady, sobbing desperation that disturbed and alarmed.

Well, so the child was crying. That was Gethin's affair. She buried her head in the bedclothes, trying to shut out the appeal.

The crying went on. 'He'll wake up the whole house,' she thought. Not that it mattered.

What on earth was Gethin thinking of? Why didn't he pick the child up, do something for it? If it went on much longer like this it would be ill.

He, not It. . . . Clem. A little boy with a comic, tufty head and a nose that wrinkled when he smiled. . . .

Suddenly Jenny got out of bed, flung into a dressing gown and slippers, and went padding along the passage into George's room.

Gethin was not there.

Her heart missed a beat, then began to hammer.

Her first thought was: Iris. Then she remembered that Iris, indignant and loudly lamenting, had been sent upstairs to sleep in Mrs. Bailey's room.

Then where was he? Had he, after all, abandoned the

child? Had he stolen away in the night and left her to cope with the helpless creature?

She picked the child up and held him in her arms; and almost immediately he stopped crying. How long since Gethin had fed him? Was he hungry, thirsty? Was he in pain? How did one find out these things?

"Drink?" she tried. But the child only gave a great sobbing sigh and shut his eyes.

Jenny walked about the room holding him in her arms. It was warm. The fire burned cosily, making shadows dance in the corners. The smell of the disinfectant she had used in scrubbing the floor still hung on the air, mingling with the aromatic smell that came in small puffs from the kettle.

The child was heavy. With infinite caution she hooked a foot under the rung of a low chair and propelled it near the fire. She laid the little boy across her knees and held him there, keeping perfectly still for fear of rousing him to further tears. He was rather an ugly little boy, she considered, in spite of his blue eyes. A sort of baby clown with that wide mouth and long upper lip, the tufts of hair standing up from the round head. But he had lovely little hands, very thin, with long fingers and well-shaped nails. His feet, too, were long and thin. Probably he would be tall when he grew up.

She hoped he was not verminous. Rather shrinkingly she parted the tufts of his hair. It seemed all right. He probably needed a bath very badly. She dared not bath him in his present state. She wondered if Gethin knew how to give a blanket-bath. Should she offer to do it? She had hated doing it for George, but this small shrimp of a body would hardly repel her. Probably the child had plenty of baths in the usual way. It was only this chill, the scarcity of clothing, the sudden change in the weather that had caught Gethin napping. Certainly his own body looked clean enough. She remembered the brown torso shining with rain, the rippling muscles of arms flexed for her admiration, the white, clean teeth, the upspringing bush of black curls. . . .

Jenny yawned and shifted the chair nearer the fire. Clem

was asleep. His chest rattled when he breathed but his head
felt cooler than it had done before. But how thin he was!
The village children were stocky, often bandy-legged with
weight. Their mothers hung over each other's prams, cluck-
'ng and poking. "Ee, my word, he's bonny! He is an' all,"
'ey would cry; and Jenny would catch a glimpse of a scarlet
pudding under the hood, and wonder what they found to
admire. They would not admire Clem, that was certain.

She sat watching him as he slept, his long, carved lips
pressed together. And suddenly he sighed and joined his
hands, folding the long, frail fingers in an exquisite gesture
of pleading, of surrender, of resignation—which? Whichever
it was, or none of them, her heart suddenly yearned over the
little boy so that she could have wept with pity and love.

"It's all right," she whispered. "I'm here. I'll look after you."

She sat very still. Rain beat on the windows. And then
there was no rain; only the wind swooping round the stout
walls and the clouds moving swiftly past the window, rag-
gedly edged with moonlight.

Away in the distance she heard the short, sharp bark of
a dog fox: one, two, three; one, two, three, four; then three
again . . . that would be over by Shaws Wood. She thought
of him running streamlined through the darkness, dappled
in moonlight and shadow; intent on his love or his hunger
or his need for rest; a shadow on shadows, fluid in the broken
light, free and fearless and beautiful. . . .

It was beautiful to be free as Gethin and the fox were
free; as she had never been free. Clem, too, he would be free.
He would get well again and Gethin would take him away
in the cart behind the rough brown pony, and they would
live their strange, unfettered lives far from her.

She tightened her arms about him, and he stirred and
sighed.

Quietly the door opened and shut.

She did not turn her head for fear of waking Clem, but
she knew that it was Gethin. He came and stood beside her,
darkly handsome in the flickering light, smelling of the out-

doors. From his hooked fingers hung a pair of rabbits, limp in death. He dropped them on the floor. Blood spread darkly on the scrubbed wood.

"For the pot," he said, and his teeth shone briefly. She looked up at him angrily, at a loss for words. "Not off your land," he assured her. "On the moor over yonder." He gestured vaguely.

Jenny realised that he had brought her a present, expected her to be pleased.

"Why did you leave Clem?" she demanded.

"I can't stop in a house for long. I never went out of ear-shot."

"That's not true. He was crying his heart out. He was crying himself sick. I couldn't stand it any longer, so I came in."

"There's kind." He smiled down at her and she dropped her gaze. Was he pleased, or just laughing at her for being officious?

"Why didn't you come back, if you could hear him crying?"

"I did. I tried the door." He kicked a coal into position and a flame shot up. "Fastened against me it was."

"Nonsense. I came up last and it wasn't locked then. People don't lock their doors in these parts."

"It was not locked when I went out. But when I came back it was locked, and bolted, too. That old woman it was. She does not like me." He laughed softly. He unwound the scarlet neckcloth and threw it into the hearth to dry. He lifted his boots for her inspection. "I am the wrong sort for a house. Making a great old mess I am, all over the place."

"If the door was bolted, how did you get in?" she said sharply.

"The window in the hall."

"You broke it?"

"I broke it and put my hand inside. Easy it was."

It was easy. Such things were easy to men like Gethin. More easy than knocking, fetching somebody downstairs to open the door for him, as other men would have done, as would have been his right in the circumstances. He would

take the easy rather than the lawful way, always. Getting
into a house, finding food for the pot, shelter for the child. . . .
He cared nothing for law and order. He was anti-social, a
rogue and a vagabond. And he was here, in her house; alone
with her in this quiet, firelit room at dead of night; nobody
else in the house but an old woman, a crippled man and a
silly girl. . . .

'I'm mad,' she thought once again. 'I must get rid of him.
In the morning he must go.'

It was the first thing she thought of when she woke to a
world of leaping light and shadow, sudden sun and sharp,
rattling bursts of rain. Autumn in a mood of April nonsense
that was more disquieting than any spring.

'He must go today,' she thought, rising with determination.

In the kitchen the atmosphere was thunderous.

Iris sulked from her enforced sojourn in Mrs. Bailey's bed.
Bailey complained of his ankle. Mrs. Bailey cooked and clattered in an ominous silence, her nose nutcrackered down over
her chin and her mouth sucked in.

When Gethin sauntered into the kitchen and flashed his
brief white smile at them they all sat speechless, staring furtively as he proceeded calmly to break eggs, fry bacon and
cut enormous hunks off the homemade, crusty loaf. He passed
his cup to Mrs. Bailey, who ignored it. After waiting politely
for a while, he poured tea for himself, spooning sugar with
so lavish a hand that when he had emptied the cup and
passed it again, Mrs. Bailey attended to it herself.

"A bit better today," he said cheerfully.

Nobody answered. Knives and forks clattered on plates,
tea was sucked noisily from saucers, arms stretched for food,
but nobody spoke. The two cats yelled for food. Bacon rinds
were thrown and Mrs. Bailey bent to give them a saucer of
milk. Gethin made a soft sound with his lips and they left
the milk and went to him, rubbing against his legs with
delight.

As soon as the food was finished Bailey dragged his ankle back to the truckle bed in the corner. He lay down and groaned a bit, to indicate that he was not well enough to do anything. He felt for his pipe, wondering how Em would take it if he had a nice smoke.

"Beds," Mrs. Bailey said briefly, and Iris flounced out of the kitchen, her underlip well out.

Mrs. Bailey began to clear the table. Gethin went on eating. He had started much later than the others. Seeing that the bread was about to be taken away he took two more slices, piling them on the edge of his plate. He lifted plate and cup and saucer so that Mrs. Bailey could whisk the cloth from under them.

When he had finished eating he carried the crockery into the scullery and smiled at the scowling old woman. "Thanks for my breakfast," he said. He chirped encouragingly at the canary and went whistling out to the stables where, presently, he could be heard talking to Posy in his singsong voice.

Mrs. Bailey banged out of the kitchen and stumped upstairs.

Jenny was giving Clem a blanket bath. She looked up briefly, said: "Shut the door, please," and went on with her job.

Mrs. Bailey stood like a miniature figure of doom, brown claws gripping each other at her waist. Her apron, as always, was spotless: she never seemed to collect dirt like other people. Her thin grey hair was strained tightly back from a forehead furrowed and brown as a ploughed field. Her small, blue eyes were sharp as gimlets.

"I'm none 'aving yon chap in my kitchen," she announced.

"So you said last night," Jenny replied.

"He were in to his breakfast, eatin' enough for three, sugar goin' in t'cup like I dunno what. I'm not 'aving it, and so I tell you."

Jenny straightened up and dried her hands on a towel.

"Very well, Mrs. Bailey, you know what to do." She began tidying the room, piling bowls and soap, cups and spoons on a tray, raking out the bars of the fire and adding more coal, adjusting the lamp's wick so that the kettle puffed its steam in less powerful jets. The child lay still and straight in the cot, his round, bright eyes staring solemnly at first one woman and then the other.

The old woman stood her ground doggedly, but she felt at a loss. She had never known Mrs. George like this before. Something had happened to her these last few days and she did not know how to deal with her. The sight of Mester's room bare and scrubbed was an affront. . . . They'd got the cot down from the attic, and the camp bed, too. They must have done it between them: Mrs. George could never have managed alone. She was letting yon chap have the run of the house. She was out of her mind—that was it, she was out of her mind! . . . They'd see what Doctor had to say to it all. He should hear all about it. Yon chap creeping about the house at all hours, going outdoors at some god-forsaken hour of the night. . . . She'd nipped down and bolted the door against him, but it hadn't been any use. Her heart had felt as if it would choke her as she swept up the broken glass in the hall this morning. . . . And all those good clothes of Mester's lying out in the shed, and all the bits of things he'd set such store by. . . .

"Owd Missus would turn in her grave," she tried bleakly; and was astounded to hear Jenny laugh.

"Oh, do let the poor soul lie quiet for once, Mrs. Bailey! You're always keeping her on the move."

Mrs. Bailey gasped, clutched her hands tighter. This was blasphemy. . . .

"A saint, if ever there was one!" she croaked.

Jenny propped the child higher on the pillow, fluffed up the newly-brushed tufts of hair with a proprietorial gesture and gave him a silver bracelet to play with. He turned it round and round in his long thin fingers, smiling with a show of minute, pearly teeth.

"I reckon you mun be daft tekkin' 'em in this road. Mucky tramps! Child might 'ave 'ad the small-pock!"

"He might," Jenny agreed, "but he hadn't. It was only a chill that went to his chest, and he's much better already. And he's quite clean, really, Mrs. Bailey. They both are."

"How long are you reckonin' to keep 'em?"

"How long will it be before Bailey gets better?"

Deadlock. . . .

Jenny went on tidying the room. Mrs. Bailey stood and glared, pushing her lips in and out, in and out.

"What do *you* know about bairns!" she threw out scornfully.

"Nothing," Jenny admitted, "except that they have to be kept clean on the outside and fed on the inside." She gave the old woman a quick, shy smile. "You'll have to help me, Mrs. Bailey."

The old woman recoiled.

"Nay, I'll 'ave nowt to do wi' it!"

The smile faded. Jenny turned her back.

"In that case, you'd better get on with your work."

Mrs. Bailey went out of the room. Slowly, as if the use were going out of her legs, she climbed the top flight of stairs and shut herself into her own room, turning the key in the lock.

Iris had not made the bed as she liked it, and there was face powder spilt on the floor; but she had no time for more than an exasperated grunt for such annoyances. With trembling hands she seized the biscuit tin and emptied the contents on to the bed. She began to count the money slowly and carefully, whispering to herself as her glazed, shaking fingers flickered among the notes.

She did not need to count them. She knew very well how much money was in the tin. She knew there was not enough— not yet. Another couple of years, maybe or even one year. . . . But it did her good to count the money. It restored her self-sufficiency, halted the creeping doubts, put courage into her.

Afterwards, she sat on the edge of the bed hugging the tin in her arms.

She did not know what to do with the money, that was the trouble.

With Bailey bedded down in the kitchen and that chap mailicking all over the place it wasn't safe to let Iris sleep alone. On the other hand, it wasn't safe to leave the biscuit tin anywhere near Iris. Bailey didn't like biscuits; he'd never dream of touching the tin. But Iris liked them only too well, she'd always have her fingers in the tin.

The money must be hidden away. But where? . . . Beneath her spare underclothing in the drawer? Thrust into the foot of a black woollen stocking? In the box where rested the "best" hat she never dreamed of wearing?

An idea struck her, and she laughed suddenly and hoarsely. Her eyes disappeared and her toothless jaws gaped to emit the sharp, unlovely sound.

Her burying clothes, of course! The long white nightgown of heavy linen tucked and frilled, with pearl buttons at neck and wristbands, given to her long ago by Owd Missus. It had never been worn. Owd Missus had brought it with her when she came to Lost Hill as a bride, but she had soon become stout, and it had lain in her drawer for years until one day, after a more than usually bitter wrangle, she had tossed the nightgown to Mrs. Bailey saying: "Here, hap yourself in that when they put you under six foot of sod—and the sooner the better!"

The nightgown was the greatest treasure Mrs. Bailey had ever possessed. She had fashioned a nightcap to match it, with satin ribbons to tie under the chin. Once every year she took the nightgown and cap out of their tissue paper, washed them with loving care, ironed each tuck and fold and frill with precision, hung them before the fire, turning them about and about until there was no possible doubt of their being aired, and laid them away once more in the cardboard box.

Iris would never touch her burying clothes; no money would induce her to. She hated to see them blowing on the line, airing before the kitchen fire. "I don't know how you *can!*" she would cry, shrinking away as she passed them. "Heathenish, I call it!"

So much the better, Mrs. Bailey thought, tucking the money into voluminous folds of linen, and replacing the cardboard box on its shelf.

She put the biscuits back in the tin and stood it on the table again. She hurried downstairs to her work. She was all behind, and dinner would be upon her before she could rightly turn around. . . .

She found her husband lying on his back, his pipe well alight, reading an old copy of the *News of The World.*

"You can get taters peeled," she snapped; but he only grinned and turned a page.

"They're done. Yon chap set to an' done 'em."

Mrs. Bailey pounced into the scullery.

It was true. A large panful of peeled potatoes stood on the copper. She saw too that the log box was filled with logs and coal had been brought in. She sucked in her lips and said nothing; but when Iris came sauntering in from the yard, she sharply bade her pump water up into the cistern.

"It's done," Iris grinned. "Gethin done it."

Mrs Bailey glared at her.

"It's your job to peel taters an' fetch logs in."

The girl preened herself complacently.

"Gethin says cartin' logs an' coal is too heavy for me." She threw a sly glance at Bailey's prostrate form. "He says it's a downright shame I've bin made to do it all these years."

Bailey turned another page, outwardly indifferent but inwardly perturbed. The girl was a slut. She lied as easily as she breathed. Her promises were pie-crust. Her laugh could be cruel as hell to a chap old enough to be her father. But her skin was white and warm, she was soft and warm and heavy to hold, full of fight and fire. He never knew when he had her; yet the thought of losing her to another chap was gall and bitterness.

He wondered if he would do better to pack up this invalid

lark and try to get his leg working again. He waggled his foot cautiously. Pain shot up into his thigh, scaring him. He really did feel pretty queer. Suppose something really serious was wrong with him? He didn't want Doctor yanking him off into the hospital and messing him about. He'd have to mind his P's and Q's with Doctor. With Em, too. Might as well keep on the right side of Em, or he'd never get a minute's peace.

Putting away his pipe he heaved into a sitting position.

"I'll shine t'brass if you've a mind," he offered. He winked at Iris, but she was staring through the window into the yard.

"Gethin's tekken a ladder to t'orchard," she announced. "He's goin' to mek a start on t'apples."

"An' you can mek a start on t'scullery floor," Mrs. Bailey snapped. "Unless Gethin's done that for you, an' all! . . . Happen we'll all be able to set back an' twiddle us thumbs, now Gethin's here!"

CHAPTER FIVE

ALL the way down from London Tod had been reminding himself not to expect too much. But as the train ran into the cutting he felt the old familiar rising of the spirits, the thrusting excitement that all his life he had felt on nearing his home.

First the black stink that was Huffley station. Then old Sanderson's dour grin and horny handshake. Then the old chap who had been collecting tickets for as long as he could remember, peering over his glasses, giving him a nonchalant "Now then!" And outside in the station yard, the shining trap with the mare whinnying between the shafts, and Sanderson grudgingly giving up the reins, warning to keep a hold on her while they got off them blasted tramlines. . . . The filthy streets crowded between factories and black, roaring mills. The prim, ugly suburbs. The long, steep climb. And at last, and so suddenly that it took your breath away, even though you had been waiting for it, the moor, pricking away into eternity under a great blowing canopy of sky. . . .

Coming home from school, from holidays with friends, from Oxford, on leave from the Army, the old magic had never failed to work. Old Sanderson had become middle-aged and grim; the old ticket collector had whitened and shrunk; the town had sprawled ever further up the moor road. But out on the moor itself nothing had ever changed. The Tarn beneath its clump of wind-bitten trees; the bell of Staving church coming faintly across the valley; scattered farms in a coloured patchwork of fields; huddled sheep under stone walls shattering the silence with sudden lamentations; the spank of the mare's hoofs and the lovely smell of horseflesh and well-polished harness. . . . Round by the orchard of Lost Hill, a sudden steep climb and a wind that blasted the breath out of you, and then the long, gradual drop to the village. The Post Office, with Mrs. Emmett waving from the window; the group of gossiping women outside the general store; the tiny Mission Hall; the row of slate-roofed cottages and the dark, creeper-hung schoolhouse with droning voices issuing from open windows across the asphalt playground marked out with lines and circles of chalk; the grey stone pub, its sign creaking in the wind. The sudden swing to the right past the wood, past Great Meadow, past the ten acres of untameable land they had christened Heartbreak, and then left, and down into the wide, welcoming gates of Shaws.

Home. . . .

Tod lit a cigarette, lifted his suitcase down from the rack and fidgeted with the new, expensive hat he had felt the occasion called for, and which he would probably never wear after today. He inhaled and blew out smoke in a long, slow stream.

No, he must not expect too much. He must be prepared for changes. Eight years was a long time. Sanderson would be eight years older. The ticket collector would be dead or retired, surely. Probably a different mare would be between the shafts. Sanderson might even have brought the car to meet him, though he hoped not: nobody at Shaws thought much of cars. You had to have the things, but they were regarded very properly as strictly utilitarian, having no relation to the amenities of life.

The house would seem different without Dad—how different, Tod did not care to contemplate. And dear old Cassie, who had looked after them for so long — she had gone, too. . . . The buildings would be shabby after eight years of war and this incredible postwar muddle. Paint would be needed everywhere, stock would be low, the farm hands too few. He was prepared for a general air of dilapidation; keyed up with longing to get down to the task that awaited him of bringing Shaws back to its former prosperity. Sanderson was good, but he couldn't work miracles. Nobody could. . . .

The train stopped with a jerk. Somebody said: "Signal's against us." And even that was good to hear. The signal always had been against them just here, as long as he could remember. His lips pursed in a contented whistling as he gazed out over the sooty sea of roofs above which, black and formidable, the mills rose like rocks.

None of Tod's fellow passengers could have guessed at the impatience that possessed him. He sat motionless; a square, stocky figure of average height with reddish hair beginning to thin back on a broad forehead; a long mouth and eyes so deeply set that laughter caused them to disappear altogether. He wore his clothes well, as so many Yorkshiremen do—in uniform he had looked really imposing—but he was no dandy. A square, solid, dependable sort of chap he looked, and such he was; taking life as it came, dealing with it honestly and without pretensions; deeply emotional but completely controlled.

Another jerk, and they were running into the station. And there was Sanderson standing in his hunched fashion, hands deep in pockets and legs straddled; pretending, the old fool, that he wasn't moved at seeing Tod home: home for the last time, he hoped; no longer schoolboy, undergraduate, dolled-up soldier, but what Sanderson and the farm and the whole of Backshaws had needed these five long years—Mester. . . .

They shook hands and grunted shyly at each other. Tod's luggage was collected and piled on a truck. His ticket was snatched disdainfully by a trousered female with scarlet nails. The mare turned her head and danced a little. Tod ran his hands over her. She was new; young and skittish, black with a white blaze and powerful quarters. He liked the look of her.

"Keep her in while we're off them blasted tramlines," Sanderson said, and Tod's laugh was filled with content.

The mills and the muddle of grimy dwellings. The shops and the town hall, the hospital, the war memorial, the new secondary school. The soot-ridden suburban gardens and the long, steep climb. The moor. . . .

Tod drew a deep breath, turned and grinned at the man beside him.

"Well, how's everything?"

Sanderson began to fill his pipe.

"Might be worse. Drought's held things up, of course."

Tod let the mare walk.

"Where's Trixie?"

"Trixie's dead. Last lot of pups finished her. I've kept the best bitch for you."

"Poor old Trix. . . ." Tod knew a prick of conscience as he remembered that eager little brown body hurling itself after the trap when he had driven away after his last leave. He had pulled up while Sanderson had put her on a lead and hauled her back; he had heard her shrill, hysterical protest long after she was out of sight. Poor little Trix. Well, there'd be no more going away now. Trixie's daughter would have better luck.

"How many hands have we now?"

"Old Carter's still with us, and Jim Pratt. Bazley was killed, you remember—Tobruk. And there's a couple of lads called Wright—old Tommy Wright's grandsons from Huffam. Young Tom's going on eighteen and not likely to be called up on account of his sight. I reckon he'll stop with us, and he's a worker. But his brother, young Albert, he's about as much use as my backside! Sooner he's called up, better it'll suit me. The Jerries went back last year, an' I can't say I cried. They knew their job, mind, and one of 'em wasn't a bad sort of lad, but the other was a proper caution. Hated our guts he did, and made no secret of it. Worked like a machine—never had to tell him owt twice!—and you could fair hear him spit the minute your back was turned! . . . But the other one, young Johan, he wasn't a bad sort of lad. A right good-looking sort of chap, an' civil with it. But of course we had trouble with the girls. . . . You'd think our girls would have more self-respect, wouldn't you? But they wouldn't let him alone, young Johan. . . . We'd a land girl at the time, Pam her name was. A very decent sort of wench, too, and a beggar for work. One day she found Eliza Good-acre's eldest setting on the water trough, and she asks her what she wants, and this girl says she's waiting for Johan, an' Pam ups an' ducks her in t'water. You never saw such a sight! Screaming blue murder she was, and water running off her head and streaking the paint on her face! 'I'll fetch me Ma to yer!' she yells. And Pam says, 'Aye, you fetch your ma—she's another as could do with a ducking.'"

Sanderson drew noisily on his pipe, chuckling reminiscently. "A proper do, that were," he said. "But do you think it cured them girls? Not on your life! You'd think they'd have more self-respect, wouldn't you?"

Self-respect. . . . Tod thought of Trudi and Else, and that little dark girl with the dimples and the red skirt. They hadn't had any self-respect either, he supposed. But how sweet they had seemed, and how grateful he had felt for their brief affections.

Old Sanderson would say that it was different for German girls; but of course it was exactly the same. And he remembered the one who called herself Gloria, just after he had joined up, and that Wren officer who had been so devilishly expensive, and had nearly got him court-martialled, and the little gypsy number he had met up in the Welsh mountain, when he was at the Convalescent Camp, back in forty-five.... It wasn't a question of whether you were English or German or Italian. It was just something to do with the war; and when the war was over, all that was over, too. You had never really wanted any of it to happen. All you had wanted was the farm, and Dad, and the moor, and the sort of life your folks had always lived.

But the war had come and you'd had to do something about it. And then Dad had died, and then there had been all that business with your gammy leg. . . .

Well, and so that was over, too. All of it. Eight years bitten clean out of your life, and nothing to show for it except a shooting pain now and again when the wind got round to the east. . . .

"Fred Emmett at the Post Office, he died last year," Sanderson was saying. "And old Mrs. Rowland, of course, you know she went three years back. Now he's gone, an' all."

"Not George Rowland!" Tod exclaimed. "Good lord, he wasn't much older than me!"

"Ah, he'd got one of them duodenals, had George. On top of the ten plagues, if you could believe all he said. The Rowland men allus died off young."

"Is Lost Hill empty, then?"

"Anything but, by what I'm told." Sanderson banged his pockets, searching for matches.

"Go on, you old gossip—give!" Tod grinned.

"Well, George married, you'll think on, 1940 or thereabouts it was. Some little body he brought home from London parts; just a bairn she looked to me. I felt right down sorry for her, stuck up there in yon house with nobody but George and his ma. And she didn't seem to mek any friends, either. Stuck-up they called her, but I don't reckon she's stuck-up, only sort of shy. Nothing much to look at, mind. When she first came she were a bonny little thing enough, but George and his ma soon put paid to that. Allus on her own she seemed to be, stalking about the moor in her old slacks an' her hair blowing all over t'place. First go off George got her a very nice grey from over Staving way. Then we heard as he'd sold it, an' it was shank's mare after that. I don't know, it were a queer setup altogether."

"I think I saw her once, on leave, but I didn't notice her particularly." Tod spoke absent-mindedly. His eyes dwelt fondly on the incomparable sweep of the moor lifting like a wave to a sky of milky blue and tenderest green, on which a moon was already palely etched. No place in all the world, he thought, was quite so lovely as this place. . . .

"Well, so then George ups and dies. I went to t'funeral, of course. Everybody went. It were a queer do, though. Widow was the only one as didn't wear black! No hat, neether. And nobody asked back to the house. . . . Rummest funeral I ever was at. She just stood there with her hands in her pockets, staring away over folks' heads an' looking sort of lost. As if she'd got mixed up in this business by accident an' she didn't know what to do about it."

"How long ago was this?"

"Two or three months, happen. End o' June, or just into July, I don't dare rightly remember."

"And she's keeping the place on?"

"Seems like it. Nobody seems to know what's going on up there, but there's queer stories."

"What sort of stories?"

"Well, it seems she's tekken up with some tinker chap. Got him living in the house with her, if you can believe what they say."

"You can't," Tod said impatiently. Really, Sanderson was getting a bit of an old woman. He suddenly wanted above all things to be alone. "When we get to the rise," he said, "I'm going to walk the rest."

"Aye, you allus liked walking the last mile or two. And your dad used to walk to meet you—remember?"

As if he could forget! . . .

He and Dad had always been closer than most fathers and sons. Partly, he supposed, because he had lost his mother so young, and Cassie had been the only woman in his life. But there had been more to it than that. They had been alike physically and mentally; two square, stocky figures striding together about the farm lands, leaning together over gates, riding side by side up the steep curve of the moor road, drinking their ale in the village pub with the same gesture of arm and toss of head. . . . Tod had known it, been proud of it. Even when they had knelt in the square family pew in Huffam church, their identical stiff, rather uncompromising attitudes of devotion had given rise to a certain pawky humour in the pews behind. "If Shaws is praying for rain," it had been said, "you might as well set to and pray for it yersens, whether you want it or not, for it's odds on that the Almighty's goin' to give it to 'em."

He had been with the Wren officer when he had opened

Sanderson's letter. "Excuse me, won't you?" he had said, running his thumb along the flap. "This is from home, and I haven't had a minute all day." And she had said: "Get me another drink before you start, my sweet. I know these home letters!" So he had bought two more drinks; and before they had arrived he had read the letter.... He remembered staring at the Wren. Her big scarlet mouth was opening and shutting, and there were a lot of large white teeth. One had a gold filling. . . .

"My Dad's dead," he had told her; and he had heard his own voice sounding surprised. She had given a silly sort of laugh. "Darling, how frightful for you!" And they had just sat staring at each other, and he hadn't felt a thing. And she had said: "I suppose this means you won't want to dance now?" And he had replied: "Why should it?" So they had danced and had a lot more drinks, and afterwards they had gone on somewhere else with lots of other people: because what did it matter what you did or where you were if Dad was dead? . . .

He had not been home since the funeral. He knew Sanderson was sore about that.

Five years. It was a long time, there would be much to relearn, a lot to catch up with. He was lucky to have Sanderson. The farm was Sanderson's life. It was more to him than the wife or child he had never had; more than Miss Ellen, the waspish little spinster sister who kept house for him in the slate-roofed lodge at the gates. . . .

Tod sighed and stretched, feeling for his cigarettes.

"Have any trouble with the war agriculture wallahs?"

Sanderson drew on his pipe with a loud sizzling sound.

"Aye," he said; and his expression was that of one who rolls a rare old brandy round his tongue. "Chap comes honking up in a bloody great car like a charry-bang. Bouncy little squirt with horn-rims and a green feather sticking up in his hat, and a plum in his gob. He says, 'Quite a well-run place you've got here,' he says. 'Thanks, I'm sure!' I says, 'an' I stares over the top of his head, which wasn't difficult, for he nubbut came up to me watch chain. 'But what are we goin' to do about those ten acres up there?' he says — meaning Heartbreak. 'What we've allus done,' I says. 'Let 'em be.' 'Nay,' he says, 'we can't do that. Every inch of land must be cultivated in these times. I'm afraid we've got to get crackin' on that hill, Mester Sanderson.'

"I says to him, 'Look,' I says, 'man and boy I've worked on this farm ever since I left school, an' that weren't yesterday. I reckon I've forgot more about farming that you'll ever know. And I tell you this: yon hill is ab-so-bloody-lutely un-re-claimable ground.' I says it slow an' loud, just like that, so's he should understand. And he gets red in t'neck and starts to stutter an' spit. 'No ground is unreclaimable,' he says. 'Heartbreak is,' I says. 'Every Shaw that's owned it has tekken a crack at it one time or another—and you see the result! There's rocks in Heartbreak,' I says, 'like Westminster Abbey.' 'Rocks can be shifted,' he says. 'Not these rocks,' I says.

"Well, he fumes and he argues, and he tells me I'm acting obstructive. That," Sanderson assured Tod, "was the very word he used. 'Your attitude is obstructive, Mester Sanderson,' he says. 'I shall have to report this.'

"'Go ahead,' I tells him, 'report it. I'd like to sit back on mer arse an' watch some o' you chaps having an argument with Heartbreak. I could do with a good laugh!' And off he goes in his charry-bang, glaring like Batley's bull!"

Tod grinned sympathetically.

"Hear any more of it?"

"Not a peep!" Sanderson snorted contemptuously. "Little pipsqueak like yon! . . . Everybody in the county knows how Shaws is run, if I do say it meself." His glance slid sideways; affectionate, a little apologetic. "All the same, I'm right glad to see you home, Mester."

The rain came in a fine drizzle. It felt good on his face. He thought he knew how the moor must feel after long drought.

He was glad he had walked, even though he must keep remembering how Dad had always come to meet him with the dogs. The dogs had always reached him a long way first. They had come streaking down the road at his whistle: Trixie tying herself into sentimental knots at his feet, Bluff and Searcher tearing back and forth between them till they met. Then all five of them together, going home.

Nobody left now but himself. . . .

Well, forget it. People died, dogs died. Life went on. He would make a life for himself. There would be work, plenty of it. A few friends. A day's hunting or shooting now and then. Very likely they'd make him a J.P. in time. Shaws had always sat on the Bench. . . . He would become part of the life of the place. Probably he would marry sooner or later. He must get sons for Shaws. He had a vague vision of somebody tall and fair waving to him from the doorway. Somebody suitable, of decent farming stock, with a bit of money and an amiable disposition. He wasn't really very interested in her. . . .

Wheels were coming up behind him and he drew aside. As the trap passed he looked up, half smiling, expecting a familiar face.

A man and a girl were in the trap. The man touched his whip to his black curls in acknowledgement, and Tod was aware of a swift appraisal, the flash of white teeth. The girl did not glance down. She was thin and pale as a flower. Her long dark hair blew untidily about her face and she sat hunched against the rain, hands thrust deep into the pockets of a man's raincoat.

Then Tod recognised old Posy. Good lord—old Posy, still going strong!

So that was George's widow, and it was true, what they were saying! The man looked the gypsy type all right.

It was true—some of it, at least. . . .

Nothing to do with anybody else, of course. Yet a sort of discomfort stirred in him.

He had never liked George, even when they were boys. There had always been something warped and unpleasant about him, even at his best. At his worst he had been a fiend. Once he had seen him cut the legs off a live frog. . . .

He couldn't remember the old man, but George's mother had been a tartar. Many a time his ear had sung beneath the weight of her hand.

Nevertheless, there had been Rowlands at Lost Hill for a hundred and fifty years. The house was part of the safe, ordered background of his childhood, and the thought of a tinker chap lording it over the good barns, the orchard and the fields was distasteful to him. The girl must be a queer type. . . .

He turned his collar up against the rain and stepped out more smartly.

As he passed Lost Hill he noticed a tent in the orchard field, an upturned cart and a rough brown pony tethered to a stake. A girl's laugh issued from the tent, coarse and shrill, and a moment later he saw her. She came running from the tent screeching foolishly, obviously inviting pursuit: a fat, ginger-headed wench with bitch written all over her. She stared boldly at Tod, smoothing her hands up her thick, white arms. Then she ran back into the tent and he heard her laughing again.

'I don't need to bother about any of them,' Tod thought thankfully.

He sloughed Lost Hill off his shoulders and began to climb. The rain stopped and a gleam of watery sun lit the moor.

He would stop in the village and have a word with Mrs. Emmett at the Post Office. She would want to talk about Fred. And about Dad, of course; he couldn't get out of it. He didn't really want to get out of it. They were his people, these dour, blunt, long-lipped Yorkshire folk. He had been away from them too long.

On the crown of Heartbreak the doctor shut off his engine. His eyes narrowed at the advancing figure. That was Tod all right: so like his father that it gave you quite a turn!

"Hullo, there!" he called, and was pleased when Tod's

pace quickened. A decent lad. He was glad he was home again.

"Not the same old Morris!" Tod shouted, yards away. "Don't tell me she still ticks over!"

"She'll tick me out," the doctor said. "Glad to have ye back, Tod. The whole of Backshaws is glad of it."

"Thanks, Doc, It's good to see you again. How's every-thing?"

"You'll soon find out. . . . Sometimes I'm glad I'm not young any more; haven't got to cope with the mess much longer. . . . You'll miss your father, Tod. Cassie, too. I wish you still had Cassie, but it was lonely for her, ye see, after your dad went. Shaws is in better heart than most of the farms, thanks to Sanderson. You've got a good man there, Tod."

"I know it."

"How's the leg?"

"So-so. Doesn't like the east wind overmuch. But I'm not grumbling. Might have been no leg at all."

"Aye, you were lucky. Or so we heard."

Tod's mouth tightened at the implied criticism.

"There didn't seem much point in coming home for a few weeks' leave now and then, and no Dad. . . . Sanderson knew more about things than I did, anyway."

"Aye, well, ye're back now. Ye'll find a lot of changes."

"I've seen one already." Tod gestured with his head.

"Ye mean Lost Hill?" Doctor Waller pushed out his lips. "You don't want to make more of it than there is. Bailey—you remember old Bailey, of course?—he came home drunk from market, as usual, and slipped on the stairs. Twisted his ankle. As a matter of fact, he's not in very good shape, but the old scoundrel's making the most of it. This chap came along just when Mrs. George was needing a man's help about the place. She'd got nobody but Mrs. Bailey, who's getting on, and that slut of a girl, Iris."

"Is that the well-developed one with the ginger head?"

"That's her. Take my tip and keep clear of that one. She's

a man-eater. I gave her a lift the other day—phew! Never again!"

"I believe you. . . . Not much point in taking this chap into the house though, was there? Sanderson said something about a child, too."

"Aye. That's what did it, if you ask me. The child was sick, lying out there in the tent, and we had some pretty bad weather when the drought broke. Mrs. George tried to make him take it to the hospital, but of course he wouldn't. You can't blame him. That sort don't take kindly to hospitals. They're pretty smart at doctoring themselves, anyroad. Still, there it was, it wasn't in human nature to leave the child lying out in a damp tent; and she needed help badly. . . . It's a rare titbit for the village, of course, but I don't believe there's anything to it. And Bailey ought to be up and about soon, unless there's something I haven't spotted yet."

"They passed me in the trap a while back. At least, I suppose it was her. Thin and dark and blown all over the place. And a man's raincoat, three sizes too large."

"That's Jenny. She's not what you'd call clothes-conscious. A strange little thing—but who wouldn't be strange, after seven years of George and his mother! I'd take it kindly if you'd be a bit neighbourly there, Tod. There aren't so many young folks in these parts, and none of her sort. After all, you and George were lads together."

Tod gave a noncommittal grunt and changed the subject. Soon afterwards the Morris emitted a series of little screams and a nerve-shattering roar and went exploding away down the hill.

Tod walked on. He met nobody else, and soon he was past Heartbreak and there, in a cup of the moor below him, was Shaws. Shaws, sprawling deep in its hollow, grey arms flung wide. The lawn, grey-green striped with silver, edged with scarlet and blue. The barns and the sober gold of haystacks. Minute white specks of geese parading downhill to the pond under the elms. A line of red Ayrshires dribbling along the side of a meadow, heads down to the rich pasture. The faint *phut-phut* of an unseen tractor. And climbing up the steep curve behind the house, the age-old pattern of two horses, a man and a plough, followed by a scatter of gulls.

There was a new housekeeper; a pale, rather sly-looking woman who called herself Mrs. Scobie, though she wore no wedding ring. Her greeting was a damp handshake from which Tod's soul recoiled. A flat, narrow woman with limp hair and long, pointed feet that splayed out sideways. She had an odd way of looking at him; furtive invitation judiciously blended with the scared threat of virginal retreat that struck him as pathetic in a woman of her age and type.

She was not a very good cook, if his first meal was anything to go by, but at least she was not a gossip. She set Tod's food before him with a nervous thump and skittered from the room as if devilish intentions were written all over his face.

Sanderson assured him he was lucky to get anybody.

"I wish to goodness dear old Cassie had stayed," Tod said moodily. "It gave me a bad turn when I got her letter. Why did she go, anyway? Surely she wasn't scared of air raids? You didn't get much trouble around here, did you?"

"Nay, it weren't air raids. . . . Cassie were scared of nowt on this earth but of losing your dad. . . . Nay, where were your eyes, Tod!"

"*Cassie!* . . . Good lord!"

"Aye. An' he might have done worse. But he never rightly got over your ma. . . . I reckon atom bombs wouldn't have got Cassie away from Shaws while ever your dad were alive; but when he died she packed her box and went to her sister in Aberdeen."

Cassie and Dad. . . . Good lord!

Sprawling before the fire with a whisky and soda, Tod suddenly felt depressed. It was very quiet. The fire crackled and Trixie's daughter snored lightly in her sleep. Rain tapped tentatively at the windows and now and then wind drummed in the wide chimney. But these small sounds only intensified the enormous silence that smothered the ancient house.

He supposed he ought to go to bed. Mrs. Scobie had gone long ago, throwing him a guarded good night from the doorway; locking herself no doubt into her room, with a chair rammed under the door knob. Definitely he did not care for Mrs. Scobie.

He stirred restlessly, poured himself another drink. Stooping, he scooped Trixie's daughter on to his knees and stroked her soft ears. "We must get fond of each other," he told her. "There's nobody else for either of us." She ducked her head and blinked agreeably. A nice little scrap. Not Trixie, of course, but someone to run at your heels, dance on the doorstep at your return. "Wendy, old girl," he murmured. He loathed the name, but Miss Ellen had christened her after a favourite niece and the damage was done.

He sat there in the silence, stroking the dog's ears, trying to get his bearings.

He had been prepared for changes, but not for the changes he had found. He had expected dilapidation, decay, an urgent necessity for making-do, inadequate staff and depleted stock. He had found them all, if hardly to the extent he had visualised. But it was the change in himself, unsuspected before, that astonished him. That he should be oppressed by the loneliness, made restless by the silence, daunted by the responsibility he had inherited—these were the feelings that had revealed themselves when Sanderson had gone stumping away for the night and Tod had turned back into the empty house.

If only Dad were here. . . .

He had always thought Dad a contented sort of chap, wrapped up in farm and son, wanting no other life. He had always believed Cassie to be as happy as she sounded, singing about her work.

Now it was revealed that neither Dad nor Cassie had been particularly happy, and he found the disclosure disturbing. Ridiculously, he felt as he had felt when he first went away to school and found himself alone in an alien and bewildering world.

His hand moved towards the whisky bottle and then withdrew. That wasn't the way. . . .

"Let's go to bed," he said aloud, and Wendy leapt from his knee, stretching and yawning.

He let her out of the front door and she disappeared into the night.

He stood in the porch waiting. It was very dark; black shapes of trees were barely discernible against the sky, but the sound of them moving in the wind, the wet smell of them was all about him. He could smell the geraniums, too, and the newly mown lawn, and the acrid aftermath of a bonfire quenched by rain.

A car ran along the top of the road past Heartbreak, its lights fanning out before it. As it swerved for the sharp decline into Backshaws, he heard the driver change gears. The crown of Heartbreak was suddenly bright as day, then lost again in darkness deeper than before.

This was home; he was here, and alone. This was life, his life, and only he could deal with it. This aloneness, this restlessness, this vague dissatisfaction must be drawn into himself, absorbed, transmuted into something worthwhile. What was good in it must be kept and fostered. What was bad must be destroyed. . . .

The dog ran past him into the house. A clock chimed eleven silver notes.

Tod shut the door of his house, raked the fire together and went upstairs. Ten minutes later there was no light in all the valley and the only sound was that of the rain tapping tentatively at the windows.

CHAPTER SIX

A CORPORATION rubbish cart came over the moor from Huffley, and all George's things were piled into it and taken away.

An hour later Bailey, loudly blasphemous, was removed in a Red Cross ambulance.

The house, Jenny thought, would be the sweeter for this double departure.

It was a field day for Iris. The Red Cross chaps were smarter than the Corporation chaps, but the Corporation chaps were the more responsive. In any case they were all men. Four in one morning. . . . That, thought Iris, would make Gethin sit up and take notice. He was a queer 'un, that Gethin. One minute he'd be all over you, making you feel like a million dollars, and the next, his black eyes would flick over you like you were a bit of summat the cat had brought home; or he wouldn't see you at all, and if you called out to him he wouldn't hear you. You never knew where you were with the chap.

As soon as the Corporation men arrived Mrs. Bailey stumped upstairs and shut herself in her room as an official protest. From behind the curtain she watched them, her face tight and disapproving.

All Mester's bits and pieces lifted up in great armsful and chucked in the cart as if they were muck! It mattered nothing that for years she had railed and grumbled at the clutter they made. Mester George was dead, and therefore canonized, and all this turmoil in the yard was sheer blasphemy.

All them lovely clothes, an' all! . . . True, Bailey and yon tinker chap had been offered their pick. But Bailey had proved a bigger man than his late master, so nothing had been of much use, and Gethin hadn't seemed interested beyond a sweater or two and a thick rug that he had taken down to his tent. Iris had begged a couple of suits for her father and had been given in addition the cloak lined with quilted satin, which she had said would make up into something for her little sisters—though Mrs. Bailey was ready to bet it would be in the pawnshop before nightfall. She had come upon Iris, the cloak thrown round her shoulders and Mester's tall hat on the back of her head, strutting round the kitchen with a watch glass stuck in her eye, to make Bailey laugh. Mrs. Bailey had fetched her a crack that had made her laugh t'other side of her face. . . .

There they went: suits and good woollens and coats and boots; pictures and stamps and coins and a bushel of rubbish that Mrs. Bailey had cursed for years, but which now seemed so vital a part of her life that pain struck and dragged at her with each loading.

And there was that Iris making a disgusting exhibition of herself with the chaps. If ever a girl asked for trouble, she did! One of the men made a swipe at her bottom as she passed, and she screeched like a donkey.

Gethin came past on his way from orchard to barn. He carried a heavy pail full of apples in either hand and he was whistling. If it was him Iris was getting at, she wasn't having much luck, the old woman thought with satisfaction; for Gethin's face never turned in the direction of the Corporation cart and its activities. He set down the pails and spoke to Posy and the brown pony who stood with their heads thrust over the stable doors, and they answered him shrilly. He stroked their noses and gave them each an apple. He picked up his pails and walked on.

Mrs. Bailey's glance followed him inimically.

That Gethin was the cause of all this trouble. Him and his sickly brat that had come driving over the moor, making a muck of decent people's lives. . . . Mrs. George going right out of her mind, seemingly; Iris that silly there was no holding her; Bailey shamming poorly so long that Doctor was sending him down to hospital for this X-ray, or whatever they called it. And herself oppressed on every side; disregarded by authority, flouted by underlings, working her fingers to the bone, and no thanks from anybody. . . . 'Sooner I'm under the sod, the better,' she thought bleakly.

And she thought of the lovely burying clothes lying in their box, so crisp and white, folded so carefully between blue layers of tissue paper.

And then she remembered what lay alongside the burying clothes. . . . They'd find the brass when they came to lay her out, and there'd be a rare to-do. Whoever had the spending of it, it wouldn't be herself. . . .

There was no comfort anywhere. A tear trickled down the side of her nose; swung, shining for an instant, and fell with an audible *plop* on to the starched bib of her apron.

When the Red Cross chaps came to take her husband away she watched without a pang. The sooner they found out he was foxing the better for everybody. They'd send him out of the hospital quick-sharp, with a flea in his ear, and then yon tinker chap could pack his traps and go.

Further than that she could not see, but for the moment it sufficed. Let things only be as they were and she wouldn't grumble.

Clem was very much better. He sat up in his cot and said two new words. "Pitty," he said, pointing at the brass fire-irons; and then, swinging his finger in a wide arc, he pointed at Jenny and smiled. "Denny," he said, quite distinctly.

Jenny was enchanted. She was awed, as if by a miracle; as if she had not been working on him for days, trying to make him say it. . . .

She hurried down into the orchard, to tell Gethin. He was high up the ladder, half hidden by fruit and foliage. He did not stop working as he laughed down at her upturned face.

"I think he's going to be awfully intelligent," she said.

"More than that he can say, when he likes!"

"I've never heard him," she said jealously.

"Ah, he's a deep one, that!"

She caught the apple he threw her, sank her teeth into its crisp flesh. Life seemed suddenly simpler and at the same time infinitely more full and rich. There was sun today, and a clean, small wind with a nip in it. George's things had all been taken away. Bailey was being dealt with. The apple was sweet, Gethin was young and friendly and Clem had said two new words. . . .

"They've taken Bailey down to the hospital, Gethin."

"I saw."

She finished the apple and threw the core away.

"I don't suppose there's much wrong with him. But just supposing there should be something. . . . how long could you stay?"

"No hurry I'm in," he said indifferently.

He did not seem anxious to talk. She found herself wandering about, picking up apples here and there, trying to appear occupied; trying to look as if she were Missus, with plenty of work awaiting her and little time to spare; trying not to look as if she wanted him to stop work and talk to her for a few minutes. 'I don't really want him to,' she thought, mystified and slightly resentful. 'I don't like him very much. But there's nobody else I can talk to about Clem. And he's young, and I don't think he dislikes me. . . .' She hovered near the foot of the ladder.

"It might be quicker if we both picked," she suggested.

"There's only the one ladder."

"I could carry, perhaps?"

"Too heavy for you."

"Well, shall I pick while you carry?"

"Falling off the ladder you'd be." She saw his white grin through the branches. "There's terrible with two of you being X-rayed in the hospital!"

She gave a small laugh.

"I haven't got anything to do," she said childishly.

"Why should you? You're Missus!"

"Clem is asleep," she evaded. "He looks so sweet."

"Out here the boy should be," he said, "in the sunshine."

"Oh, no!" She was horrified. "He isn't well enough for that. We shall have to take great care for a time."

"Coddling never did anyone any good."

"But Gethin, that's not coddling. It's just common sense." She peered up anxiously into the branches of the apple tree, but his face was hidden from her. "It's like flowers," she persisted. "You wouldn't plant out young plants before the frosts were finished."

"Flowers!" he said, and laughed.

He came down the ladder slowly, balanced and sure, holding the pail heaped with russet-cheeked fruit before him. He scrubbed juice from his hands with a handkerchief of fine white linen embroidered with his initial, G. . . . Of course, it was one of George's!

He had said he wanted nothing but the turtle-necked sweaters and the rug.

Suddenly Jenny was furiously angry. Why must he do these things: break in rather than ask for admission; steal rather than accept; lie, in all probability, rather than admit the slightest truth about himself? How would she ever be able to understand or trust him?

She never would, of course.

But there would be no need for trust. His work here would soon be over. Clem would be well. Bailey would be back. He would go away out of her life for ever. And good riddance. . . .

He picked up his two pails, heaped with colour, and smiled at her.

"Flowers don't matter. But people matters. People has got to be made hard, so they stand up to anything. If not, they're never free. Better dead they are if they are not free."

He went off with his long, loping stride. The pails swung, glinting in the sun.

She could not follow at his heels like a chidden spaniel. She could not stand here and wait for his return. Blindly she began to climb the hill beyond the orchard. The sun had not yet dried the grass and she slipped and stumbled, dashing away the ignominy of tears with hands stained by earth and fruit. The goats moved towards her with loud cries, rattling their chains along the ground; but she passed them by, un-noticing.

When she reached the top of the hill she began to run.

Tod's leg was giving him trouble. He did not need a wet finger in the wind to tell him it was east. He wished he had not walked quite so far.

All morning he had been with Sanderson; tramping round the fields, inspecting ditches and hedges, gates and fencing; looking over the stock and talking to the men; listening to endless anecdotes about war-time conditions, market prices, and the superiority of Shaws over all other farms in the district.

He had lunched with Sanderson and his sister at Miss Ellen's pressing invitation. He was not sure how Mrs. Scobie was going to take that. He had sent her a message by Albert; nevertheless he had the liveliest forebodings. "What about lunch, Mr—er—" she had said before he left the house. She seemed quite incapable of remembering his name. He had assured her that anything would do, though Tod was fond of his food. "I thought a nice bit of fish—that is if the fish-man calls in time—and a semolina pudding?"

He had replied with overemphatic heartiness that it sounded fine, fine! Whereupon she had given a nervous titter and backed out of the room muttering something that sounded like "one o'clock"—but might have been anything.

He hadn't got through with Sanderson until a quarter to two. And there had been Miss Ellen waiting for them, waspish and dictatorial as ever, just dishing up the most delicious pie he had seen or smelt for years. He had fallen for it uncondi-tionally. Mrs. Scobie would have to learn that, on a farm, you couldn't be tied down to ten minutes. She could make fish cakes for supper, and heat up the semolina pudding. And if she didn't like it, he thought valiantly, she could lump it.

Afterwards, he had parked the car at the far end of the village and struck out across the moor to the Tarn. This had always been his first walk after long absence.

It was grand up there, the water glittering in the sun and the marshy verges emerald from recent rain. Heather rippled in the wind; the unforgettable smell of it took him back to his boyhood. When the clock on Staving church struck four he found himself turning almost guiltily for home, wondering if he ought to run for it. 'A good job I don't have to,' he thought as his leg gave a twinge that made him blink.

It was only then that he noticed the girl.

She was leaning back against a tree, hands thrust deep into the pockets of a man's raincoat, battered and stained by age and weather. The collar was turned up and above it dark hair blew about her face. She wore brown slacks. The end of a brown scarf hung from her neck.

So colourless she was, so motionless, so much a part of the landscape, he would have passed her by unseeing had not the wind caught at the scarf and set it flying. The tiny movement halted him, jerked a muttered exclamation to his lips, and their eyes met.

It was the girl he had seen in the trap. George's wife: the girl Doc had asked him to befriend.

At this moment he was not in the mood to befriend anyone. He wanted to be alone as much as she, obviously, wanted to be alone; but their proximity, their utter isolation, made silence an impossible affectation.

"Hullo!" he said. "I'd no idea anyone else was here."

Her great eyes stared at him above the upturned collar, but she did not speak.

"You quite startled me," he added. His laugh sounded inane but it brought a wan smile to her mouth. He moved a few steps towards her. "You are Mrs. Rowland, aren't you?"

She nodded. She kept her back to the tree but stood more upright, smoothing ineffectually at her blowing hair. He could see that she had been crying: crying, he judged, without benefit of handkerchief, for her cheeks were grimed and smudged and the hollows beneath her eyes were still wet.

"I'm Edward Shaw—Tod to the entire village! I farm the place just beyond Backshaws, so we're really neighbours. I expect you've heard of me from your husband." He paused a moment and then added awkwardly: "I was sorry to hear of George's death. We . . . we were boys together." For the life of him he could find nothing nice to say about George. "If I can be of any help to you, please don't hesitate to call on me at any time."

"Thank you," she whispered. She looked as though she might take to her heels and run. Her mouth dragged down unsteadily, as a child's mouth drags, resisting tears.

Tod felt a sort of tenderness overlaid with impatience. She had no business to look and act like a child. She was adult, married for seven years, experienced and—if he knew George —disillusioned. So what was she crying for? George? Hardly. Or was even George better than being alone? And what about that tinker chap she was supposed to be carrying on with?

He felt awkward, impatient. Yet how could he walk on and leave her crying, alone on the moor!

He found himself asking: "Haven't you got a handker-chief?"

"I think I must have dropped it," she said vaguely.

His leg gave another twinge.

"I must get back. Better come along with me, hadn't you? It's rolling up for rain again."

Obediently she turned and walked beside him.

"I don't cry very often," she said.

"Does it help much?"

"No. No, I don't think it does."

Any other woman, he reflected, would be dabbing at her face, peering into a little mirror, fumbling for lipstick and powder. She seemed quite unconscious of her appearance.

"Does it help to talk?"

"I don't know. I've never talked to people very much."

"Hadn't you any family—I mean before you married?"

"No. At least, there was my father, but he wasn't the sort of person you talked to. Unless, of course, you wanted to talk about old pottery, or pictures, or thirteenth century carving. Things like that. And then he did the talking."

She laughed suddenly, and Tod turned and looked at her with sudden pleasure. She had an attractive laugh, very light and clear. Tears were still wet on her cheeks.

A queer, disturbing sort of girl, he thought. She walked well, too, carrying her unfeminine attire with unconscious grace. Very long legs, he judged, and not an ounce of superfluous flesh on her. Not enough flesh in fact. He liked them thin, but she was going to be scraggy if she didn't look out.

"Tell me about your father," he said.

"Oh . . . well, he was rather old, you know, and so clever that he hadn't much patience with people. . . . He kept a shop in Soho. He collected things. Old things: some of them very valuable, some just rubbish. He sold the rubbish in the shop. Sometimes he would part with a valuable piece if he found the right sort of buyer. He couldn't bear people who didn't understand them. . . . That's how I met George, you see. He used to come poking about among the rubbish. He was a very good client," she added simply.

"And you lived there—at the Soho shop?"

"We had a flat above it. I kept house for my father. There wasn't much to do. He liked the very simplest sort of food, and we very seldom had visitors."

"A bit lonely for you, wasn't it?"

She considered this a little.

"I don't remember feeling lonely. I used to go out a lot. I used to walk all over London by myself, and go to theatres and art galleries and museums. . . . I loved the zoo. I used to go there twice a week. Some of the animals knew me. I thought so, anyway. I often took them food. . . ."

She drew her hand over a wet cheek. Without a word Tod handed her an enormous khaki handkerchief. She thanked him in a small voice and blew her nose loudly.

"You had no mother?" Tod asked.

"She died when I was quite small. I was brought up by an aunt, and then I went to a convent school in France. I stayed there until I was seventeen and then I went to keep house for my father at the shop. We didn't know each other at all, you see."

"No school friends? Cousins?"

"Nobody I cared about. My aunt died while I was at the convent and she had no children of her own. The only cousins I ever heard of were in Canada. . . . There was a French girl in my form, but of course she stayed in France. I heard she was killed by the Germans. . . . Most of the English girls were awfully rich; there was nobody I could have kept up a friendship with after I left school."

"So you married George Rowland. . . . Why!"

She did not seem to resent the question.

"There didn't seem to be anything else to do after Father was killed."

"Killed?"

"He had a business appointment at the hotel where a client was staying. While they were talking there was a raid. The hotel got a direct hit."

"I see. . . . So there was nothing for it but marrying George?"

She was frowning, as if concentrating on this question of why she had married George; as if she had to make the reason clear to herself as well as to him.

"Well. . . . George was *there*, you see. I mean he was at the shop when I heard about Father. He was waiting to see Father, and it got later and later and he didn't come. And then there was the telephone message. . . . So he didn't like to leave me all alone, I suppose. And then there was the business to sell, and hundreds of things to see to. He really was awfully kind to me then. . . . So when he said I'd better marry him, I—I just did. He'd often talked to me about Lost Hill. I thought the moor sounded lovely. . . . Of course, we weren't in love with each other, or anything like that, but—well, I didn't think that would matter."

"And you found it mattered a hell of a lot! No, don't answer that. I'd no right to say it. I've only known you half an hour, and here I'm dragging the whole story out of you. . . . Please forgive me, Mrs. Rowland. You seem very young to me, and people are apt to take liberties with the young."

"I'm twenty-seven," she said simply.

"Years have nothing to do with it." He smiled at her and offered his cigarette case. When she refused he lit a cigarette for himself and closed the case with a snap, as if that disposed of the topic. "Here comes the rain. The weather's making noble amends for the months of drought, isn't it? My car is parked just along the road. I'll run you home."

But once safe in the car Tod showed no inclination to hurry. He fiddled with the choke and windscreen wiper, rubbed mist from the windows, lit another cigarette. And at length, clumsily enough, he got it out.

"How are you managing without Bailey?"

He had not meant to look at her. It was none of his business. But suddenly he had to know; not only what she said but how she said it.

He saw at once that she guessed his purpose and resented it. Her great eyes held reproach. But she answered candidly enough.

"I was lucky. A man—a tinker, I suppose you'd call him—camped in the orchard field because his little boy was sick. I offered to give them both house-room if he would take on Bailey's job for a few days."

Tod let in the clutch. The car moved slowly forward. Rain streamed against the windscreen, danced on the bonnet. The wiper hummed backwards and forwards, giving little relief.

"He's a very good worker," she added. "Much better than Bailey."

"All the same, I don't think it was a very good idea," Tod said slowly.

"What else was I to do?"

"You could have asked me. I could have spared one of the men, or found somebody to help out."

"You were not home. Anyway, I didn't know you then. And the little boy was ill."

"There are hospitals."

"Oh, no. If you put people like them in hospitals, they die."

"That's what he told you, I suppose?"

"Gethin? Yes, he said that."

"I thought so. It isn't true, of course. You mustn't let yourself romanticize those people. They'll say owt but their prayers, and them they'll whistle, as we say in these parts. I've met a good many of them, in the Army and in Wales, as well as around here. I was at a Convalescent Camp in the Snowdon district back in '44; they were always camping in the valleys. Believe me, there's nothing romantic about them."

"Gethin was in the Army, right from the start."

She said it defensively. 'Good lord,' Tod thought, dismayed. 'I believe she really does like the chap!'

He turned in at the gates of Lost Hill. The tyres crunched up the ill-kept drive. He hadn't been so near the house since his boyhood. The paintwork, he noticed, was bad, and everything had a neglected look. The house was solid, admirably built of local stone: it would stand up to years of ill-treatment. But it no longer looked impressive as it had done in Old Missus' time. George, he guessed, had grudged even the small outlay of money it had been possible to spend upon repairs during the war years. Old Bailey, of course, wouldn't consider it his business, and the girl could hardly be expected to understand about such things. . . .

"Have you made any plans?" he asked diffidently. "I mean, have you considered selling the house? It's a bit too much for you to manage, isn't it?"

"Doctor Waller thinks I ought to sell it," she said doubtfully. "I haven't made up my mind."

"You're fond of the place?"

"No. Oh, no! I expect you'll think it sounds silly, but I've never felt as if the house liked me. . . . But I've nowhere else to go, you see, and I love the moor so much."

"But you love London, too."

"You mean buy a house there?"

"Or take a flat. Or you could live in an hotel."

He had a sudden vision of her drifting about the grey London streets, alone, in her brown slacks and George's old raincoat. Staring in shop windows at gay clothes it would never occur to her to buy; mooning in art galleries; leaning over the embankment watching the busy water; sitting at her table for one in some dreary little hotel, with a book propped against the cruet: an uncomplaining, unregarded guest, having nothing in common with the card-playing women or the smart young city gents or the old fogies who monopolised the comfortable chairs. And alone, always alone. . . . 'Great heavens!' he thought, suddenly exasperated by the whole thing, 'why should *I* worry? She's plenty of money—must have—and she's not a child. I can't help it if she hasn't got a clue. . . .'

The rain slackened and the sun came out.

As he turned the car the man she called Gethin came into the yard carrying a load of apples. Tod saw him speak to the girl, shake rain from his shoulders, smile with a white flash of teeth. A well set up fellow with a lot of black hair. Tod thought he knew the type.

'She didn't even know enough to ask me in for a drink!' he thought as he turned for home.

Clem was not in his cot.

Jenny could hardly believe it. Absurdly, she lifted the covers, as if it were possible he could be concealed beneath them. Even more absurdly she opened a cupboard door, looked behind a chair.

Her heart pounded heavily, rather frighteningly. She was angry and at the same time humiliated.

Where had he taken Clem? She had no authority to forbid his moving the child—but why had he wished to?

She remembered what he had said. *"People has got to be made hard, or they're better dead. . . ."*

If Clem had been out in that rain he might easily be ill

again. He might die. . . . Such a small, fragile creature. Such an uncertain hold on life. . . . She was frightened—oh, she was frightened! For Clem, because he might die. For herself, because she suddenly knew how much it meant to her that Clem should live. 'I mustn't care like this!' she thought, dismayed. 'I mustn't care what happens to Clem.'

But she knew that it was too late. She loved the little boy.

She heard Iris laughing out in the yard. She went to the window and saw her standing there talking to Gethin. In her arms she held Clem bundled up in blankets. . . . Iris was used to children: there were half a dozen younger than herself at home. She held Clem with an accustomed ease that Jenny envied.

But she was angry, too. It was odious that Iris should hold Clem in her arms; worse that Gethin should stand there laughing down at them both, satisfied to leave his child in Iris's care. . . .

She turned and ran downstairs, out into the yard. Her cheeks were red with anger, her movements urgent. Tod would have been astonished to see the change in her.

Gethin had gone. Iris was strolling up and down with the child in her arms. She was talking the inane baby-talk of her kind. Every few steps she did a clumsy dance, tossing the child up in the air and stamping her feet. Clem laughed delightedly every time she did it.

"Give him to me," Jenny said curtly.

Iris stood her ground, her fat, white face defiant.

"Gethin said to take him out into the sunshine. He asked me to."

"In my house you will do as I say!" Jenny's voice was out of control.

"He said he didn't want him coddled."

"Common sense is not coddling. The air is too damp, it's been pouring cats and dogs." She reached out and took the child into her own arms.

"I had him in the tent then. He never got a drop on him—did you, luv?" Iris clucked amiably, her face pushed close to the child's face, and Clem laughed loudly. "Ee, he's a little duck, isn't he!" she cried. "But he don't talk much. Our Albert Edward's three months younger'n him, an' he can say anything. You should just hear him swear!" Her great mouth opened in a bellow of mirth.

Jenny stepped back, holding the child closely.

"Well, get on with your work now."

"It's me half-day," Iris said blandly.

"Then you should have gone home."

"I'd as soon stop here."

The girl grinned insolently, turned and walked away in the direction Gethin had taken.

Jenny took Clem indoors, carried him upstairs and sat before the fire nursing him.

"Pitty!" he said, holding long, delicate fingers to the fire.

"Say Jenny," she pleaded.

"Pitty," he repeated, watching the flames.

"Jenny. Say Jenny, Clem."

She turned him round, forced him to look at her. She smiled at him, tickled him, jogged him up and down on her knee. He regarded her with a faraway expression.

> To market, to market, to buy a fat pig.
> Home again, home again, jiggety jig,

she sang, jigging her knees energetically.

He gave her a faint, polite smile and belched briefly.

Finally, shamefacedly, she made the uncouth noises Iris had made; tossed him up and down; brought her face close to his and babbled nonsense. He strained away from her, struggling round towards the fire again, reaching for it.

"Pitty! Pitty!"

"You can't like Iris as much as me," she said jealously. "You can't. You must love me better than anybody else. Nobody has ever loved me best. . . ."

As if sensing the loneliness in her Clem turned and laid one hand against her cheek.

"Denny," he said softly. "Denny."

Her heart leapt.

"Say you love me, Clem. Say it!"

"Yuv you." He dropped a cool, moist kiss on the point of her chin.

Her arms tightened about him. Her heart felt as if it would burst.

She had never received anything she valued so much.

CHAPTER SEVEN

As soon as he was well enough Jenny took Clem into Huffley and bought clothes for him. A belted overcoat with cap and leggings to match. A cardigan embroidered with rabbits. Shoes and socks and gloves and minute pyjamas, and overalls to keep him clean. The price of these tiny garments astonished her, but she bought on, undismayed.

Clem kicked and struggled. He bellowed with wrath at being forced into one garment after another. But Jenny was adamant. She took him into the toy department and soothed him with a grey wool rabbit that squeaked and a tiny tricycle with a bell of piercing shrillness and bright red wheels.

Gethin was waiting outside with the trap. Pacified by his presents, Clem strutted in his new clothes. Gethin grinned at him derisively.

"Why didn't you get some clothes for yourself?" he said to Jenny. "A red dress to show up that hair of yours, and a blue one to put stars in your grey eyes. You need clothes, and the kid's better without 'em."

"I've got plenty of clothes," Jenny said in surprise. But she turned and looked at herself in the window of the shop, and what she saw was not reassuring. She had thought of this tweed suit as her best. Now it occurred to her that she had so regarded it for at least five years—probably longer. 'I must get a new suit one of these days,' she thought, vaguely resentful.

"I have to see Bailey now," she told Gethin. "The hospital is along this road: first turn left after the railway bridge. I'll show you."

The hospital stood in a rather sooty garden, where she left Gethin and the child.

"Don't let him get dirty," she said anxiously.

"Why not?"

"Well. . . . I just bought him all those nice clothes!"

"I didn't ask you to." His stare was derisive, challenging. Jenny moved away uncertainly. 'I'm being such an awful fool!' she thought helplessly.

She went through echoing corridors, down polished wards between rows of tidy beds covered in red blankets. There were bright flowers and sunshine. A girl's high laugh came from an open door along with the smell of cooking cabbage.

Bailey looked almost shockingly clean and rather pathetic. A very young probationer put a chair for her, twitched at the bedclothes, said, "Behave yourself, Gorgeous!" and hurried away resettling her starched cap.

"I'm bahn to get out o' here, Missus!" Bailey said hoarsely.

Jenny said: "I'm afraid it's going to be longer than we expected. They won't keep you longer than they can help, because they're short of beds."

"I don't like it 'ere." He began to grumble about the food, the draughts, the noise at night, the favouritism, the inconsiderate treatment by doctors and nurses alike. . . . "An' I feel right poorly, Missus. They're allus pulling and pokin' at me. I don't get no rest."

Jenny wondered what Clem was doing, and if Gethin was keeping an eye on him. The hospital gates stood wide open, and the road was thick with traffic. . . .

"I can only stay a few minutes," she said. "What was it you wanted to see me about?"

Bailey regarded his knotted fists resting on the red coverlet.

"I want to see Iris," he growled.

"Oh. . . . Well, I'll tell Mrs. Bailey," Jenny promised doubtfully.

"That ain't no good—you know that. I've got to see Iris. I've got to speak to 'er, quick. There's summat I've got to tell 'er. It's important. . . . Sitha, Missus, send the lass down 'ere with a message or summat. *You* say as she's got to come. . . . I got to speak to 'er, I tell you!"

"You know I can't do that, Bailey. If anyone comes it must be your wife."

"I don't want the owd buzzard!" he protested violently. "It's yon lass I've got to speak to."

"I don't mind taking Iris a message, if it's really so important. But I won't send her down without Mrs. Bailey's permission. You should have more sense than to ask."

"What's wrong wi' me talkin' to Iris?"

"You know that better than I do," she suggested.

He blinked vindictively at her.

"You're a nice one to talk—ain't you!"

After a moment Jenny got to her feet.

"I brought you some tobacco," she said evenly. She laid the package on the red coverlet and stood regarding him with a shrinking distaste.

"I don't want yer ol' bacca!" Bailey shouted. He grabbed at the package and flung it away. It slid across the polished floor and a cackle of laughter came from an adjoining bed. "All I asks is, send the lass down 'ere for a word wi' me. Ten minutes 'll do. Five minutes. . . . It's not much to ask. I've worked for Lost Hill a good many years, both for Mester George an' Owd Missus, too, an' yon's all t'thanks I get! You can tek yer bacca away an' give it to yon fancy man o' yourn!"

The probationer dashed out from behind a screen, picked up the package and gave the furious old man a smart slap.

"Now then, Gorgeous, give over, do!" she said brightly. "See, you've made your girl friend blush. You're a dirty old man!"

Jenny fled down the ward, thankful to escape. She stood still in the white, empty corridor smelling of antiseptic, trying to regain composure before she rejoined Gethin and the child.

Your fancy man. . . .

Was that how they all thought of her: Mrs. Bailey and Iris and Doctor Waller and all the folks at Backshaws? Was that what Tod Shaw was thinking? And Gethin himself? . . . She pressed cold fingers over her eyes.

"Are you all right?" a voice asked.

She took her hands away and rainbows flashed briefly. A young man in a white coat stood beside her. A stethoscope hung from his neck and his hair stood up in a red bush.

"Yes, of course," she said brusquely.

"Righty-ho!" The young man strode away whistling, and Jenny went out through the swing doors into the sooty, Huffley air.

They were sitting on an iron seat, waiting for her. Gethin was smoking a cigarette but Clem sat motionless, staring at the asphalt path. His stillness was remarkable in so young a child. She had observed this quality of stillness in him before. It lent an air of defeat, an almost tragically patient acceptance to the small figure that made her want to run to him, put her arms round him and shield him from life.

But she turned her back, crossed the asphalt to where old Posy drowsed between the shafts. Footsteps followed her: Gethin's long, easy stride, Clem's quick patter. Without a word she handed the reins to Gethin and climbed into the trap. Gethin lifted Clem up and they pulled out of the hospital grounds into the stream of traffic.

The child sat between them, his head bowed. Jenny looked at him sharply.

"Why has he been crying again?" she demanded.

A car honked impatiently behind them. Gethin motioned it to pass.

"He was dirtying his fine new coat."

"Yes, but—Gethin, you didn't punish him?"

"I fetched him a crack."

"Oh, Gethin, how could you! He's so young—so small!"

He turned and looked at her sullenly; a stranger's glance, faintly contemptuous.

"You're hard to please, lady. . . . Time it is we went, the child and I."

Jenny's heart jerked painfully.

He was right, of course. It was time they went away. High time. . . . They should never have come to Lost Hill; never have stayed, even for a night. Just when freedom had seemed assured these two had come riding over the moor, bringing new chains. . . .

She lifted the child on to her knee. He resisted her for a moment and then leaned against her breast. Almost at once he fell asleep, worn out by excitement and tears.

She held him tenderly, loving his weight, his limp abandon, the swing of small heels against her leg.

They must go, of course. But not yet—surely not yet? And then a thought that had glimmered more than once suddenly leapt to a blaze.

If only Gethin could go, and Clem remain. . . .

They drove through the crowded streets in silence. There was nothing to say that could with decency be said at this time.

They did not go unremarked.

The wife of the innkeeper at Backshaws saw them. She nudged the friend with whom she was shop-gazing, and they indulged in a series of shocked and gratified noises. Doctor Waller, hurrying towards the hospital with his old-fashioned black bag, saw them, and his lips shot out. The undertaker who had buried George lifted his eyebrows and grinned to himself. Susan Scales, driving her father in the smart, brand-new Sunbeam, said sharply: "Look, isn't that the Rowland woman over at Lost Hill?"

"So it's true!" her father commented. "By gum, that'd mek Owd Missus turn in her grave!"

And Councillor Sellers, coming out of the Royal after a quick one with Councillor Ramsbottom, stood stock still on the pavement staring after them with open mouth. "See that?" he demanded of his crony, with whom he had just transacted a highly profitable piece of graft. "Yon's Mrs George Rowland, of Lost Hill, if you please! Her wi' t'gyppo up beside 'er. . . . You an' me was at t' poor chap's funeril nobbut a few weeks back!"

"Well, I don't know!" exclaimed Councillor Ramsbottom, peering after the trap.

And these two highly respectable city fathers hastened home to their wives with the succulent titbit.

Tod, standing in the doorway of the grain merchant's, saw them go by. The handsome, dark chap with the scarlet scarf round his neck; the girl looking down at the child asleep in her arms. . . . He surprised himself by feeling murderous. Sanderson, who was with him, muttered: "Nay!" but Tod pretended not to hear.

"Well, I'll go along to the bank," he said. "Meet me at the Royal and we'll have one for the road."

He followed the trap up the High Street. It was moving slowly because of the traffic. It would not have been difficult to catch up with it.

But then what? Drag the girl out by that soft, untidy hair of hers? Bash the fellow up in the middle of the High Street and get run in for assault? Make a damn fool of himself before a crowd of grinning Huffleyites? . . .

He swung round impatiently, walked back down the street and bought himself a large whisky and soda at the Royal where, presently, Sanderson joined him.

"Did you get to see t'Manager?" Sanderson asked.

"What? Oh, I didn't go to the bank, after all. It can wait a few days."

Sanderson downed his drink in silence. There were summat up with Tod, that were a sure thing. He hoped it was nothing to do with Lost Hill. Anyroad, he wasn't meddling—not him!

The River Huff was a shining curve between the two hills. The hills soared upwards on either side of it. Fifty years ago, so Old Missus had told Jenny, the hills had been a bonny sight; bright with gorse and heather, scented with hawthorne white and red, carpeted with innumerable wild flowers, alive with the white scuts of rabbits and the songs of birds. There had been no made-up roads across the hills then; only a stony track winding down Hawks Hill, whose back was humped against the east, climbing up over Huffam Hill to the village on its crest. Once a chap called Abel Gurney had dreamed of making a fine road, but had succeeded only in making a mess of his life and the lives of those nearest to him.

But with passing years others had made Abel Gurney's dream come true, and now a wide roadway thrust up Huffam Hill, houses sprawled among the green, the gay little wild creatures, the sweet hawthorne and the silence were all gone, and Huffam village was a thriving suburb, just as Abel Gurney had visualised it, with two great cinemas, five churches, a secondary school and a recreation ground.

The trap stood in a traffic block on the bridge over the river, and Jenny gazed regretfully at the ruined hills. How lovely they must have been fifty years ago! How short a time it took to despoil a lovely thing and make it ugly. . . .

So much ugliness everywhere, she thought; in people's minds, in their sly gossip, their cruelty and self-righteousness. So little beauty, comfort, kindliness and understanding. . . . Even her love for Clem must be viewed by jaundiced eyes, fouled by unfriendly tongues. . . .

"Come up!" Gethin gave Posy the whip. Startled, she plunged a little, her ears flat with resentment.

"Go easy!" Jenny said sharply. "She's old."

He grinned, shooting a glance at her averted face.

"With you it's always too young or too old, isn't it? What happens to the in-between ones? Like you and me?"

"We can take care of ourselves, I suppose."

"Not much success you make of it, do you?"

"You're impertinent!" she flared.

"I'm only an ignorant fellow," he jeered. "I don't know no better. You'll have to excuse me."

When they reached the moor Gethin let Posy amble along at her own pace. He whistled softly between his teeth as he rolled a cigarette. Jenny watched him covertly. Thin, broad,

clever hands he had: hands that would tackle any job effi-
ciently, whether it was picking a pocket or nursing a young,
delicate plant or tending a sick animal. Hands that could hit
a little child. . . . And then, in all fairness, she remembered
they were hands that could wash and cook for a child, doctor
it, hold it more expertly than she could hold it. . . .

"It seems there's something wrong with Bailey," she told
him. "They may have to operate. It will be weeks before he's
able to work again."

"Bailey will never work again," he said impassively.

She turned her head, startled.

"Why do you say that?"

"A very sick man he is. I knew that, soon as I clapped eyes
on him."

"What is it? How could you tell?"

"I dunno what it is. I just think he's going to die. Written
all over him it is. They'll find out soon, down in that hospital.
He's had his chips, that old man."

Jenny felt troubled and remorseful. She had never liked
Bailey: only this morning she had been furiously angry with
him. But she didn't want him to die.

Gethin was probably wrong. What knowledge could he
have? Even Doctor Waller had been vague about it. It was
no use worrying yet, anyway.

"Will you be able to stay a few weeks longer?" she forced
herself to ask.

He took the drooping cigarette from his mouth and blew
out a thin stream of smoke. He whistled a few bars of a tune,
as if he had not heard her speak.

"Please stay, Gethin. I can't manage without you."

"If I had not come, somebody else you would have found."

She was silent. And presently he threw away the cigarette
and shifted round so that he was looking full at her.

"Often I am thinking it would have been better if I had
not come."

Jenny held Clem closely; clinging to him rather than sup-
porting him.

"Why *did* you come!" she cried.

"The child was ill."

"But Shaws was only a mile or two further on. That's where you were making for, wasn't it? Iris said you were asking the way to Shaws."

After a pause he said, "Is that what she told you?" and began to whistle again. He clicked at Posy. And this time she responded willingly enough, for her stable was near.

"You're not wanting to part with the child, isn't it?"

Jenny looked at him helplessly. And suddenly he smiled at her, quite gently, as she had never seen him smile before.

"Nothing more than a child you are yourself!"

"I'm twenty-seven!" she whispered.

"Yes, indeed. But you're still a kid with a new toy. Something you've got that you've been wanting for years, and now you've got it you can't let go, not for a minute. . . . Only a borrowed toy it is, but you won't let yourself remember that, will you?"

"Give it to me, then!" she wanted to cry. "Let me keep Clem. I'll pay you well. I'll give him a wonderful life. I'll love him, guard him, educate him, make him safe and rich and important. . . . Go away and leave Clem with me!" But she dared not say it. Not yet. It must be the right moment, the right mood. . . .

Suddenly she felt him closer. She looked up, startled.

"Keep your toy you shall a little longer," he said. "Poor Jenny bach!" He bent and laid his mouth very gently against her cheek.

The public bar of The Bell was nearly empty. It was early yet, and Ben Bugle, the landlord, leaned on his elbows gossiping with a few cronies. Behind his grizzled head rows of coloured bottles gleamed in the last rays of the sun. A log fire blazed in the hearth, and along the white-stoned window sills miniature fires of geranium blazed as brightly. A large ginger cat was hunched in the middle of the hearthrug, rumbling content. Everything was polished and tidy, the scrubbed floor still smelling faintly of soap, the high stools in an orderly row, the red serge curtains folded back.

By closing time the floor would be patterned with mud, the fire a grey heap of ash, the mahogany bar smeared, the stools all over the place, the air blue and asphyxiating, the landlord and his buxom wife scarcely on speaking terms with each other. Only the ginger cat would still lie humped on the hearthrug, imperturbable and unchallenged. Customers who wished to warm themselves could stand behind him or beside him, straddle above him or group themselves in a respectful halfcircle around him. It would be a brave man indeed who removed Mrs. Bugle's ginger cat from his time-honoured place, and nobody within memory had attempted it.

Bassett of Drakesdown emptied his tankard and slapped it on the mahogany.

"Filthy muck," he remarked mildly. "When are they goin' to give us summat worth supping? Fill her up, Ben. No good askin' you!"

Mr. Bugle sucked his teeth in concurrence. He drank very little until late in the evening, and this early abstinence gave him a feeling of rectitude as a temperate man.

"Watter," agreed Joe Clynes of Reetly. "Nobbut watter, an' weak at that!" He also demanded a fill-up. The two drank in silence and Bugle watched them, sucking his teeth.

"Queer sort of setup ower at Lost Hill," he remarked, and his listeners' heads jerked expressively. "They was down in Huffley a week back, driving together up t'High Street as bold as brass. She were holding t'little 'un on her knees. The Missus saw 'em with her own eyes. I couldn't 'ardly believe it, but she says, 'I saw it with me own eyes,' she says, 'and Mrs. Garrett was with me, and she'll bear me out.'"

"Nay!" said Bassett.

"Owd Missus'd turn in her grave," said Clynes.

"Well, but I mean to say—it's a bit thick!"

"That's what I said to the Missus. 'It's a bit thick,' I says. I mean to say, I weren't all that set on George Rowland, but there's such a thing as decency, all said an' done."

"Ah!" chorused Bassett and Clynes.

"I mean to say, chap's not been in his grave above a few weeks. Bad enough if she'd tekken up with some chap from round these parts; one of us, as you might say. But yon tinker chap. . . . Nay!"

Jackie Bates from out Huffam way propped his bicycle outside the window and came in grinning.

"Evening all!" he said heartily. "Pint of the usual, Ben. And how's Ben?"

"None the better for seeing you," Bugle retorted. He slapped the drink down, juggled with change. "We were just talking about Lost Hill."

Bates sucked noisily at his tankard and drew the back of his hand across a froth-ringed mouth.

"Then you was talkin' of the devil—an' you'll see his horns come round the door any minute now. I passed yon chap on me bike not five minutes since."

"Might not be coming in here," Clynes objected.

"Wheer else would a chap be headin' for, this time o' day!" Bassett said reasonably.

"Tekken a nice walk, happen." This was intended as a joke and accepted as such, for Jackie Bates was the local card.

"I'll just tell the Missus," Bugle murmured, and disappeared through a door. The others took up strategic positions between bar and window.

" 'Eigh-up!" Jackie hissed. "Here he comes!"

Gethin came in, gave them a civil "Good evening" and stood at the bar, waiting. The head of Mrs. Bugle, one half still bristling with steel curlers, came round a door and instantly withdrew. Clynes and Bassett and Jackie Bates contemplated their tankards and discoursed in artificial tones about the weather.

After a moment or two Gethin rapped on the mahogany with a coin.

Bugle came back, and Gethin ordered a pint of mild. He walked over to the fire and set his drink on the high mantelpiece. With one foot he stirred the ginger cat from somnolence. He made small, secret noises with his lips and the cat rose up, stretched and mewed, looking up into his face. He bent and lifted it to his shoulder. It purred loudly, kneading his shoulder with fat, ecstatic paws. And presently, of its own accord it curled round his neck like a massive collar and lay there, limp and blissful, still rumbling praise.

A silence had fallen on the room. The drinkers stood petrified, tankards midway to open mouths. The landlord glowered, hovered uncertainly and finally slipped through the door behind the bar. "Min!" he could be heard calling urgently.

Instinctively Clynes and Bassett and Jackie Bates drew together, for Mrs. Bugle's temper was notorious: it could make or mar the entire evening.

Gethin drained his tankard and took it back to the bar.

"Nice drop of rain," he remarked, flashing his sudden smile at the apprehensive group. They stared out of the window, at their beer—anywhere but at this upstart gyppo with his white teeth and his scarlet neckerchief, who came swaggering in where he wasn't wanted, upsetting honest Yorkshiremen and thinking he could get away with it. "It's clearing," he added. "In for some good weather now we are."

We! . . . Just as if he was one of themselves; just as if he belonged here. Nay! . . .

The door to the back premises flung wide open and Mrs. Bugle came in. She was dressed for the evening. The steel curlers had given place to tight, stone-coloured sausages arranged symmetrically across her head. Her blouse of pink satin was embellished with a massive brooch glittering with red and blue stones. She wore two diamond rings, a lace apron and an expression of such malignancy that a little man in a bowler hat, who was just coming in, went out again with some agility.

"Put that cat down!" Mrs. Bugle said loudly.

Gethin's dark gaze ran over her from curls to apron, and he smiled brilliantly.

"Okay," he agreed. He threw the cat lightly to the floor.

Immediately it leapt to the bar and back again to his shoulder. It rubbed its fat ginger face against his neck and started the kneading process all over again.

"Put 'im down!" Mrs. Bugle shrilled. " 'Ere—give 'im to me!"

"Okay." He handed the cat across the bar and Mrs. Bugle gripped it to her satin bosom, glaring at Gethin.

"A fine cat," Gethin said pleasantly. "There's beautiful his coat is. Well, good night all." He smiled at the stricken group and strolled out, leaving the door ajar.

"My word, of all the nerve!" Mrs. Bugle exploded. "He'd have nipped off with 'im if I hadn't come in! He'd have had 'im flayed within the hour, an' t'skin sold in Huffley market. . . . And what was you doing!" she demanded, turning on the shrinking men. "What was all you lot doing, letting 'im mess about with the cat! Four great 'ulking fellows, and not one on you man enough to look after a poor innocent cat as never 'armed nobody! I wonder you're not ashamed!"

She bore her darling back to his rightful place upon the hearthrug.

" 'Eigh-up, Missus!" Clynes shouted. "He's off!"

Mrs. Bugle grabbed, but too late. The ginger cat had streaked out of the door in search of Gethin. Whereupon arose such a hullabaloo that the little man in the bowler hat, who was lurking outside, decided to call it a day and went home, frustrated.

Quite unconscious of the enormity of his crime, Gethin went swiftly along the road in the sweet, rain-drenched twilight. He went past the wood, past Heartbreak, and turned down the lane leading to Shaws.

He went slower now, hands in pockets, whistling between his teeth. The farm lay below him, folded between the shadowed hills, strong and square and secure. Windows blossomed into light as he watched and a chimney sent up a thick column of smoke as if someone had just mended a fire. There was the muffled bark of a dog, the slam of a door, the clanking of pails on stone and, from some warm, dim interior, a cow's contentment bellowed forth, long drawn-out and muted.

A nice place, the man thought. A warm, tidy, rich place; the best for miles around. So they all said, and so he could believe.

There would be money in that place; money to save and money to play with, and money to buy whatever was needed to be bought—even silence. The owner of such a place would surely set a high price on his good name. . . . It was this hope that had brought him across England from the narrow valleys of Wales to this bleak, upland Yorkshire moor.

But then, he reflected, he had never heard of Lost Hill and of the girl, Jenny; the nice, silly, frightened creature. . . .

Avoiding Sanderson's cottage near the gates Gethin climbed a stone wall, dropped on turf and went with his quick, light stride across two fields and a paved rose garden to the wall of the house.

He was not sure why he went. Curiosity perhaps, that killed the cat, he thought, grinning. . . . He had seen Shaw driving about the place. He had seen him bring Jenny home that day. He had seen him glaring at them from the shop doorway, down in Huffley.

He wanted to see him in his own place, by his own hearth, alone and off his guard. He wanted to see what Angharad had seen in this stolid Yorkshire type.

It was nearly dark now. He stared through a window into a square, lamp-lit kitchen floored with red flags. A woman bent over an ironing board. She was not young but not very old. She had a face like a sheep and long, narrow feet that splayed out sideways. She did not interest him.

He saw her hang a man's shirt over a line and then stand still, her head cocked sideways, listening. Presently she went to the inner door and listened again. She came back and peered at herself in a small mirror hanging on a wall. She bent closer, examining her skin, her teeth, the roots of her hair. She rubbed her cheeks vigorously, then dabbed at them with a powder puff she took from the dresser drawer. She went back to her ironing.

Grinning to himself in the darkness Gethin moved noiselessly round the house. He had no interest in the house apart from a magpie curiosity. He often examined the exteriors of houses. He would guess at, even test out their vulnerability, as another man might browse along a bookstall or pause before a picture in a gallery.

There was a side door which he found locked. Jenny was wrong when she said folks didn't lock their doors in these parts. . . . There was a window in what was a sitting room, as far as he could tell, though it was unlighted save for a gleam from an inner door that stood ajar. He got an impression of pale, padded chairs and sofas, mirrors and pictures, flowers in a glass bowl. It all looked rich and stuffy. He tried the window, found it unlatched and clicked his tongue. There was careless! Anybody could get in, easy as falling off a log.

Now his hand was on a stretch of creeper-covered wall. Old, strong creeper with stout, twisted stems that would take a man's weight. . . . Now the wall turned, forming a right-angle with the front of the house. Here the creeper was even thicker. It gave off a strong, musty smell that surprised a sneeze out of him.

He stood quite still in the angle of the wall, listening.

Suddenly the light of a torch flashed in his face and Major Shaw stood there, his square form black against the dimness.

"What are you up to?"

"Nothing." Gethin's gaze was blank.

"What are you doing skulking round my house?"

"Trying to find the front door I was."

The torch played over him from head to foot.

"You're from Lost Hill, aren't you?"

"That's right."

"Then you should know the front of Shaws from the back. What's your business? Have you brought a message from Mrs. Rowland?"

Gethin thought swiftly. He could make up some sort of

message and get away with it easily enough as far as Jenny was concerned. But this man was a different kettle of fish. He knew this type: there had been plenty like him in the Army. He was the sort that took everything you said seriously and proceeded to sift it to the very bottom.

"Looking for a cat I was," he said softly. "It followed me out of the pub and the landlady will be worrying. A big ginger cat. I thought it ran this way."

Tod looked at him keenly. The story was so improbable that it could be true. The fellow didn't seen frightened, not even apologetic at being discovered in such doubtful circumstances. . . . Yet with all his forthright nature Tod distrusted that inscrutable black stare, the silky voice, the unnatural immobility of the man.

"Come into the light," he said abruptly, gesturing him out towards the front of the house where lamp-light flooded a close-cut square of lawn. "Why did the cat follow you?"

"I picked it up and the landlady was very angry with me. So I put it down again. But it took a sort of fancy to me, see? It followed me out of the pub. I couldn't make it go back. Followed me it did right across those fields."

"You don't expect me to swallow that yarn, do you?"

"Why not?"

Tod took a grip on his temper.

"You may have lost Mrs. Bugle's cat for her—but that's not why you were creeping round this house in the darkness. Don't try those sort of tricks with me. I've seen you hanging round here more than once. What's more, I understand that you were enquiring the way to Shaws, the day you arrived. Is that the case?"

"It might be," Gethin said impassively.

"Why? Speak out, man, if you've got any business with me. Come on, let's have it."

Gethin lifted his shoulders.

"Everyone spoke of this good farm. Maybe I just wanted work."

"Why didn't you come and ask for work, then?"

"The weather broke, and the child was sick. And the lady at Lost Hill was very kind. . . ."

It was no good, Tod thought impatiently, you never got the truth out of this sort. He was just wasting his time yapping out here in the dark, and his supper was getting cold.

"There's glad I was to work for her, so kind she had been to me and the child," Gethin continued softly. "And the poor old man dying down there in that old hospital."

"Dying? . . . He only sprained his ankle!"

"Dying he is," Gethin proclaimed sombrely.

A bat dipped between them, circled round them: Tod felt a fan of air from its wings. And another breath, faint and fleeting as the bat's wing, stirred his memory.

"You're Welsh, aren't you?" he said harshly.

"I have lived in Wales," Gethin admitted. And added: "In a valley that is not far from the mountain they call Siabod."

Angharad. Tod remembered suddenly. That was her name— Angharad. . . . Short and rather squat, but filled to the brim with what it took. . . . Not that it took much when you were let loose in a Convalescent Camp after months of bedridden pain and misery. For a week, he recalled, he had been intrigued by her dark, animal vitality. They had met by that crazy bridge across the waterfall with the unpronounceable name. Every day she had waited for him. He remembered the quick warmth of her smile, the black silence of her anger, her greed and her easy generosity, her childish delight in his paltry gifts. Then one day she had not been at the bridge and that had been the end of it. She had never come again. It was over, and he had been rather relieved. He had rarely thought of her since. . . .

"Do you still want to work here?" he asked sharply.

Gethin said slowly and consideringly, "No, I don't think I do, thanking you all the same, Major. I likes working at Lost Hill. Very kind to me Mrs. Rowland is, and so fond of the child. . . . Well suited I am at Lost Hill, I think."

"Then there's no point in hanging around my land, is there? If you have any reason to speak to me in future, I shall be obliged if you will come through the gates in a proper manner. Good night to you."

"Good night, Major." Gethin gestured with his hand; half wave, half salute. He turned and loped away along the drive, and Tod stood watching him until he was out of sight. Then he went indoors to his supper, for which he suddenly had small appetite

CHAPTER EIGHT

As THE car ran into the yard a scutter of indignant hens fled before it. Their squawks brought Mrs. Bailey to the back door.

"Nay, it's Mester Shaw!" she exclaimed, as Tod stepped out, smiling at her.

"Don't you Mester me," he said. "You've boxed my ears too often for that. The name is Tod—remember?"

"And well you earned it," she retorted. But her expression was softer than usual. Owd Missus had been fond of Tod.

Tod shook hands with the old woman, enquired after her health and her husband's progress in hospital, and listened to a long recital of her woes, in which "that Iris" and "that tinker chap" figured prominently. He listened with patience and courtesy, for he had the true landowner's appreciation of old and well-tried servants. She was a tartar, this old woman, but she was a part of Lost Hill; her roots were deep in this soil.

"What's to become of me?" she lamented. "Bailey's none so young as he were, an' old bones is queer things to mend. When I clapped eyes on 'im down in t'hospital you could 'ave knocked me down wi' a feather! Right-down poorly he looked, an' feelin' poorly, an' all. Allus pokin' and pryin' at 'im they are, and won't give 'im no peace. Happen he'll nivver be worth his salt again."

"Don't worry. Lost Hill has a wide roof," he comforted her. But the old woman bristled angrily.

"You think I want to share a roof wi' yon Gethin?" she shrilled. "Poor I may be, but I've allus lived respectable, an' so I hope to die!"

"It's not for long. He'll be on his way soon."

Mrs. Bailey laughed caustically.

"An' her so set on the child? . . . Do you think I've got no eyes in me head, Mester? I tell you she's besotted wi' t'bairn. She'll nivver give 'im up, not without she's forced. Not even if she was to wed yon chap to get 'im. . . . Oh, I can see as far through a brick wall as most, I tell you, and I see that coming, plain as the nose on me face. . . . An' what's me an' Bailey going to do then? Ee, I can't get me sleep for thinking of it."

"Don't cross your bridges before you come to them," Tod told her. "Now, don't you think I might have a glass of that famous elderberry wine of yours, seeing I'm not a lad any more? I always longed to taste it, but you never would give me a drop."

"It's nowt to crack on," she grumbled, immensely gratified. She bustled away and Tod went in search of Jenny.

He was deeply disturbed by Mrs. Bailey's prediction; the more so because it was the echo of his own unacknowledged fear.

'She couldn't be such a fool!' he thought angrily. 'Any woman would know better than to take on a packet like that!'

But Jenny was not just any woman. Tod had never known a woman like her. He had known so few, really. . . . He could just remember his mother. She had been plump and pretty and she had laughed a lot. She had worn her hair in plaits over her ears, like shining platters. He hadn't bothered much with girls at Oxford. There had been none of the traditional incidents with tobacconists' daughters or female undergraduates. He had been young and happy and completely heart-whole, wrapped up in work and play. It had been different in the Army, of course.

War always made things different. You were going to be killed any minute, so what the hell! . . . So there was a girl in a red skirt, whose name he never could remember. And there were Trudi and Else in Cologne, and Angharad in the Welsh valley, and the Wren officer, and possibly others whom he had forgotten entirely. . . . None of them had meant very

much to him. They had been the creatures of his loneliness;
vain amulets against the inescapable fear; meretricious jewels
that had sparkled for an hour in the artificial light of a forced,
wartime gaiety.

And of course, vaguely at the back of his mind there had
always been the blonde, pleasant, healthy creature who would
wave to him from his doorstep, order his house, bear his
children, look well on a horse, and take her place beside him
in the life of the county. . . .

So where did Jenny fit into his scheme of things?

The answer to that, of course, was—nowhere. He had no
use for a girl like Jenny, with her childish inconsequence, her
fierce, adult stubbornness, her maddening disregard of con-
vention and all that made for law and order, the traditional
stability in which he had been reared.

Iris admitted him; told him with a stealthy stare that she
had not the slightest idea where the Missus was.

"Then please go and find her," Tod said briefly, and took
up a rather aggressive attitude on the hearthrug. *'Women!'*
he thought.

He was not in the best of tempers. Mrs. Scobie's early
promise as an indifferent cook had been dismally fulfilled. He
had risen from his midday meal feeling that one more semolina pudding would send him berserk. Only the knowledge
that the alternative would be yet another Tinned Mixed Fruit
swimming in tepid custard made him hesitate to complain.
He had made the initial mistake of saying airily that anything
would do, and he had only himself to blame. 'But good
heavens,' he thought, 'are there no eggs on the place? No
fruit? No cream?'

But her culinary lapses caused him less dismay than the
sudden and violent blooming of Mrs. Scobie which was taking
place daily under his very eyes. That which had been pale in
Mrs. Scobie now richly blushed; that which had hung limply
round her skull, despite numberless pins and kirbygrips, now

rose from her forehead in a pompadour of such brassy brilliance that one was obliged to glance again to make sure. Sanderson said it made his eyes water. And that which had been flat had now assumed such rich and provocative curves that imagination boggled at the methods by which they had been achieved.

Mrs. Scobie had suddenly become ubiquitous. He ran into her round corners. He fell over her on the stairs. Whichever room he chose to be in, that was the room Mrs. Scobie wished to dust or air or shut up.

Besides being visual Mrs. Scobie had become vocal. She sang about the place all day long; even at night after she had shut the door of her bedroom (but now, Tod guessed apprehensively, neither locked nor barricaded it) her dragging contralto could be heard. *Eileen Alannah* she sang and *I Passed By Your Window*, and a dreadful dirge about someone called Melisande, who was much given to the unhealthy pastime of kneeling beside dark pools in forests.

If, Tod thought impatiently, Mrs. Scobie had fallen a victim to his charms, as seemed dreadfully indicated, why could she not take the way proverbially quickest to a man's heart—through his stomach? Why offset semolina by rouge and uplifts and all this dim caterwauling? . . . 'Oh, Cassie!' he mourned.

He gazed round the square, solidly furnished sitting room of Lost Hill. He had not been in this room since he was a boy but, as far as he could remember, nothing was changed. The Victorian sofa and chairs that were surprisingly more comfortable than they looked. The Axminster carpet in red and green, the worn patch between door and table a little more worn, but still with years of life in it. And that enormous blue-and-white vase containing honesty—surely it had always stood in that very position! It took him back, it took him back. . . .

George and himself playing Ludo on that table and Mrs. Bailey shooing them off because she wanted to set the tea. George showing him a filthy book he had obtained from heaven knew where, and George's mother coming in unexpectedly, demanding to know what they were sniggering about. And the wet, steamy afternoon when he had kicked George most heartily in the pants because of the deliberate and loathsome things he was doing to the flies on the window-pane.

George had taken a knife to him on that occasion. . . . Yes, now he remembered with a curious sense of shock that George had actually come at him with the knife he had been employing on the flies. While his back was turned, too. . . .

They had disliked each other fundamentally; drifting together on the long school holidays from boredom more than anything, from propinquity.

After prep school their ways had parted; holiday encounters had been little more than a wave from a passing vehicle, an occasional drink in the pub.

'Good lord!' Tod thought, dismayed, 'fancy forgetting that! Came at me from behind, the little beast!' And he wondered with a sharp stir of compassion for Jenny what sort of man the young George had grown into; what sort of husband. At its best the marriage could have been no picnic. At its worst. . . .

He paced restlessly about the room. He drank the elderberry wine Mrs. Bailey brought him, praised it extravagantly. He glanced at the clock ticking solemnly within its glass dome. He had an appointment in Huffley in an hour. It was rather an important one; but suddenly it did not seem to matter whether he kept it or not. What mattered was that he should see Jenny, find out if she were well and happy; assure himself that she had not been crying again, alone up on the moor; convince her that she was not friendless and without help; that he, at least, having known George, could understand her need for love.

After all, what more natural than that she should love this child whom fate had thrust into her loneliness?

And Gethin himself, perhaps? . . . Oh, not that! At least not that, he thought violently.

He could stay in the quiet room no longer. He would go

and find Jenny for himself. He felt lightheaded. Perhaps it was Mrs. Bailey's elderberry wine, but perhaps not. Was it an even headier brew born of memory, of pity and, a little perhaps, of his own loneliness?

Well, the treatment for that was fresh air and action, not mooning about in this old house thick with old memories. . . .

As he passed the drawing room door he paused. A small sound came from the room, and for a moment he wondered absurdly if Jenny were hiding there; hiding from him.

He pushed the door open and went in.

The rear portion of a little boy dressed in blue jeans protruded from an open cupboard whose contents lay scattered about the floor; china, mostly, and good china at that; Old Missus' treasured and seldom used Spode coffee set.

Not one piece was broken. Even as he watched, the child emerged from the cupboard, breathing hard in concentration, his tongue showing between his teeth, a beautiful little cup held carefully between long, thin fingers.

He set the cup on the floor beside the other pieces. He moved them about so that they formed a circle. He placed a saucer in the middle of the circle and on the saucer he stood the cream jug, and on the top of that another saucer, then a cup. He sat back on his heels and laughed softly to himself: a satisfied sound.

Then, like a little animal sensing danger, his eyes flicked across the room and rested on Tod. They stared at him appraisingly, summing him up; wide, blue eyes made bluer by the colour of his overalls and wider by the short, thick fringe of lashes several shades darker than the daffodil hair that stuck up tuftily on his head. Why was it, Tod wondered briefly, that the term "inscrutable" was used only for dark eyes? Nothing could be more inscrutable than that light, bright stare.

Fearful for the china, Tod stood quite still and smiled.

"Hullo," he said pleasantly. "Building a house?"

The child stared at him silently, warily: he might have been carved in stone.

"What's your name?" Tod asked, taking a cigarette and flicking his lighter. After a moment he added, "Haven't you got a name?"

The stare never wavered.

"I think your name's Clem. . . . Come here and talk to me."

No sound. No movement.

Tod flicked open the old-fashioned gold hunter that had been his father's, held it out invitingly.

"Come and listen," he tried.

The blue stare was steadfast. Tod put the watch away, feeling a fool. He stood and smoked in silence and the little boy crouched on the carpet, silent, too. 'Where do we go from here?' Tod thought. One step forward, one unexpected movement, and that small, silent, watchful animal would be away into some hole, probably kicking the poised china to blazes in the process.

On the other hand, he couldn't stay here all day. . . .

A finger of sun wandered across the carpet, touched the black, empty fireplace, the silent clock. Outside, a brash October wind flung handfuls of brown and yellow leaves across the heavily curtained windows. From the distant kitchen the muted shrillness of the canary monotonously rose and fell.

He heard footsteps running, questions sharply put and indistinctly answered, and a moment later Jenny pushed past him into the room. She snatched the child up in her arms, pressing his head into the hollow of her neck.

"Where have you been?" she cried, her voice sharp with relief. "I've been looking everywhere for you!" Her foot touched the piled Spode. It tottered and fell and the handle of the cream jug snapped off. Jenny pushed it impatiently aside with her foot. She looked across the room at Tod, as if aware of him for the first time.

"I thought I'd lost him! . . . I've been looking everywhere. Gethin's searching, too. Iris said she saw him going down to the gates and I was so afraid he'd get out on the moor alone. I was afraid. . . ."

"Sit down," Tod said quietly, pulling up a chair. "You mustn't let yourself get so upset. He would have taken no harm for an hour."

"He might have got lost."

"A child of two isn't hard to find on an open moor," Tod said reasonably. "He couldn't get as far as the Tarn, and there are no adders about, this time of the year."

"It's the being alone that's frightening," Jenny said. "It's a terrifying thing to be alone and lost in a world you don't understand. I don't suppose it's ever happened to you."

"Why should you suppose that? I have been alone and lost many times. Afraid, too."

Their eyes met over the child's head.

'She could be pretty,' Tod thought, surprised. 'With that colour in her cheeks and her hair groomed and properly dressed. . . . She'd look nice with it done in plaits over her ears.' "Why don't you wear your hair in plaits over your ears?" he asked abruptly. "It would suit you so much better."

She looked at him with faint surprise.

"Do you think it would?"

"I'm sure of it. It's very long, isn't it? And thick?"

"It's a perfect nuisance. I never know what to do with it."

"Try it that way."

"All right," she agreed docilely. And suddenly she gave her small clear laugh. "Is that what you came to see me about— to tell me how to do my hair?"

"Good lord, no!" Tod's ears were red. "Please forgive me, it just slipped out."

"It was kind of you to say it," she assured him earnestly. "You are a very kind sort of man, I think."

What an afternoon, Tod thought in sudden exasperation. He had spent over an hour hanging about, wallowing in memories; he had been snubbed by the child, laughed at by the girl; missed an important appointment. And he hadn't yet said what he had come to say.

He would say it now, and be gone.

"I called to tell you that I've heard of a chap who could

take on Bailey's job. A decent sort of chap, name of Watts;
John Watts from out Huffam way. He wants an outdoor job
for a month or two. I've spoken to him about you, and he's
willing to start next week if that suits you."

He saw her arms tighten about the child. After a long
moment she said in a curiously flat voice: "It doesn't suit me."

Tod stood on the hearthrug looking down at her. She lifted
her head and stared back at him. The child stared at him, too.
He could not read either of their faces.

He schooled his voice to gentleness.

"You mustn't get too fond of the boy, Jenny."

"It's too late to tell me that!"

"Very well then, so you're fond of him. But you must let
him go. This man Gethin must go away and the boy must go
with him. Get it over and done with before it's too late."

"I don't know what you mean—too late," she cried defensively.

"Yes, you do."

Her brows drew together.

"I know all the beastly sort of things they're saying about
me in the village, if that's what you mean. I saw them staring
and gossiping when we drove through Huffley. Do you think
I care how they talk? What do they know about me, and what
I feel and what I need?"

"Do you know yourself?" he asked quietly.

"I want Clem," she cried passionately. "I want him more
than I've ever wanted anything in my life. I've never had anything of my very own—only Grey Boy, and they took him
away from me. I've never had anyone love me or need me
or depend on me. I want him, I tell you. I can't let him go!"

Tod was appalled by her intensity.

"Look," he said, "be reasonable. Is it likely Gethin will
agree to your adopting him? I take it that's what you want?"

"Why not? I could give him so much." She gazed at him
imploringly. Her arms held the little boy so tightly that he
whimpered and struggled. She let him slide from her knee
and he trotted back to his pile of Spode. Jenny pushed the

untidy weight of hair from her face and leaned her head back against the chair. The flush had faded from her cheeks and her eyes were shadowed. "You don't understand," she said wearily. "I suppose it's hardly possible that you should. I I expect you think I'm crazy. Maybe I am. . . . Yes, I think I am crazy. I wanted to be free, to have a life of my own. . . . When George died I had the chance. . . . I've lived an unnatural sort of life. Thwarted, I suppose you'd call it. I've never told anybody about it. . . ."

"Tell me."

Suddenly prim, she said: "Thank you, Major Shaw. I'm sure you don't really want to listen to the story of my life."

"The name is Tod," he said. "Go ahead!"

"All right," she said awkwardly. "You asked for it!" She smoothed the faded slacks over her knees with long, nervous fingers, her eyes lowered broodingly. She seemed at a loss for words. "You see," she said abruptly, "I wasn't very happy at school." She stopped again, watching her hands going over and down, over and down. Then she folded them in her lap, as if the movement distracted her thoughts. "I don't want to give you the impression that I wasn't understood, that they were harsh or unkind in any way. It was just that I didn't fit in. It was an expensive sort of school and most of the girls came from rich homes. My aunt paid the fees for me, and it didn't seem to occur to her that anything more was needed. Pocket money, and pretty clothes to wear on the days when we were allowed out of uniform, and special classes for music and dancing and elocution. All that sort of thing. . . . It set me apart from the other girls. They were nice enough girls, quite ready to sympathise and share with me, but I suppose I was proud or shy, or something. I wouldn't take anything from anyone. . . . There was Yvonne—the French girl I told you about—who lived quite near the school; she often asked me to go home with her for week ends, and the Sisters would have given me permission, but I never would, although I wanted to more than anything in the world. I thought Yvonne was wonderful. She *was* wonderful. She had everything I had not: beauty, grace, a happy home and a big, generous nature. And courage, too. Oh, she had such courage! . . . They shot her, you know." Her voice was suddenly hard and brittle, the glance she sent him fleetingly held bewilderment and horror. "First they raped her. Then they stood her up against a wall and shot her to pieces because she tried to save her father and mother. . . . I found out through the Red Cross. . . ."

"Go on," Tod said in an ordinary voice. She opened her fingers that had been clenched together, stared at them as if they hurt. She gave a sharp sigh.

"Well, so when I left school I went to live with my father; and I thought that now I should have someone who needed me, somewhere I really fitted in. . . . But it wasn't like that. Father didn't need me. He had managed perfectly well without me for years. We had nothing to give each other. I think I embarrassed him in some way. . . . It sounds so stupid put into words. . . . And then, you see, there was George. . . ." She sat quite still for a long time, staring at the carpet, silent. Tod shifted uncomfortably.

"Don't rake up anything that hurts too much," he said.

She appeared not to have heard him.

"George," she repeated in a flat voice. "I don't know what George was like when you knew him, when he was a boy; but as a man he could be . . . terrible. Frightening. And somehow pitiable. . . . I wouldn't have minded his cruelty if he had ever loved me, if he had needed me. I could have put up with almost anything just to know that I was wanted. But he didn't want me. He tired of me so quickly, just as he tired of his stamps and his pictures and his tarnished old coins. . . . I think his mother was sorry for me in a way, but I didn't want that. The girls at school had been sorry for me. Father, too, I think. I wanted to be absolutely necessary to somebody. I wanted to be depended on."

She paused again. Very softly the voice of Clem said, "Pitty!" their heads turned towards him.

The Spode was piled high, it swayed precariously. He

crouched beside it, watching intently, his thin, delicate fingers fanned out. "Pitty!" he breathed.

Tod took a step towards him but Jenny waved him back. "Let him alone," she said curtly. "He's happy."

"A box of bricks would come cheaper," Tod said dryly. But she only shrugged and said again, "He's happy."

They watched him silently. He had an extraordinary delicacy of touch and sense of balance. He was utterly absorbed in his building, quite oblivious of their presence.

"I didn't want him at first," she said. "I didn't want anything or anyone. I wanted to get away from this house and be free. I had never known any children, I didn't understand them. And he was ill, and so dirty—I had to force myself to touch him! But when I picked him up he clung to me, and he smiled. He was a bit scared, I could see that, I could feel it. He wasn't sure of me. But he smiled and clung to me tightly.... I didn't want him, and yet I loved his wanting me. I was all muddled up inside.... And I made him well. I did everything for him and, he looked to me to do everything. That was it, you see—he depended on me. And he put his arms round my neck and kissed me—oh, it was so sweet...." She brushed impatiently at wet eyes. "I expect you think me a fool. I *am* a fool! But nothing so utterly sweet had ever happened to me before, and I knew that I wanted him...."

"And if Gethin won't give him up?" Tod asked.

She did not answer, and her eyes refused to meet his.

"Don't tell me," he said roughly. "I know!"

"Tod...." she said uncertainly.

"You fool," he said, and his voice was sharp and rough. "You blind little fool! Have you thought what you'll let yourself in for? Haven't you any imagination at all?"

"Now tell me Old Missus would turn in her grave!" she flung at him. "Say your piece properly while you're about it."

They stared at each other; poles apart, yet so near that they could touch.

Tod knew the brief, extraordinary sensation that time rushed round them like a vortex, creating a nothingness in which this thin, dark, frightened girl and himself were trapped, inescapably alone together. 'I must get out!' he thought in numb astonishment. And knew in that instant with a sober and fearful joy that from this moment his life was bound up with Jenny's life. Whatever happened to her must happen to him, also. Whom she loved he must love. What she strove for he must strive to attain, as long as they both should live.

The feeling passed, leaving him shaken.

He reached out and took her hand. It was cold. He pressed it between his own hands, warming it, loosening the rigid fingers.

"Jenny," he said urgently.

A sound came from the open doorway and they both turned, startled.

The man Gethin stood in the doorway, dark and unsmiling, watching them. He breathed quickly as if he had been running.

"All over the moor I have been," he said, "looking for the child. And all the time he is here."

Jenny pulled her hand away from Tod's.

"I just found him here, Gethin. He wasn't lost at all. Iris must have been mistaken."

"She is a liar, that girl," he said sullenly. His eye fell on the broken handle of the cream jug. "He has broken something?"

"No," Jenny said quickly. "I broke that. Clem has been as good as gold, haven't you, Clem?" She held out her hand and the child went to her immediately. She stroked his pale head, pressed it against her thigh.

"Come here," Gethin told him.

The little boy hesitated, then he pressed closer to Jenny, circling her knees with his arms. From under the pale thatch of his hair blue eyes gazed up at her, flattered her with smiles. She flashed a triumphant glance at the dark figure in the doorway.

"He wants to be with me."

"He will do as I tells him," Gethin said softly. "Outside he should be. Grand parlours are not for such as him."

"But it's cold, Gethin. The wind is treacherous."

"There is treachery everywhere; indoors as well as out," he said sombrely. "Come, Clem."

Jenny knelt swiftly and hugged the blue-overalled figure to her breast.

"Kiss me before you go, Clem. Tell Jenny you love her. Say it, Clem!"

Tod turned away, stared out of the window at the blowing October afternoon.

"Let him go, Jenny," he entreated softly.

"Yuv you, Denny," Clem sang. With one eye on Gethin he kissed the point of her chin, stroked the backs of his fingers up her cheek in a deliberate, unchildlike gesture.

"There, you see? He loves me!" Jenny cried; and her laugh came sudden and harsh and very close to tears.

"Come, Clem," Gethin repeated impassively.

Without another word or glance the little boy went to him. Their footsteps went down the stone-flagged hall and a door slammed with finality.

"He does love me," she whispered. "You could see that, couldn't you, Tod? You could see he loves me." She shivered suddenly.

"My dear, you're cold," he said pitifully. "Come into the other room where there's a fire."

For a long time after Tod had gone Jenny sat crouched over the fire. She was very cold: cold to the heart. She yearned towards the fire as if she would draw it into herself, possess it in the frozen emptiness that was her body. Behind her the room gathered shadows about it; withdrawn, inimical, rejecting her and her problems.

Outside the October day languished and died under the hand of the wind. And then the wind died, too, with an abruptness that provoked disquiet.

The sudden silence sent her to the window, peering uneasily across the darkening farmyard heaped with fallen leaves. She could hear the goats complaining up on the hill. Had Gethin not milked them yet? What was he doing, leaving them so late? Where was he? Where was Clem? Out in that chill dampness of evening; without a coat or the rubber boots she had bought for him?

Had Gethin gone; really gone, this time, and taken Clem with him? . . .

For an instant it seemed that her feet were frozen to the floor. Then life rushed back along her limbs; she flung on a coat and ran out across the yard, down to the orchard field. It hurt her to breathe.

It was all right. It was all right! . . . The tent was there and there was a light in it. She heard Clem's laugh, shrill and excited, and a shout from Gethin, and the dull thump of a stick.

At the door of the tent she halted, shocked and repelled. Her hands flew to her face.

By the smoky flicker of an oil lamp she saw them; Clem crouched on his heels motionless, Gethin standing in the middle of the tent, one arm holding a heavy stick above his head. Facing them, cornered and desperate, was a large brown rat. Its eyes shone with hate. To Jenny's outraged sight the thing was as big as a rabbit.

"Don't move!" Gethin said sharply, not turning his head. And suddenly the stick came down again with a mighty thwack; the rat kicked convulsively and was dead; loathsome, but robbed instantly of all terror.

"He's a goner," Gethin said. There was blood on the end of the stick.

Clem sprang up and down, shrieking with delight.

"'S a goner!" he shouted. "'S a goner!" He ran towards the dead rat, but Jenny snatched him back and held him, struggling.

"How could you, Gethin!" she cried. Her whole being revolted at the scene, but she dared not say more. Gethin was angry with her already. She was afraid of saying too much, of going too far. At any moment he might put Clem in the cart and go away as silently and suddenly as he had come. . . .

He was grinning at her over his shoulder.

"We don't like rats, Clem and me."

She turned her eyes from the dead rat, feeling sick.

"Come Clem, it's time for bed."

The child resisted her, his underlip pushed out. Gethin threw the stick down, ran his fingers through his dark thicket of curls.

"He does not need sleep yet. Coming with me he is to milk them old goats."

"The goats should have been milked an hour ago," Jenny reproached him.

"No harm they will take. I have been busy, fair play, looking for Clem on the moor."

"I know," she conceded quickly. "But he must come in now, Gethin. It's too cold for him out here. We don't want him ill again."

"He must get used to the cold."

The little boy's head was flung back, watching them; first Gethin's face, then Jenny's. He wanted to go up to the orchard field with Gethin, into the dark, strong-smelling shed, with the eyes of the goats flaming in the lamp-light and the sound of their jaws crunching and the thin *swish-swish* of the milk spurting into the pail. And he wanted, too, to go back with Jenny into the big, warm house, and play with the yellow duck that bobbed in his bath water, and sit on Jenny's knee while she told him stories or showed him coloured pictures in a book. He wanted all these things. And he could do nothing about it; only look from one angry face to the other and wait to see what was decided for him. . . .

"Let me take him, Gethin."

"Coming with me he is."

Gethin held out his hand, and the child pulled away from Jenny and went to him.

She was defeated. There was nothing she could do but submit. It was no good arguing any more.

"I'll get him a coat," she said quietly.

"He can wear this." He picked up a length of sacking and wrapped it round the little boy. "Proper old farmer you are now, Clem bach!"

Clem hugged the sacking, grinning with pleasure, but Jenny exclaimed in disgust.

"Gethin! That filthy old thing!"

He laughed with real amusement.

"Filthy, you say! Only earth it is on the sack. Good, honest earth, that we all come from and all go back to. . . . Come you, Clem, or them old goats will get sore throats bawling."

"Please, Gethin, don't keep him out too late."

She left them and went back to the house. The air smelled strongly of rotting leaves. The yard was slippery with them. Her shoes were stuck with earth and leaves.

She went upstairs in stocking feet, shut herself into her bedroom and lit the lamp.

Her face stared back at her from the old, blotched mirror.

Why don't you wear your hair in plaits over your ears? It would suit you so much better.

Who had said that—Gethin?

No, it was Tod.

Tod. Tod. . . . Funny little name. Nice little name. Like a warm rock on which you could sit in the sun and feel safe.

And Gethin. . . .

She gave her fancy full rein, whispering the name to herself, watching her lips whisper it in the dim circle of the mirror. Gethin was a forest of whispering leaves. A dark forest, full of unknown paths and bottomless pools flecked with pale weed, stirred by secret slither of unseen life. . . . And enchantment? Wasn't there supposed to be enchantment in forests? If you were not alone in the forest, say, but held the warm, loving hand of a little boy close in your hand? Wouldn't that be enchantment enough? . . .

She began to brush out her long, dark hair. It began to crackle and cling round her cheeks. Perhaps it was not such bad hair, after all, she thought. She brushed until it shone like a river at night. Then she parted it down the middle, plaited it into two long ropes and wound the ropes into circles, one over each ear. It made her look astonishingly different.

'I could be almost pretty,' she thought. 'I need more colour. And some nicer clothes. . . . I must get some clothes. It is so long since I bought anything for myself. . . . A red dress,' she remembered, 'to show up my dark hair; and a blue one to put stars in my eyes. . . . It was Gethin said that.'

She rummaged in the wardrobe and found a dress of dark red stuff that she had seldom worn. It hung loosely on her, she had grown so thin, and the style was outmoded. But the colour was right.

'I must get some clothes,' she thought again. 'Dresses, and proper things to wear underneath. And shoes and stockings. I haven't got any nice stockings at all. All that money, and I haven't any stockings!'

Words began to float through her memory: alien words, but faintly exciting, echoes from another world. . . . Nylons. Mink. Suede. Chiffon. Brocade. . . . She remembered herself wandering down Bond Street, a thousand years ago; drifting from shop to shop, a solitary figure, staring at silks and furs and fine leather; revelling in colour and sheen; in the folds of a gossamer nightgown thrown across a gilt chair, the bloom of a fur cape, the trim jauntiness of tweeds and the flower-garden radiance of summer silks. . . .

She had admired without envy—for what beggar really covets the Koh-i-noor? But now, she remembered with a sudden pleasurable shock, she was rich. Rich—and she had nothing to wear but slacks and gum-boots and a tweed suit with torn pockets and lining!

She laughed quietly; and the woman in the mirror laughed back at her.

'Gethin said I ought to wear red,' she thought, 'and Tod told me how to do my hair. They don't think of me as a real woman at all.'

But if she had no reality for these two men, why had Gethin kissed her cheek? Why had Tod taken her hand, saying, 'Jenny!' in that strange, urgent tone?

'I am real,' she thought. 'I do know what I want. It's only that I don't know how to get it.'

She heard Clem's shrill treble out in the yard, the clank of a pail, Gethin's voice speaking to someone: to Iris, of course! That loud, meaningless burst of laughter was unmistakable.

From her window she could dimly see the little procession. Gethin, milk pail in one hand, lamp swinging in the other; Iris, walking close at his side, the shifting light making her face into a silly, upturned moon; Clem's tiny form, grotesque in the sacking cloak, trailing and slipping on the fallen leaves behind them. . . .

'He's tired out!' she thought angrily. 'Poor baby, he's tired to death. I *will* have him now. He must let me have him.'

Running into Clem's room she lit the lamp, pulled the red curtains close, made up the fire, drew the tin bath before it and the low chair and the tray of toilet things.

When she was half-way down the stairs Gethin came along the passage with the child, already half asleep, in his arms. He paused with one foot on the bottom step, looking up at her.

"There's pretty!" he exclaimed softly in genuine pleasure.

Suddenly conscious of the red dress, the shining plaits, Jenny retreated to the top of the stairs. She held out her arms for Clem.

"It's very late," she said, nervous under that black, appraising stare. "Much too late for him to be out."

"There's pretty!" Gethin said again. His hand reached out to touch a shining plait. "Here's a present for Jenny. Pretty Jenny!"

The little boy half opened his eyes.

"Pitty Denny," he murmured sleepily.

"Give him to me," she said shortly, her cheeks flaming. She

gathered him into her arms and went into the room, closing the door with her foot. Leaning against the door, her breath coming quick and shallow, she listened to his footsteps as they went down the stairs, very slowly, and along the passage to the kitchen quarter.

The leaves of the forest whispered all about her: whispered and promised and threatened. . . .

❉✲❉✲❉✲❉✲❉✲❉✲❉✲❉✲❉✲❉✲❉✲❉✲❉

CHAPTER NINE

THE last leaves had been stripped from tossing branches. The bones of the trees, bare and beautiful, were stretched against a steel-grey skyline. Patient ploughs crawled up and down the patchwork fields and white drifts of gulls followed the ploughs. The moor stared frozenly at a frozen sky. Ice filmed the surface of the Tarn. Sheep huddled plaintively at the troughs for fodder and from the shadowed corners of barns, brown owls hooted incessantly on moonlit nights. The hum of the threshing machine continued all day long, and the old year stirred in her sleep, dreaming of her youthful lustiness.

Tod had been home for three months. It seemed incredible. Twelve weeks of tramping aimlessly round the fields with Sanderson; of driving down into Huffley on unimportant errands; of eating in solitary state on the end of the dining room table; of sitting alone before the fire, drinking too much whisky and watching the hands creep round the white, implacable face of the clock until it was time to go to bed again. Twelve weeks of enduring Mrs. Scobie's slipshod meals, her terrifying advances and coy withdrawals; the suffocating smell of the perfume she lavished on her person; the revolting sight of her long, scarlet nails, her brassy hair, the rouged scragginess of her face; the perpetual menace of her siren-singing. Twelve weeks of worrying about Jenny and the whole setup at Lost Hill. Twelve weeks of doing nothing about it, because there was nothing he could do, or anyone else could do, as far as he could see.

Twelve weeks. . . .

And now it was nearly Christmas.

The children at the tiny schoolhouse in Backshaws had given their annual concert at which Tod, embarrassed but genial, had presented a number of prizes and made the sort of speech that was required of one on such occasions. Shrill little boys had sung carols. Self-conscious little girls had recited *It Was the Schooner Hesperus* and *Christopher Robin Is Saying His Prayers*. Prinking babies in pink tulle had danced on their toes with fingers touching above crimped heads. A lanky youth in spectacles had played the violin surprisingly well and a stout little five-year-old had forgotten her lines and retired in tears, to the accompaniment of kindly laughter and loud, clucking commiseration.

Afterwards there had been a party; a stodgy, peace-time tea followed by games in which Tod had joined with a certain shy enjoyment. He had stood in a hand-locked ring of children and parents singing *Auld Lang Syne*, and had gallantly kissed the flurried little school-mistress under the mistletoe.

And then it had all been over, and the hard, bleached road had rung under his feet as he had returned to yet another lonely evening with the whisky bottle and the distant strains of Mrs. Scobie's love-laments. There was not even Wendy to keep him company; for Wendy had transferred her not very stable devotions to Mrs. Scobie and now spent her evenings by the kitchen fire. "I reely can't think *why!*" Mrs. Scobie had protested in arch apology. "She seems to have taken quite a fancy to poor little me. Two lonely women, aren't we, girlie?" This with a languishing glance at Tod followed by a gusty sigh, both of which he had ignored.

He had a shrewd suspicion that large plates of food and a firmly shut door had a good deal to do with Wendy's new allegiance, but he did not really care. Trixie's daughter had never taken her mother's place in his affections. One of these days he'd get himself another dog. A golden retriever, perhaps, or an Alsatian—though that was rather a chancy business in sheep country. Or he might get a small, compact Cairn that he could tuck in beside him everywhere he went and have sleeping on the end of his bed. One of these days. . . .

Mrs. Bugle had decorated the bar of The Bell with a lavish hand. Holly outlined each picture, stood stiffly in vases along the window sills. Mistletoe swung coyly from the central lamp. Paper chains festooned the walls, and everywhere bells of coloured paper swung soundlessly in the draughts from opening or shutting doors. Immense fires blazed, before which the ginger cat slept in unmolested majesty.

Three days before Christmas Tod went in for a pint on his way home from Huffley.

"Morning, Ben," he said. "How's tricks?"

"Mustn't grumble," Mr. Bugle replied impassively.

"Proper weather for the Season!"

"Might be worse," Mr. Bugle admitted.

In the rather strained silence that followed, Tod sensed reproach. Since his return he had seldom been into The Bell, and he guessed that they thought him stuck-up and stand-offish—not the man his father had been. Too much of this gadding about and drinking in the big places in the town. . . . His father had been a temperate man, but he had liked his tankard of old-and-mild amongst his friends and neighbours. 'And what better place,' thought Tod, 'to strike a bargain or settle a debt or discuss the points of a new mare? . . . I must come in more often. I'm missing something.'

"What will you drink?" he asked; knowing that Bugle made a fetish of not drinking before the evening, but hoping the olive branch would be accepted.

For a moment the landlord continued his task of polishing a glass. Then, surprisingly, he poured himself a half-pint of mild.

"All the best, sir," he said in stately forgiveness.

"Cheers," Tod murmured.

They drank deeply. Tod began to fill his pipe.

"How's Mrs. Bugle?"

Bugle pursed his lips and looked profound.

"She 'as 'er ups, you know, and she 'as 'er downs." He pondered darkly on these switchback aspects of his wife's well-being, seemed on the point of divulging some information and then appeared to change his mind. He began polishing again with great vigour. "Tekken' it by and large," he summed up, "we mustn't grumble."

Joe Clynes of Reetly came in with Jackie Bates. They nodded with elaborate nonchalance to Tod, made the usual enquiries for his health and admitted that, for their part, they mustn't grumble.

"Settling down, like?" Clynes asked him.

"More or less. It's taking a bit longer than I expected."

"Ah. You'll miss yer dad, I reckon."

"I do that," Tod said sincerely. "The place doesn't seem the same without him."

"Ah. One of the best, yer dad were."

"He were that," Bugle and Jackie Bates agreed.

Tod warmed to them. They were good fellows; good, solid Yorkshiremen, born and bred to the land. He must get to know them better. . . . He bought them drinks, renewed his own and the landlord's glasses—which latter circumstance caused Jackie Bates to accuse Bugle of going to the dogs. "Nay! Two 'arf-pints of mild, before 'is dinner, an' all! It's the thin edge of t'wedge, Ben, my lad!"

"Christmas," Ben announced, "comes but one a year." Easy laughter rang between the lounging men. The bar was brightly warm and cheerful. Pots and bottles gleamed and wood shone, and the good smell of roasting pork and boiling greens came pleasantly through the half-open door from the kitchens.

A little man in a bowler hat propped his bicycle outside the window and came in, blowing on his hands.

"Morning all," he piped. "Half o' mild, Ben."

"On me," Tod said benevolently.

The little man's eyes popped. He muttered "Cheers!" and hid himself behind his mug, hoping this did not mean paying for a round himself. His wife kept him very short of money and he wanted to buy a Christmas present for his little girl.

Mrs. Bugle came in from the house premises. Her hair was wound into steel curlers, her buxom curves, unrestrained by corsets, were encased in a flowered print pinafore. She seemed a little put out to find Tod there, and her eyes flicked the promise of a few words with her husband on his lack of initiative. But Christmas came for Mrs. Bugle also, but once a year; and presently, after the correct amount of persuasion and protestation, she allowed Tod to buy her a small port, which she sipped genteelly, eyebrows arched and little finger delicately lifted.

"I'm not dressed for company," she apologised. "You'd think anyone could manage to be dressed and out of the kitchen by midday, with two great girls in the house, not to mention Ben here and yon lad that reckons to help in the yard an' that. But don't you believe it, Mester Shaw! If I don't see to every mortal thing meself, nowt gets done. Every mortal thing I have to see to meself. It's a crying shame, that's what it is."

Tod said that it was, and that he could well believe it, and that it did Mrs. Bugle credit.

"And never abed before half-past eleven—more like twelve or after! And up at six every morning of me life," Mrs. Bugle continued, sipping away at her port. "I often say to Ben, I say, 'I don't know how long I shall last at this rate,' I say. 'But this I do know, you'll never get nobody else to do it— not if you go down on your bended knees you won't!' I say. I've said that to you many's the time, haven't I Ben?"

"You 'ave," said Mr. Bugle sourly.

"Two great girls skulking round the 'ouse all day long," she went on, her face reddening with port and indignation. "And not a hand's stir out of either on 'em, without I push 'em to it! It's a crying shame. I said to Ben this morning, I said, 'Thank yer stars you're not a woman,' I said. Didn't I, Ben?"

"You did," Mr. Bugle agreed sucking his teeth.

"I said, 'A woman's work is never done,' I said. An' that's the truest word as ever was spoken!"

Jackie Bates opened his mouth to be funny about this, but Joe Clynes kicked him sharply on the ankle. Being funny with Mrs. Bugle was not a paying proposition and he wished to drink in peace.

The little man in the bowler hat sidled towards the door, murmuring excuses for leaving the company, and pedalled thankfully away to his dinner. Tod made a few gallant remarks to his irate hostess and insisted on her drinking another port. He bent to tickle the ginger cat under the chin.

"Been fighting, has he?" he remarked, noting one lascerated ear.

"Fighting?" Mrs. Bugle echoed indignantly. "That cat never fought in his life! As mild as a lamb my Tommy is. No, that's the work of yon tinker chap over at Lost Hill, that is. An' if ever he dares to show his face in yon door again, he'll get the length of my tongue, he will that! . . . Enticed 'im," declared Mrs. Bugle, setting down her port as if she could not trust herself to hold it while the awful tale was told. "Deliberately enticed that poor creature out o' the door an' off to heaven knows where, an' got 'im lost for best part of a day an' a night. Not a wink of sleep I got—did I Ben?—not one wink of sleep while 'e come limping 'ome again, thin as a rail, 'is ear all torn an' bleeding an' one foot lame. And filthy!" Here Mrs. Bugle's powers of description failed and she could only roll her eyes and flap her hands. " 'Well,' I said to Ben, I said, 'Let yon chap show 'is nose in this bar again,' I said, ' 'an' I'll pull it off with me own hands,' I said. Didn't I, Ben?"

At this point a tousled female head came round the door and was understood to mention that the greens were boiling over. Whereupon Mrs. Bugle tossed off the remainder of her port, exclaimed, "What did I tell you!" to Tod, and vanished, slamming the door behind her.

The four men stood motionless, eyes downcast: almost, Tod thought, as if they were observing a two minutes' silence.

Then, still silently, Mr. Bugle drew four tankards of mild-and-bitter and set them on the bar.

"On the 'ouse," he murmured.

They all drank, drew gusty breaths of relief and grinned sheepishly at each other.

"Fact, though," said Bugle, nodding a portentous head. "Moment he come in yon door, cat wouldn't let 'im be. Up in 'is arms, purring fit to bust. Layin' round 'is neck like a perishin' tippet. An' no sooner had chap gone than he were after 'im like a streak o' greased lightning! Wheer he went I don't know an' never shall know. All I know is he come home in a shockin' state. Shockin'! . . . We had the Vet to 'im. Twenty-five bob, if you please, an' no guarantee as 'e wouldn't go septic. My word," Bugle ended reverently, "I've seen the wife spitting mad a time or two, but never like yon! Nor," he added frankly, "I never wish to."

Tod rubbed the toe of his boot along the overfed sides of the pampered animal. He did not for a moment believe that Gethin had harmed one hair of the creature. If he could have believed it he would have been more hopeful. Cruelty to animals was something you could cope with.

There was no doubt that, when he chose, the fellow could charm. Tod had seen it for himself. Old Posy whinnied wildly when she heard his step. The brown pony followed him like a dog. Mrs. Bailey's two cats forsook her immediately he came in sight: it was not the least of her complaints against him. And on two occasions when their paths had crossed, Wendy had run to him fawning and whining with pleasure.

He had remarked it in the child, Clem. In Jenny herself. . . .

A couple of centuries ago it would have been called sorcery, he supposed. The villagers would have ducked him in the pond, or strung him up to a stout oak limb, or burned him at the stake. And very nice too, he thought savagely. In this enlightened age, of course, you stood politely by and watched your dog or your girl charmed away from your side. . . .

"Joe, here, he'll bear me out," Bugle was saying. "You was here, wasn't you, Joe? You an' all, Jackie—you both saw it 'appen."

"That's right," they chorused. "Never knew the beggar could move so fast," Clynes added.

"Never knew the beggar could move at all!" Bates contributed, seeing that Mrs. Bugle was not present.

Three or four newcomers joined in the discussion.

"I hear owd Bailey's pretty bad."

"Poor owd sod! Go in with a twisted ankle, an' come out with 'arf of yer insides cut out. . . . It's a caution, yon!"

"Lucky if they let him out at all—without it's in a box!"

"I reckon his number's up."

"Aye, well, we all come to it, sooner or later."

Everybody drank and edged away from the subject. After all, Christmas came but once a year, and nobody present but had his own troubles. Speculation as to the actual status of yon tinker chap at Lost Hill opened up, and promised to become ribald. . . .

Tod had suddenly had enough. He excused himself from further conviviality and left the company discussing the juicy subject from every angle with unabated gusto.

The air was sharp and still. Sounds came clearly from a very long way off: the curt commands of a sheep dog, the clanking of a pump handle and, somewhere, a girl's voice dragging out, *"I'll see you again. . . ."*

After the warm stuffiness of the bar the air stung the nostrils pleasantly. Pale sunlight washed the frozen road and a robin, tossing on a frosted twig, puffed out his scarlet breast and voiced approval.

Starting up the car's sluggish engine, Tod sloughed off his sudden depression.

What, after all, had Lost Hill to do with him? Old Doc had asked him to be neighbourly. Well, he had been neighbourly. He had tried his best to help and she wouldn't be helped, and there was nothing more he could do about it. Let her marry the fellow if she'd no more sense than that. Why should he mess up his life worrying about it! . . . He whistled a soft accompaniment to the invisible girl's song, slammed the door and turned her nose for home.

As he slid cautiously down to the gates he saw that he

had visitors. A large, expensive looking car was parked in the drive and a stout, elderly man stood beside it talking to Sanderson. Even at that distance, and after years of absence, Tod recognised the portly figure, the loud, confident laugh, the general air of affluence belonging to Alfred Scales, mill owner and local bigwig whose ornate and execrable dwelling dominated the once green and solitary slope of Huffam Hill.

Both men turned at the sound of his engine. Scales sketched a jocular salute in the Nazi manner. He called something in a loud voice, and a girl came out of the house and stood smiling and waving on the doorstep.

She was big and blonde and healthy-looking. She would, undoubtedly, look well on a horse. In all probability she was the potential mother of fine children. And she was waving to Tod from his own doorstep. . . .

There she was. Old Scales' youngest girl—Sadie, Sally—something like that. He knew her at once, though she had changed from a pigtailed schoolgirl into a fashionable young woman.

Looks, health, money and, he seemed to remember, amiability. And there she was waving to him from his own doorstep. . . .

Tod stood quite still, staring.

The plump, near-matronly figure. The blonde permanent wave. The frank amiability. The abundant health. . . . Strange sensations ran through him: an unwilling pleasure half obscured by a swift, secret pain. . . .

He waved back; not so much in greeting as to stop her waving to him. He went forward and took her hand; made the usual exclamations at her altered appearance; teased her kindly about her abandoned pigtails; reminded her of small, ridiculous incidents of the past. That time she fell through the ice into the Tarn. The week-old puppy she had smuggled into church, and which had screamed for its mother until the pair of them had been marched down the aisle in disgrace.

She laughed loudly at his badinage: too loudly. She opened her eyes too widely, showed too many of her nice teeth, agreed with him too eagerly, flicked him with an over-manicured hand when his remarks became too pertinent.

Her father shouted with laughter, slapped Tod on the back and gave him a cigar, pressed him to visit them at the earliest opportunity. This, he said, was the third time he and Susan had called on him. They'd begun to think he was dodging them and, if so, they wanted to know why, didn't they, Susie lass?

Susie lass giggled, opened her mouth and her eyes wide and said that now they had run him to earth they weren't going to let him escape again, were they, Pop?

"Won't you come in?" Tod suggested, wondering what Mrs. Scobie's reactions would be to two extra people for lunch.

But no, they would not come in. They were late as it was.

"Just wanted to know what you're doing for Christmas," Scales boomed. "You don't want to stop here, cooped up alone, you know. You come to us, lad, an' have a bit of fun. The Missus'll be delighted. She doesn't go out and about a deal hersen, but she likes to see the young folks about her. We shan't mek a stranger of you. Liberty Hall, that's us! Tek us as you find us, but there'll be a crust an' a swally o' beer, I'll be bound!" His laugh wheezed richly at this superlative joke, and he smote Tod once again between the shoulders.

Tod laughed, too, in duty bound. He edged, not very skil-fully, round the invitation, saying he would let them know if he could manage it, dispensed some of his father's fine old sherry, and watched with relief as the great car climbed away from the gates.

"Well, there you are," Sanderson said, "all fixed up for Christmas, and very nice too!"

"Who says I'm fixed up?" Tod snapped.

"Don't mean to tell me you'll not go?"

"I think it's extremely unlikely."

"You're daft!" Sanderson told him grimly.

"I've promised to lunch at his club tomorrow, and I'm com-mitted to cocktails with Susan the day after. That seems to be enough for a start."

"Now sitha, Tod, you're Mester here, and I'm man. But I've known you since you was born and I couldn't be fonder of you if you was my own lad. It's time somebody talked straight to you, Tod. I reckon you'll be barmy if you don't go to Scales' for Christmas. They'll mek you right welcome, an' you'll have a champion time. House'll be full of folks, young and old, and there'll be plenty to eat and drink—never mind where it come from!—and that's nowt to turn your nose up at, times like these! You want tekkin' out of yourself, Tod. I don't like t'way you're going on. Moonin' about alone, avoiding the right folks, an' no interest in t'farm. . . . Oh, don't try to tell me! I wasn't born yesterday. I can see as far through a brick wall as most, an' a bit farther than some. . . . You've no heart for t'farm. You can't settle to your work. Best part o' three months you've bin back, and the men still calling me Mester. . . . It's not good enough, lad!"

"I shall settle down," Tod said irritably, "in my own time and my own way."

"Go to Scales's for Christmas, for a start! Alfred Scales may not be everybody's cup o' tea, but he's a smart enough chap in his own way. He knows everybody, goes everywhere. You'll meet folks as'll be useful to you. Mek yourself friendly an' folks will be friendly to you. Shaws has allus tekken their rightful place in t'community, an' you don't want to be different from yer dad, and them as went before him. Pattern's bin a right good one. Don't spoil it."

"The pattern is changing of its own accord," Tod said. "Who cares two hoots, nowadays, whether Shaw of Backshaws is on the Bench or not, or chairman of this and that committee! The Council is made up of the local Toms, Dicks and Harrys—and good luck to 'em! Let them shoulder the burden if they want to, and find out what it's like."

"Yer dad would never have talked that road," Sanderson muttered sombrely.

"The King is dead. Long live the King. . . . That sort of thing doesn't work any more, Sanderson."

"Nor never will while chaps like you mek no effort to put

things to rights. . . . Aye, well, I'd better be gettin' back. I've me own dinner to get. Our Ellen's gone to Huffley to buy hersen a new hat. Lord knows why, for she's getten a cupboardful, an' never claps one on her head!"

"Have dinner with me," Tod said. "I'd be glad of your company, you old termagant, you!"

Sanderson grinned and followed Tod indoors, where an aggrieved Mrs. Scobie made a loud, clattering display of setting another place at table, and a resentful explanation of the dried-up condition of the grilled cod steaks. "One o'clock, and everything was done to a turn!" she moaned. "And now look at it!"

They looked at it. Sanderson poked at his portion with a gloomy fork.

"Never mind," Tod told him maliciously, "I'm sure Mrs. Scobie has a nice semonila pudding to make up for it!"

"Well, there!" Mrs. Scobie exclaimed, "However did you guess? . . . I was going to make an apple pie, only what with one thing and another. . . . And then that young lady inviting herself in the way she did, and me with only the one pair of hands. . . . 'I'm frozen stiff!' she says. 'Can I come in an' get meself warm?' And into my kitchen she comes, though I'm sure there was a lovely fire in the sitting room, and shooting off questions enough to make your head spin! Did Mr. Shaw like this or that or the other? And was he partial to so-and-so? And what did he do with his week ends? . . . Well, I mean to say, who could make an apple pie under those conditions?"

"Who, indeed!" Tod said smoothly. "Mr. Sanderson must take us as he finds us. Liberty Hall, that's us, and always plenty to eat—never mind where it comes from—which is not to be despised, times like these. Right you are, Mrs. Scobie, I'll ring when we're ready for the semolina."

"Tod," Sanderson said when they were alone again, "if you was a few years younger, I'd upend you an' tan yer backside!"

"Get on with your nice cod steak, you old ruffian," Tod grinned, "and thank your stars Susan Scales put the stopper on that apple pie, if you value your digestion."

Because they were hungry, they ate the cod and the semolina and drowned their sorrows in some of the port Tod's father had put down at his birth. It was past its prime, but still good, and the tempers of both men were mellowed appreciably.

"Y'know, Tod, yon's a grand lass of Scales'. Handsome woman she's going to mek."

"I believe you. Looks well on a horse, I'll be bound."

"A fair treat!" Sanderson said eagerly. "A good breeder, an' all, I'll tek my oath. There'd be no lack of sons if she was Missus here."

Tod twiddled his port glass backwards and forwards, watching the light catch and gleam in the rich colour.

He suddenly saw the old house alive with children. Sturdy boys with clattering feet, graceful little girls laughing together, their blonde heads gleaming in sunlight. He saw Susan, groomed and competent, sitting there across the table from him, dispensing hospitality with a lavish hand. He saw the old house renovated, refurnished; clean as a new pin under the ministrations of well-trained maids. He saw the end of cod and semolina, burnt chops and muddy coffee; the end of doubt and confusion; the end of loneliness. . . .

"Always supposing, of course, that she'd have me," he suggested with an attempt at lightness.

"Aye," Sanderson replied dryly. "Allus supposing. . . ."

When he had got rid of Sanderson Tod went out, striking across his own land in a circuitous route for the Tarn. He did not imagine that the ice would yet be thick enough for skating, but he wanted to see for himself. It was many years since he had done any skating. Tomorrow he would poke about in the attics and see if his old skates were still in existence.

Susan skated well. He remembered her as a child, gliding effortlessly round and round, cutting figure eights, shooting in between timid novices, delighted if she caused panic. He remembered how her pigtails had shone in the sun. He remembered one time when he had tried to catch her, and how she had screamed and laughed as she circled round and round his more cautious figure. . . . She had been a jolly little kid.

He wondered if Sanderson were right, after all.

She had been a jolly kid. She was a jolly girl now. She would be a jolly, laughing, comfortable woman; large and loud, yet not without dignity. She would look after him. She would look after his children, his house, his interests. Her ambition would urge him on, and the money old Scales would leave her would back up her ambition, making a solid defence against any retreat. . . .

'Oh, lord!' Tod thought, 'It's just as if I'd stumbled headlong over a hidden hoard of gold that I don't want, and yet don't like to leave untouched. . . .'

A flicker of scarlet caught his eye and he stood still, watching with narrowed lids until he identified the object. A scarf, of course. It must be that fellow from Lost Hill mooching about on his land again. Well, he'd put a stop to this, once and for all!

"Hi, there!" he called. Keeping his eyes on the scarlet patch he made his way towards it.

The scarlet ceased to move. And presently the form of the wearer detached itself from the background of trees and was revealed as Gethin, dark and smiling, and not at all abashed by the furry burden hanging limply from his hand.

"I thought I warned you off my land?" Tod said loudly, as soon as they were within speaking distance.

"I don't remember that," Gethin said politely.

"Then your memory is pretty poor!"

"I remember, Major, that you told me to come in at the gates if I wanted to speak to you."

"Very well, then."

"But I didn't want to speak to you, see?"

"I can imagine that," Tod said, eyeing the two rabbits hanging from his hand.

"Ah, you won't be missing a couple of rabbits, with all the hundreds you've got! Proper old nuisances they are, rabbits.

But good for the pot." His cigarette glowed against his dark mouth. Smoke issued from his nostrils in thin streams. With his free hand he hitched at the khaki slacks belted about his hard, flat waistline. He made Tod feel lumpish and heavy, conscious of the weight he had put on since leaving the Army. Conscious of being a stone heavier, two inches shorter and probably five years older than this insolent hound, damn him!

"Take those rabbits down to Shaws and give them to my housekeeper," he said curtly. "And from now on, keep off my land."

Gethin said softly: "For Jenny I got them."

Tod took a grip on himself.

"I hardly think Mrs. Rowland instructed you to come poaching on my land. And keep a civil tongue in your head when you speak of your mistress." He cursed himself for using that particular word as a smile played briefly round Gethin's lips.

"Her name it is, fair play. Jenny. A pretty name, I think. Pretty Jenny. . . ."

Tod's fist glanced off the point of Gethin's jaw. Gethin dodged nimbly, came up behind Tod. An excruciating pain shot up the length of Tod's arm. He could neither move nor free himself. He heard the fellow laugh softly behind him; the warmth of his breathing was on Tod's neck.

"I shouldn't do them sort of things, Major. You're older than me, and not in fighting trim, what with your leg and all."

"Let go," Tod said harshly.

Gethin immediately released him, stooped to pick up the rabbits that lay between them on the frozen grass.

"Jenny wants me to stay." Gethin's voice was quiet, his expression thoughtful, quite devoid of offence. Tod turned to go, then swung round again. He looked Gethin straight in the eyes.

"Why did you come to this place?"

"Asked me that before, you did," Gethin answered slowly. "I told you."

"Bunkum! You didn't come all the way from a Welsh valley

in order to find work on this particular farm without some
reason. Now then, out with it!"

Gethin ground the butt of his cigarette into the frozen,
rutted earth.

"Always on the move I am," he evaded. "That's my life."

"You were asking the way to Shaws."

"Why not?"

"*Why?*"

In the last few moments the sun had dropped behind the
western hills. A chill wind blew down the valley. A black line
of rooks beat across the leaden sky, making for home. Tod
shivered involuntarily. He felt cold to the marrow. His leg
began to ache; the arm Gethin had twisted ached, too. 'Don't
ask, you fool,' he thought. 'Go home and let well alone.' But
he had to know, and he knew he could make Gethin tell him.
Tod had been trained to command and Gethin to obey, and
that training was still too recent for either to reject.

"Come on, let's have it, man!"

Gethin shifted uneasily.

"Looking for the child's father I was."

Tod's hands clenched in his pockets.

"The boy is not yours?"

"No."

Tod's throat hurt when he tried to swallow.

"Why pick on me?"

Gethin's glance followed the rooks out of sight.

"Angharad told me about you," he said softly.

"I see. . . . And you hoped to make a nice little packet?"

Gethin shrugged his broad shoulders.

"I thought his father might be glad to know he was well
cared for."

"Well cared for! The child was ill, he had no proper
clothing."

"All children get ill sometimes. All children grows out of
their clothes. He hadn't needed clothes in all that hot weather
we'd had. . . . I got him clothes as soon as I could. I looked
after him okay."

"What proof have you that the child is mine?"

"No proof at all, Major. I just took a chance."

"You believed what Angharad told you?"

A faint smile came and went on the man's thin lips.

"Ah, you couldn't believe a word she said, Major."

"Where is Angharad now?"

"She died more than a year back. Her lungs was rotten and they took her away to the hospital and she died."

Tod took a deep breath.

"You, I take it, were living with Angharad at the time?"

"That's right, Major."

"And how long had you lived together?"

Gethin shrugged again.

"Six months—ten months—under a year, anyways. . . . . Took up with her I did soon after I was demobbed. The boy was a few months old then. After a bit she was ill and they took her away and then she died, see?"

Tod looked at him consideringly.

"You realise that I can check up on all this?"

"Okay."

"What you don't seem to realise is that blackmail is a serious crime and carries heavy punishment."

Gethin smiled suddenly, brilliantly.

"I haven't asked you for a penny, Major!"

"But you came here for that purpose."

"Ah, I wouldn't say that! Things has turned out different from what I expected, anyways."

"You mean you don't want to get rid of the boy?"

"Whyever should I!" The words were spoken in such genuine astonishment that Tod's animosity lessened in spite of himself. "We're kind of fond of each other, Clem and me. Brought him up from a baby I have, fair play."

'What a preposterous conversation this is!' Tod thought. He felt suddenly tired, discouraged and rather old. The east wind bit into his bones, right through the Army overcoat, right through the heavy tweeds and the knitted pullover he wore. Gethin wore nothing but his sweater and khaki slacks, and precious little underneath, Tod surmised. His lean body was braced against the wind but he did not look cold or tired. He did not look in the least furtive or ashamed. . . .

"Take that lot down to my housekeeper," Tod said curtly. "And from now on, keep off my land."

He walked away trying not to let his limp show. He would have been glad to go home, but that would have meant taking the same path as Gethin. It was too far, after all, to the Tarn. He would go to the Tarn tomorrow. He cut across the fields to the road, climbed the stile clumsily and stood staring uncertainly through the frosty twilight at the lighted windows of Lost Hill.

And after a while his feet seemed to move towards them of their own accord. Slowly, even reluctantly, but quite inevitably he made his way to Jenny.

The house was quiet and warm. It smelled of wood smoke and furniture polish and the cakes Mrs. Bailey had just pulled out of the kitchen oven.

He went into the kitchen for a moment to ask after her husband.

The old woman peered at him over the spicy load. She was in one of her tempers. Her toothless jaws worked up and down and her head trembled on its sinewy stalk of neck.

"They're sendin' him home!" she cried angrily. "Cut half of his insides out, an' then send 'im back for me to mend. As if I 'adn't got enough on me 'ands without!" She shot a baleful glance at Iris who was sulkily cleaning silver at the end of the table. "What's hospitals for, that's what I say!"

"I expect they're short of beds," Tod said mildly.

The old woman snorted.

"They were sharp enough giving 'im a bed when there were nowt amiss wi' him but a twisted ankle. I could 'ave put that right mesen wi' a poultice—but no, he mun be took down to t'hospital! An' then they pokes round in 'im while they finds summat they can tek a knife to. . . . It's not good enough,

Mester!" she shrilled. "My Jos were a strong, healthy chap. Ten good years of work in 'im there were. An' now what? What am *I* going to do, an' nobody to work for me when I'm past it?" Her head trembled uncontrollably and her brown, wrinkled face worked and puckered.

Over the heavy cruet she was polishing Iris stared at her contemptuously. Her eyes slid round to Mester Shaw, hoping to share the joke. But Mester Shaw, it seemed, was not amused. He was looking soppy at the owd buzzard, as if he felt sorry for her. He ought to live with her for a week, Iris thought viciously, and see how that suited him! As far as it was in her to hate a man, Iris hated Tod. He had never for one moment looked at her as if she were a woman. . . . He wasn't a patch on Gethin, in spite of his brass and his great farm. He wasn't a patch on Bailey, if it came to that. . . . Iris smiled reminiscently and perhaps anticipatorily. Bailey might be an owd 'un, but he knew a thing or two that Iris had found worth knowing. She attacked the cruet again with a secret relish.

"There were nowt wrong wi' him at t'start," Mrs. Bailey was reiterating sharply.

"There's nowt wrong with that cake," Tod said guilefully. "I don't get cakes like those nowadays."

"Oh, *her!* . . . I've heerd as she uses lard for 'er cakes, an' throws her drippin' in t'dustbin! You want to get shut on her, Mester, afore she 'as you in t' Poor House. Tek the lamp an' show Mester Shaw into t'room," she added sharply to Iris.

"No, no. I'll find my own way."

"I'll bring thee a sup of tea."

"And some of that cake—the crusty one?"

"Get along wi' you!" she grumbled, hiding a grudging pleasure.

He stood for a moment before opening the sitting room door. Jenny was reading a story to the child.

So Father Rat and Mother Rat and the baby with the long brown tail all went down to the river together to teach the baby how to swim. And Mother Rat thought no other baby had such a handsome tail as her baby had, or such bright, black eyes, or such a glossy coat. . . .

"Gessin killed a wat," Clem said loudly. "Bang! Bang! He's a goner!"

"Yes, well, listen to the story, Clem, and sit still. . . . 'So when they got to the river, Mother Rat said to her husband—'"

"What's 'usband?"

"Husband means the baby's father."

"What's farver?"

"The big rat that the little baby belonged to."

There was a moment's silence. Then Clem said fretfully, "Where's Gessin?"

"Gethin's coming soon. Now listen to the story, Clem, and then we'll have tea."

"Want Gessin!"

Tod opened the door and went in.

Their heads were close together, the dark head and the bright. The coloured picture book had fallen to the floor and Clem was knuckling his eyes, inclined to tears. Jenny's arms were tight about the thin little body, her gaze brooding and compassionate.

Caught between lamp and fire, they were ringed with light; like a holy picture, he thought. The red of Jenny's garment, the blue of the child's, the bright pages at their feet stood out against the shadowy background with a strange and poignant beauty.

She put the child down and rose to greet him; nervously, he thought, but not without pleasure.

"I'll ring for tea," she said.

"It's on its way. I've been gossiping in the kitchen. I hear Bailey's coming home."

"Yes. He's had a bad time."

"Lucky he hurt his ankle, or maybe they wouldn't have known he was ill until too late."

"Gethin knew," she said slowly. "He told me Bailey was going to die."

"Want Gessin," Clem fretted.

"He's coming soon, darling."

"But he didn't die, you see," Tod pointed out. "Which only goes to show."

"To show what?"

He shrugged impatiently.

"Bailey was due to die in the natural order of things," she said somberly. "Gethin knew that. . . . Modern science happened to save him, that's all. Won't you take off your coat?"

His arm gave a sharp twinge as he shrugged at the sleeve.

"You're obsessed with this man, aren't you!" he said angrily.

"I'm not, I'm not!" she cried, and her voice was sharp, almost anguished, so that he looked at her more keenly, first in surprise, then with a dawning delight.

"Your hair," he murmured. "You've got it done in plaits, like I said!" His eyes travelled over her with pleasure. "And that red dress . . . it suits you. You look beautiful, Jenny."

"Oh, do you think so?"

"I do think so."

"Pitty Denny," Clem said loudly. He put his arms round Jenny's knees, glowering up at Tod in sudden jealousy.

Jenny laughed rather nervously, but Tod did not laugh. While Jenny went to see about tea, he stared in sombre perplexity at the child who stared back resentfully at him.

"Come here," Tod said, holding out his hand.

Clem did not move. He stared fixedly at Tod, legs planted apart, the long line of his mouth set in stubborn repudiation. No beauty, Tod thought, yet there was something attractive about the little beggar. There was character there and plenty of it, whether good or bad. Those very bright blue eyes, deeply set and far apart; the long upper lip; the delicate hands; the pale hair. . . . There was little of Angharad in him, so far as he remembered Angharad. The hair might darken with age, the figure broaden and thicken; you never knew with children. . . .Was there anything of himself there? The mouth was not unlike. And those shoulders—were they rather high and stiffset? It was easy to imagine things, once you started. He was beautifully dressed in pale blue woollen jersey and knickers edged with some furry white stuff. His socks and shoes were white and his tufty hair shone with brushing. His skin was healthy looking, quite free from blemishes. Jenny was looking after him well.

"Go away," Clem said clearly and very deliberately.

Tod sat bolt upright in surprise.

"I'm doing nothing of the sort," he replied. "I'm going to stay for tea, and if you don't like it, you can lump it."

Clem spat suddenly and violently. His aim was good but the distance between them was too great to affect Tod with more than a surprised distaste. For a moment he could think of nothing to say. They just stared at each other across the lamplit room. 'What on earth makes him hate me so?' Tod wondered.

"It's a pity to do that," he suggested coldly, "on such a nice carpet. Jenny's carpet," he added. "I don't think Jenny would like that very much."

Clem's gaze lowered itself to the carpet. After a moment he came forward stiffly, warily, rubbed the toe of his shoe into the carpet and retired again. The blue eyes never ceased their inimical watchfulness.

With an attempt at friendliness Tod flicked his lighter several times. "Blow!" he invited, kindling and extinguishing the flames. Clem never even glanced at the performance. Tod put the lighter away, pulled his chair nearer to the fire and ignored the child.

After a few moments Clem squatted on the floor, drew the picture book into his lap and began to repeat the story of the rats word for word, as Jenny had read it. " 'Mother Rat thought no other baby had such a handsome tail as her baby had, or such bright, black eyes, or such a glossy coat. . . .' "

He glanced obliquely at Tod's averted face. He brought his thin little fist down on the picture with a sudden thump. "Bang! Bang!" he shouted. "He's a goner!"

Tod paid no attention to these histrionics. He inserted the poker between the bars of the grate, so that flames shot up, crackling, and heat came out. 'He can talk well enough when he likes,' he thought. 'What a secretive little beggar!'

"' So when they got to the river Mother Rat said to her 'usband. . . .'" And here Clem had to stop, defeated.

Diffidently Tod held out his hand for the book.

"Shall I go on?"

Clem shut the book with a bang. He flung it from him violently. Scrambling on hands and knees he reached the half open door. Tod heard his feet pattering down the passage, his shrill voice shrieking for Jenny.

Presently she came back alone carrying the loaded tray. She shut the door with her foot, forgetting how often she had scolded Iris for doing this.

"Clem is having his tea in the kitchen."

"Does Mrs. Bailey allow that?" Tod exclaimed.

"She doesn't mind. Actually," Jenny admitted grudgingly, "she rather likes him. Iris, of course, is the sort that makes a fool of herself over anything young—especially if it happens to be male. . . .You do take sugar, don't you?"

"Please."

"And here's your cake. I've never known Mrs. Bailey cut into one before Christmas. You must be popular here!"

"It doesn't seem to work with Clem, anyway."

The silver knife bit through the cake.

"Clem needs understanding," Jenny said shortly.

"You're telling me! . . . And how clearly he can talk now."

She stared at him, frowning astonishment.

"He just talks baby-talk, like other children of two. I can understand what he says very well."

Tod set down his cup with a click.

"Don't deceive yourself. He spoke clearly enough just now. He told me to go away."

"He didn't!"

"And then he started showing off with the book, pretending to read the story you were reading aloud when I came in. He enunciated every syllable clearly and correctly. He remembered every word. I offered to finish it for him, and he chucked the book across the room and scrammed. . . . He hates me, that kid! I've tried to make friends, but there's nothing doing." He laughed shortly and bit into the spicy cake. "I don't seem to be such a howling success round these parts, after all."

The fire leapt and crackled and shadows jumped in the corners of the quiet room. Tod went stolidly on with his tea. Across the lamplit pool of tablecloth Jenny looked at him with troubled eyes.

"You have been so kind," she said uncertainly. "I shouldn't like you to think I don't appreciate it. . . . Please don't think that, Tod."

"I haven't been kind at all," he said carefully. "I have not been allowed to be kind. I've merely offered you advice—which you have chosen to reject. That's all there is to it. Anyone can offer advice."

"I plaited my hair to please you," she said; so childishly that his heart melted and he longed to smile forgiveness. But he kept his eyes down.

"So you did. And I think you'll agree my advice was good there. It might be worth your while to take a little more of it, don't you think? . . . Do you mind if I smoke? And I should love another cup of tea if there's one going."

She made no answer, no movement; just sat still staring down at the linked hands lying in her lap.

Tod lit a cigarette, shifted his chair round so that he could cross his knees. Deliberately he began to think about Susan Scales.

Blonde, healthy, simple, uninhibited. With no past that he could not compass at a glance, no future he could not mould to his own pattern.

Susan would make his home come alive with her laughter

and the voices of children; with rich smells of well-cooked foods and bright gleam of polished furniture; with the crunch of wheels on the drive, the loud welcoming and speeding of many guests. Susan's father would pull strings and the puppets would dance as they were directed. Susan's money would oil the wheels of Shaws, and money would beget money. Susan would want to be a Councillor's wife, so he would be on the Council. She would fancy herself as Mayoress, so in a few years he might well become Huffley's Mayor. Very possibly he would get a Knighthood: you could buy anything with brass. . . . Sir Edward Shaw. And after that—why not?— Lord Shaw of Backshaws. . . .

But all that, he reflected wryly, was hardly himself moulding Susan's future. It was Susan moulding his. . . . What did it matter? You could only live your life once. It was not himself that mattered. Tod Shaw was only a link in the chain. But the chain mattered; and the chain was Shaws. Shaws would go on and on, long after he and Susan and Jenny were little heaps of dust in Huffam churchyard. . . .

He stole a glance at Jenny.

Her head was down on the table, hidden in her arms. He thought she was crying but he could not be sure. One of the dark plaits had come uncoiled; it hung across her shoulder almost to the floor.

What thick, heavy hair. And what frail, childish shoulders sharply outlined beneath the red stuff of her dress.

His heart gave a tug of compassion. Such an absurd, exasperating, appealing creature! She had no defences against life, this girl, this child who had been denied womanhood; this groper after substances who grasped only shadows. . . . He had a sudden, immense urge to drop on his knees beside her, take her in his arms and say: 'Marry me, Jenny. I'll look after you. I'll give you a house that welcomes you. I'll give you children of your own. I'll bring life to you gently, so that you'll learn to love living for its own sake. . . .'

But he went on sitting in his chair, conscious of all that stood between them: the shadow of Shaws and its ceaseless, traditional demands; the small, stubborn shadow of Clem; the dark, equivocal shadow of the man Gethin. . . .

From the circle of her arms her voice came softly, with a note of apology, of pleading.

"Tod. . . . I think you ought to know that I'm going to marry Gethin . . . if he wants me to."

Tod threw away his cigarette and stood up. Suddenly he was furiously angry. His anger swept away all his tenderness for her, all his pity.

"When?"

"We . . . we haven't spoken of it yet."

He forced himself to restraint.

"You know the sort of man he is? Thief, liar, lecher? . . ."

She lifted her head and looked at him. Her eyes were troubled but her mouth was firmly set and there were no tears upon her cheeks.

"A lot of men who are called respectable are all these things underneath," she said slowly. And Tod thought: 'What about me? Have I never lied, never taken what was not mine to take?' But the flash of self-revelation did nothing to lessen his anger.

"Look here, Jenny, does this fellow sleep in the house?"

"No. For a few nights he did. I gave him a bed in Clem's room. But soon he went back to sleeping in the tent. He said sleeping in a house stifled him."

"You know about Gethin and Iris—your own servant?" he insisted cruelly. "It's common talk in the village."

"It's not true, Tod. How can you listen to the village gossip!"

"You don't choose to believe it, that's all," he said angrily. "You deliberately blind yourself to the truth."

"It is not the truth," she said with a weary dignity that stabbed at his heart. "Iris is a slut. She gives him no peace. But there is a good side to him, Tod, as well as the one you know."

"Do you imagine you are in love with him?"

"No. Oh, no, I don't think so. I want Clem, that's all."

Tod shrugged himself angrily into his coat.

"You don't even know that the child belongs to Gethin. You don't know anything about either of them, do you?"

He saw a flicker of fear in her eyes; but her lips were pressed stubbornly together.

"You said you wanted to be free," he went on harshly, "and you are deliberately selling yourself into slavery!"

"I said free to do as I wished with my own life, Tod."

"And this really is what you wish to do with your life? Think, Jenny! Look at the thing straight. Face up to it."

"I want Clem," was all she could say.

Tod shut the door and went out into a night of blackness and bitter cold. From behind the glowing red curtain of the kitchen window the high-pitched laughter of the child came clearly to him.

Bending his head to the wind he began the long walk home.

CHAPTER TEN

THE Christmas tree stood in a dark corner of the drawing room; mysterious, beautiful. Its fingers touched the walls. Its delicate head reared up nearly to the raftered ceiling. The silver globes, the bright, brittle ornaments of red and blue and green, the frosted streamers hung from bough to bough, caught at the light and held it, so that the tree dominated the room, so that there seemed nothing in the room, but the tree and the brightness it had drawn into itself. . . .

Clem stood by the doorway, his mouth open, his eyes wide with wonder. He would not go near the tree, would not touch it, but he could not tear himself away. It was the most exciting and beautiful thing he had ever seen. From time to time he would stretch out his hands towards it, long, thin fingers fanned out, and make stroking movements in the air. His lips would move as if he whispered to the tree. But he would neither approach nor touch it.

When Jenny had first opened the door and let him in he had gone very pale and his hands had flown together under his chin. He had made a small, whimpering sound, as if something hurt him.

"Come along, Clem, it's all right. It's only a tree with pretty things hung on it. Look!"—and she had gone forward to touch the tree, to reassure him.

He had screamed with sudden violence, so that she had halted, rather appalled by his reaction to the lovely thing.

"Don't touch it," he had whispered.

He had gone running from the room to find Gethin; and presently they had returned together, Clem slung over Gethin's shoulder. He had set the child down and they had stood together hand in hand, staring and fascinated, dark eyes and blue gleaming with awe and admiration.

"There's pretty!" Gethin had said softly. "There's pretty indeed, Jenny bach! . . ."

"Clem won't touch it," she had told him.

"It is not for touching. Enough it is to look at it."

All day long Clem had stolen in and out of the drawing room, standing by the door to stare and whisper and make his soft, stroking movements in the air. There had been presents at the foot of his cot when he woke that morning: a book, a box of barley sugar, a little red cart with a long handle. He had accepted these calmly and without question. Christmas meant nothing to him. Even to Gethin, Jenny suddenly realised, Christmas was nothing more than a brightly-coloured word. . . . The revelation at first had shocked and appalled her.

But what, after all, did Christmas mean to herself? . . . She stood by the window, staring out across the frozen yard, trying to recall the half-forgotten.

As a very small girl in her aunt's house, she vaguely remembered a great many grown-ups eating a great deal of hot food. And there had been new clothes, an orange in her stocking, a suitable book. . . . At school Christmas had meant end-of-term exams, chocolate biscuits for tea, Yvonne taking her to peep at the lovely little crib the Sisters had made in the chapel. The Sisters themselves had been extra kind, in this season of Christian kindness, to the poor little Protestant. *Pauvre petite!*. And then the dreaded Channel crossing, the bustle of the lighted London streets and the shut-in quietness of her aunt's house. . . . In Soho Father had never taken the slightest notice of Christmas, nor encouraged her to do so. And anyway, the war had come so soon. . . . Here, at Lost Hill, while Old Missus was alive there had been food and yet more food; mince pies hot from the oven for visiting tradesmen, for carol singers, for any and all who called at the house. There had been a goose, chicken, sauces and stuffings of all kinds, rich black puddings flaming in brandy, trifles snowed under whipped cream. . . . Somehow Old Missus had managed it, war or no war. Food and bustle and extra housework—these had been Old Missus's sole conception of Christmas. Since her death there had been nothing save what Mrs. Bailey chose to provide. . . .

Jenny had never known the true, inner happiness of Christmas; never been drawn into its deep wonder, its mystery and simplicity such as she had sensed when peeping at the crib with Yvonne in the dim, incense-smelling chapel. She had made the tree partly for herself and partly for Clem, so that they should stand on the threshold of beauty and glimpse it together, even without understanding. . . .

She had taken immense pains over the tree, searching for hours in the Huffley shops to find the small, expensive ornaments that seemed in such short supply; hanging and rehanging the shining, fragile globes until it seemed quite perfect to her. It had been nearly midnight when it was finished, but she could hardly bring herself to go to bed, hardly wait until morning to watch Clem's pleasure in the tree. . . .

She put on a thick coat and went out to feed the chickens.

Gethin was sawing logs down in the orchard field. She could hear the rasp of his saw as it bit into the wood. Sometimes there was a pause; and then she could imagine how he straightened up, bracing broad shoulders, hitching the khaki slacks higher. He would whistle a few bars of a tune, and then the sawing would begin again. He was a worker.

When she had fed the chickens she went slowly down to the orchard field.

He saw her coming, threw down the saw and grinned, stretching his arms and drawing a long, deep breath.

"Gethin, do you really think Clem likes the tree?"

"He likes it," he replied.

"He seemed—frightened of it."

"He is not frightened."

"He won't go near it. He won't touch it."

A robin came bouncing lightly about on the frozen ground, its head cocked warily, first to one side, then the other. A lorry thundered past along the road and it flew up to a near-by branch uttering a few clear notes.

"It is not for touching," Gethin said. "There's some things, you see, that's too beautiful for touching. Spoil them it would, bring them too near, see what I mean? Make them too ordinary."

"A child would not think like that, surely?"

He hitched the khaki slacks higher and tightened his belt. "Children knows the hell of a lot of things they're liable to forget when they're growed up."

Jenny stared at the log pile, frowning. What extraordinary things this man said! Would she ever understand him? . . .

"What a lot of logs!" she murmured.

"Nothing to do I have but these old logs, so I keep on." He rolled the sleeves of his sweater higher up his long, sinewy arms, still brown from the summer's sun. He took the stump of a cigarette from behind his ear and lit it. He never asked permission to smoke in her presence, whether inside or outside the house. "Soon," he added slowly, "that old Bailey will be back again."

Jenny's heart gave a jerk.

"He won't be fit for work, Gethin—not for a long time. I shan't be able to manage without you."

He blew smoke in a long, steady stream.

"He will never work again, that Bailey. Time for him to die it was, but they wouldn't let him die, down in that hospital. They cut him an' patched him an' sewed him up again, and they'll send him back to the old woman alive, and think themselves clever. But he'll never work no more."

"Well . . . supposing you are right . . . that's all the more reason for you to stay, Gethin. Isn't it?"

He put his foot on the glowing end of the cigarette. His dark eyes rested on her consideringly.

"What is it you want me to do?" he said slowly.

Jenny felt the hot tide flushing her neck, her face; pricking up into the roots of her hair. Now it had come. Now she must face it. . . . She drew a quivering breath and tried to swallow.

"I want you to stay, Gethin."

"An' how long will you be wanting me?"

Staring at him helplessly, she could find no words to say.

"How long?" he insisted. "For always? . . . Is that what you are wanting, girl?"

Now the hot tide receded and she was suddenly cold, so that she must clutch the coat more closely round her body. Even so she shivered. The bare bones of the orchard trees shivered with her, and were still. . . .

He came close to her. His hands were not ungentle, but there was no resisting their strength as he forced her chin up until her eyes met his.

"Is that what you're wanting? For me to be master here, an' you my woman, an' us to live here together for always?"

Her lips parted but no words came. She felt as if she were frozen to the iron ground.

"If you love me, my girl, you'll leave this house an' come along with me in the cart. . . . And you know what that'll be like? . . . Cold you'll be at night unless I keeps you warm. There'll be no shelter from the rain or from the sun, and never stopping long in any place. . . . You'll work when there's work to be had, an' go hungry when there's no work. Coppers'll move us on an' women'll slam their doors in your face, an' your children'll wear what clothes you can get for 'em. . . . There'll be lucky times," he went on, "an' then we'll eat our bellies full an' be warm an' dry. And there'll be bad times when you'll be glad of a crust from a dustbin. . . . There'll be days you're glad to be alive, an' days when you'll wish you was dead. . . ."

His arms came round her and she felt herself pulled close against the hardness of his chest. Something beat furiously between them—his heart or hers: she could not tell which. The bitter smell of sweat-soaked wool was in her nostrils, and the clean, dry smell of the sawn wood. One of the logs fell from the top of the pile with a small crash. She heard the goats bellowing forlornly up on the hill, and the hoarse sound of a distant car changing gear far down the road.

His mouth came down on hers. His kiss was hard and slow and infinitely revealing. When it was finished she would have fallen had not his arms held her.

"Is that how you love me?" he said roughly. "Will you come away in the cart with me an' the boy because you love me like that?"

Her mouth was trembling so that she could not speak. 'I asked for it,' she thought dimly. 'It's my own fault, I asked for it. . . .'

She pushed her hands against his chest, but he would not let her go. She felt weak and frightened. New and astonishing sensations shot through her body and she trembled from head to foot. His dark eyes were watching her intently.

"You've never been kissed like that before, have you?" he said. "You didn't know anybody'd kiss like that. . . . What sort of chap was that husband of yours, anyway?"

"Let me go," she whispered. "Take your hands away from me. Please let me go. . . ."

He pushed her from him suddenly, so that she staggered back against the log pile.

"No," he said, "you don't love me at all, do you? You don't know how to love. . . . Hate it, you would, to come away in the cart with me. An' you don't want me to stay, neither. All that about needing me was lies, wasn't it, Jenny? . . . Even if we got married in a church, an' all respectable—that's not what you're wanting, is it, Jenny? . . ." His face screwed up into a grimace of silent, mirthless laughter. He bent and picked up the saw, bending it back and forth in tense fingers. Light flashed brightly from the blue, supple steel. "I know well enough what it is you want. You want Clem. You want me to go away an' leave Clem with you. That's what you want, Jenny bach, isn't it?"

Her glance was shamed but eager.

"Oh, Gethin . . . if you would only let me have him!"

The goats were bleating again. He turned and stared at them as they pranced and circled on their long chains up on the hill's crest.

"An' what about me?" he demanded, swinging round on her again. "What do I get out of it?"

"I'll pay you well," she said in a low voice. "I'll give you anything you ask if you'll let me have Clem. I can give him so much, Gethin—things he'd never have if he stayed with you. I'll send him to a good school. We'll travel, see the world. He could go to a university, be trained for some profession. . . . It's such a chance for the boy, Gethin. You must see that."

"Book learnin'!" he said contemptuously. "What good to a man is that!"

"He's quick, Gethin. He's a clever little boy. I've only to read him a story once or twice, and he can repeat it word for word."

"So can a parrot."

"If he stays with me he need never be cold or hungry again, never be without a roof over his head."

"So much the worse for him!"

"That's only your way of thinking," she cried, angry and desperate. "You think only of yourself. It's Clem you've got to think of, not yourself. His life, not yours."

"*You*, to say that to *me!* . . ." His voice was quiet and deliberate, heavy with scorn. "You say you love the boy, but you don't know what it is to love anybody. . . . Why don't you marry your fat farmer an' have half a dozen brats of your own, an' find out what life's all about!"

He laid the saw across the log trough. His narrowed eyes glanced at the sky which was grey and solid-looking. He sniffed delicately at the air.

"There's snow coming—plenty, by the looks of it. Better it would be to bring them old goats down the hill. A job it will be to get fodder up to them if the drifts is deep."

He began to move towards the hill. The ground crackled sharply as he trod the wheel ruts, the frozen hoof marks of the brown pony. The short grass of the hill was stiff with frost. On the windward sides of the trees each bough, each branch and smallest twig was delicately rimed with white.

Over all the land lay the strange, penetrating light that heralds snow, and the expectant hush that comes with it.

Jenny watched him go a few steps; then suddenly she ran after him, calling him sharply by name. He swung on his heel, unsmiling, waiting for her to speak.

"Gethin . . . if you did stay here . . . I mean for always, like you were saying just now . . . would you like that?" Her voice was small and breathless, her eyes enormous with apprehension. Her face, tilted at a sharp angle above the hunched shoulders, looked pinched, blue-shadowed. He gazed down at it impassively.

"I dunno," he said slowly. "A bit of thinking about it would want, that."

"You won't go yet, will you, Gethin? Not until you've . . . thought about it?"

"I won't be going yet awhile."

As she turned to go he reached out and fastened the storm collar of her coat high up round her face. His fingers rested a moment against her cheeks. "Frozen you are," he said with a rough tenderness. "Better you get back into the house right away."

Tod thought he had seldom heard so much noise in so confined a space.

There were twenty people in the room talking at the tops of their voices, laughing immoderately, shouting to each other, singing the silly words to the tune a young and exuberant redhead was pounding out on the grand piano. Several couples —he and Susan amongst them—were pushing each other backwards and forwards, trying to dance on the deep, dragging pile of the fitted carpet. A young subaltern in uniform was playing a mouth organ. Two excited grandchildren who should long ago have been in bed were running round and round, blowing shrill blasts on instruments they had received from the colossal party favours Alfred Scales had obtained from heaven alone knew where.

The heat of the room was unbelievable. Everyone was smoking too much, drinking too much. Everyone was hoarse with laughing and shouting. Alfred Scales was in his element. At any sign of flagging he was on his feet immediately, filling up glasses—"Nay, Christmas comes but once a year, lad!"—opening fresh boxes of cigarettes, being gallant with the girls and matey with the men and loudly contesting any suggestion that it was time his grandchildren were in bed. "Christmas comes but once a year!" he shouted over and over again; and everybody laughed loudly, as if he had newly coined the phrase.

The only quiet person in the room was Alfred's wife.

She was small, grey-haired and dumpy. She sat with tightly-folded, beringed hands in a corner of the room, and spoke when she was spoken to. If a grandchild ran to her she would smile and hug it fondly. If a guest, remembering his manners, included her in a joke, her grey head would duck in laughter and her fat little hands beat on her knees. "Go on with you!" she would cry. "Go on with you!" But she seemed content to be ignored. Her small, bright eyes followed Alfred about the room. 'How can she bear the great noisy brute!' thought Tod, whose head felt like a balloon filled with concrete.

"Oh, stop it, Tod!" he heard Susan saying. "You're giving me a pain!" She pushed him sharply, gasping with laughter and wiping her eyes. He realised with a sudden shock that he had been clowning stupidly, making a fool of himself. People were staring, laughing, calling encouragement.

The redhead sprang up from the piano.

"Somebody else play," she shouted. "Tod and I are going to do an exhibition dance. Come on, Tod, loosen up, we'll give 'em a basinful of jitterbug!"

She began throwing herself about, posturing absurdly. She was little more than a child; rather pretty, scarlet-cheeked, bright-eyed, silly with excitement. She had thrown herself at Tod the whole of the evening. She wagged a finger at him, advancing and retreating, arching her back and waggling her immature hips. "Whoops, dearie!" she cried. Tod imitated

her movements, wagging his finger and arching his back in a
sheepish attempt to play up. 'Oh, lord,' he thought, 'I'm making a fool of myself! I'm too old for this sort of thing. . . .'

A ring formed round them. Hands clapped, voices chanted
and feet stamped rhythmically. The young subaltern had
taken over the piano. He was grinning as he sang the stupid
words. Susan was stamping and clapping with the rest, but
Tod was suddenly conscious of the displeasure underlying
her smile.

Susan was jealous, he realised with a shock of dismay.
Jealous of the little redhead; of anybody he spoke to or smiled
at or touched, other than herself.

What had he done? What had he said? . . . He cursed himself for coming to this party.

Still clowning, he fought his way out of the ring, resisting
all the redhead's screeching encouragements, and flung himself down on the floor between the wall and the armchair in
which his hostess sat enthroned.

"Phew! . . . I'm much too old for that sort of thing!"

She gave a little squeal.

"Go on with you! . . . I know how old you are. I remember
you being born."

"Do you really?" He shook his head at the offer of a cigar,
waved away a drink that was being thrust upon him. "Well,
that was a long time ago!"

"Ee, yes, I remember. . . . A great big boy you were, and
your poor ma had a hard time of it. Right upset the whole
house was, and your poor dear father very near out of his
mind. . . . Ee, I shall never forget that night, never! . . . She
were a lovely woman, your ma. A grand wife and mother,
an' the best mistress any girl could wish for. We all loved her.
Aye . . ."

He stared at her rather muzzily. Had she been a friend of
his mother's back in those old days? He suddenly realised
how little he actually knew of this family. He could remember
this house being built; recalled his father's ironic comments
on it and its owner. The figure of Alfred Scales had been

familiar enough, striding and shouting about the place in everincreasing opulence. He was known all over the countryside as a warm man, a go-getter; a figure of fun that yet compelled reluctant admiration. He had been on more or less friendly terms with the older children. But he had been away so much. The small, laughing, confident child that Susan had been was his only clear memory of them all.

"You knew my mother?" he asked.

Mrs. Scales regarded him with surprise.

"Ee, well, I should just about think so! I were in service at Shaws six years before I married Alfred. We was married just after you was born." Then her pudgy face crimsoned and her fat little hands moved nervously up and down the arms of her chair, sending out shimmering sparks of jewelled light. Her glance darted guiltily about the room. "Ee, there, now! I didn't ought to have said that, did I? The girls are always on at me, but my tongue always was my downfall. . . . Not as I'm ashamed of it, luv. But with Alfred's position, you see, and the girls married so well, happen I ought to keep mum about them old days. . . ." She laughed self-consciously and blew her button of a nose. "Ee, my word," she said simply, "I nivver thowt when I were scrubbin t'kitchen floor of Shaws as I'd ever be sitting here like what I am, with everything heart could wish for! . . . I didn't want to leave your ma, but Alfred wouldn't be said nay. 'It's now or never, Annie,' he said. He said, 'I'm going to get on, Annie, and I shall want a woman behind me—and if it's not you,' he said, 'it'll have to be somebody else.'" She blew her nose again, replaced the handkerchief in a satin bag with a diamant clasp. "So you see, luv, I hadn't a deal of choice, had I?" She laughed uncertainly and her eyes sought out the burly figure of Alfred, who was giving his youngest grandchild a piggy-back round the room.

Tod patted her hand. He liked this little woman. If Susan took after her mother there wasn't much amiss with her. Of course, she might take after her father. Well, that might not be such a bad thing, either. . . . You had to be sensible about these things.

He took a cigarette he didn't want, lit it irritably. Susan made no secret of her liking for him, but he wasn't going to rush his fences. Women were the very devil. . . .

"Aye, a chap needs a woman behind him, luv." Annie Scales folded her hands again contentedly. "Alfred knew that. And of course, my bit of money came in handy at t'start. I always like to remember that." Her eyes twinkled, seeing his surprise. "Oh, aye, I'd got a nice little bit put by! Eighteen pounds a year your ma paid me the first three years, an' twenty pounds after that. Good money that was in those days. My folks didn't need help, so I saved most of it, what with your ma being generous with uniforms an' that, and me not being one for gadding about. Best part of eighty pounds I had when I married Alfred: enough to furnish the three rooms we had."

"That damsel who took my hat and coat tonight would turn up her nose at it, I'll be bound!" Tod grinned.

"You never spoke a truer word!" Mrs. Scales said tartly. "Two pounds a week I have to give that girl, if you'll believe me, and about as much use as me knife half shut! Answering t'door and a bit of dusting's about all she's good for. And on top of that," she added, her voice rising in wrath, "she wants me to call her Miss Pollitt, if you please! I soon put t'stopper on *that!* 'Maud your name is, an' Maud you'll be called while you're under this roof' I said. 'And if you don't like it, you can lump it!'" She fumbled with the clasp of her bag and her eyes glanced uneasily round the hot, smokewreathed room. "But there, I mustn't keep you listening to an old woman's nonsense, luv, or I shall get into trouble."

A grandchild hurled itself weeping against her knee and she turned her attention to comforting it.

Tod rose to his feet, pulling at his waistcoat and flexing his knees. Susan was talking animatedly to the young subaltern, but he was uneasily conscious that she observed his every movement. He felt trapped in this hot, bright, noisy room. He longed for fresh air, darkness, quietness.

Cautiously maneuvering, he slipped out of the room, shut the door silently behind him and crossed the thick pile of the hall carpet. He opened the front door with a deep sigh of thankfulness. Stars hung coldly in a tranquil sky and the smell of frost came sharply on the unmoving air. The lights of Huf-fam Hill lay below him, terraced down to the dark ribbon of the Huff. Across the valley the lights of Hawks Hill rose as steeply. The two hills, once so wild and beautiful, stood tamed and patient, like oxen in harness, under the jewelled chains that man had laid upon them.

Would it be thus with Shaws some day? Tod tried to visual-ise it. The farm turned into Ye Olde Roadhouse. The south pasture boasting a super-cinema, a car-park complete with Ladies' and Gents' and a snack-bar in technicolour. The forty-acre sprouting rows of bungalows with pink asbestos roofs. Even Heartbreak, perhaps, would at last be tamed; hacked and hewed and drilled into submission, crowned with a row of shops, a garage ringed with petrol pumps, a red brick Methodist Chapel. . . .

A melancholy fell upon him. He breathed deeply, trying to dispel it. 'It'll be all the same a hundred years from now,' he tried. But that didn't work, either.

He wondered if it would matter very much if he found his hat and coat and slipped away now; he could apologise later, blame his wound. . . .

He knew he could not treat that nice little dumpy woman so shabbily.

In any case it was too late. The door behind him had opened and shut, and Susan's voice was saying, "Are you all right, Tod?" Her hand came thrusting through the crook of his arm. It had a vaguely proprietary touch that was not unpleasant. He could smell the perfume she wore.

"Just hot," he smiled.

"I know. These family do's are terrible. It wouldn't be so bad if we could dance properly, but Mother won't have the carpet rolled up. She's afraid the parquet might get scratched." She laughed with a tolerance that jarred.

"I like your mother," Tod said.

"Oh, she's a poppet, of course, but you know how people

get when they're old. .... I saw you both nattering away in the corner nineteen to the dozen. What on earth was it all about?" The brightness of her voice was edged.

His eyes rested on her, watched her narrowly.

"Oh, the servant problem, marriage, children, economics . . . life in general."

"Goodness, quite some ground you covered!" She shivered elaborately. "We shall both get pneumonia if we stand here, anyway." She shut the door firmly and leaned back against it. "Do you want to go back?" she said. "Would you rather be quiet for a bit? There's a good fire in the morning room and we could talk in peace." Her chin tilted at him invitingly and Tod thought how easy it would all be. She was young and handsome and vital, dazzlingly sure of herself; and she was like a ripe plum, ready to fall into his arms at the lightest touch. Without smugness he was sure of it. . . . She longed to be married like her sisters, to have her own background, scope for her own ambitions, and there were not so many eligible young men in the district: none, in fact, so eligible as Shaw of Backshaws.

And why not? He might do a great deal worse. . . .

And then he remembered Jenny looking at him across a lamplit pool of tablecloth, dark eyes troubled, thin shoulders hunched beneath the red stuff of her shabby dress. "*I plaited my hair to please you. . . .*" And one plait had come unbound, had hung nearly to the floor in a shining rope. And then, from the circle of her arms, the pleading note, the apology: "*I think you ought to know that I'm going to marry Gethin. . . .*"

His heart gave an odd lurch. He thrust his hands deep into his pockets.

"We must go back," he said briefly. "They'll be wondering what's happened to us."

The party went on and on.

Incredibly, Tod ate more food, drank more drinks, smoked more cigarettes, joined in a variety of stupid games and laughed as loudly as any of them. People slapped his back and he slapped their backs in return, all good fellows together. Girls flirted with him and he responded gallantly. The red-head kissed him under the mistletoe and he returned the kiss with good measure and then smacked her bony little behind, to the general merriment.

'I suppose I'm having a good time,' he thought. 'I suppose I could get used to all this quite quickly.'

And there'd be electricity at Shaws; well-trained servants; good food; people coming and going all the time. . . . And so what did it matter if a thin, dark, frightened girl married a gypsy type and made a muck of her life? She would have Clem. That was what she wanted, wasn't it? Clem. . . .

He wondered what Susan's reactions would be if he suddenly said, 'It is just possible that I have an illegitimate son.'

Would she be shocked, horrified? Would she refuse to have anything more to do with him? That would be the natural reaction of any girl brought up as she had been brought up.

And yet he was not sure. Susan would fight for anything she wanted. And she wanted him. She had made that abundantly clear from the first moment of their reunion. She had frankly confessed to a childish passion for him. She had laughed about it; had said, "I expect I made myself an awful little nuisance, hanging round you all the time." And he had told her, "I always thought you were a jolly little kid."

Well, there it was. She had offered him a generous springboard for any jump he cared to make.

But an illegitimate son. That would be a facer for any girl. . . .

They were pushing the chairs back against the wall for Sir Roger. Faces were slack and flushed and clothing disordered. Yawns dragged resonantly. Mrs. Scales was bustling about in the hall in an aura of hot soup.

Tod went out and bowed to her with smiling ceremony. "Will you give me the pleasure?"

Her face creased into embarrassed delight.

"What—me? Ee, I never heard such nonsense!" But she relinquished her soup to the resentful Miss Pollitt and allowed

Tod to lead her to a place in the dance, where she gave a lively enough account of herself. "Ee!" she gasped, "I've right enjoyed that! Thank you very much, luv. And I enjoyed our little chat, too. We must have another one some time. My girls tell me I talk too much, an' happen they're right. But I like to remember the old days now and again."

Bustling and smiling, she attended to her guests.

Tod went out to start his car, which was fractious in cold weather. A dozen cars were parked on the curving gravel. Owners were laughing, grumbling, swinging handles, revving reluctant engines.

"Who'll take little me home?" shrilled the redhead, languishing at Tod over a huddle of furs.

Tod determinedly ignored her. Enough was enough. He wanted most urgently to be alone. An idea had suddenly been born: an idea so obvious that it seemed incredible it had not occurred to him before.

The young subaltern beat the redhead briskly in the rear. "You know damn well you're going home with me." He bundled her unceremoniously into a vicious-looking M. G. and shot away into the night, exploding loudly.

"Come again soon, lad," Alfred Scales said, smacking Tod between the shoulder blades. "What about New Year's? We allus have a bit of a do at New Year's."

"We're making up a party for the Panto, Tod," Susan called from the lighted doorway. "You mustn't miss that."

"Oh, aye, we allus go to t'Panto! It's got to be a regular institution. I tek the two front rows of t'stalls, an' anyone can come who's got a mind. Your clutch wants seeing to, Tod, that's what it sounds like to me. I reckon you could do wi' a new car. Any time you feel like running to it tip me the wink, an' I wouldn't say as I couldn't do summat about it." He nudged Tod in the ribs. "Under your hat, of course!"

Tod got away at last.

His lights fanned out before him, feeling their way along the switch-back, stone-walled lanes; startling a huddle of sheep into lamentation; scattering and bobbing white scuts of rabbits in all directions; throwing into transient relief the motionless, intricate design of a tree outlined with frost, the low, lightless roofs of sleeping houses, the sharp, alien intrusion of pylons. . . .

He shut the garage doors and stood in the immense, comforting solitude of the night. He filled his lungs with clean, ice-cold air; listened contentedly to the small, intimate sounds of darkness: the muffled stamp of a stabled hoof; the hoot of an owl in the south pasure; the rustle of some minute, predatory body in the long undergrowth of the ditch. A star shot in a falling arc across the sky and was gone. The moon was just climbing up behind the forty-acre. It turned a trailing scarf of mist into shining silk and threw a diamond into the water trough.

Suddenly the whole thing clicked into perspective and life seemed simple again.

He knew what he must do. He must go to Wales and find out for himself about this child.

If Clem really were his son he would claim him.

The whole place would be scandalised, of course. He could imagine the righteous horror with which he would be regarded; the knowing leers and nudges he would have to suffer; the studied airs of unconcern; the uncompromising snubs.

The offence would lie not in his having fathered Clem, but in his admission of it: illegitimate sons were no rarity; one simply did not acknowledge their existence to the extent of foisting them on to decent society. . . . One could not, for instance, expect to sit on the Bench or aspire to the Mayoral chair, while one's by-blow unashamedly played on the lawns of one's home for all the world to see. . . .

Well, he could take it.

He would have Jenny. . . .

CHAPTER ELEVEN

BAILEY lay in the bed and groaned. Not because he felt pain, for the pain had died now to an occasional rumbling reminder. He groaned because of the weakness that made his limbs feel like lead, that made him utterly dependent on others for every smallest thing.

In health he had been a bed-loving man; but this enforced immobility had none of the sweet luxury of idleness. He could not wash himself or feed himself or attend to his own bodily needs. There were newspapers and books by his bed, but when he had held them for a few minutes they grew heavy and unmanageable and dropped to the floor. The food they brought revolted him and he was not allowed the food he liked. He slept from time to time, but when he was not asleep he had nothing but his thoughts, and they were not pleasant.

He lay in a small room on the ground floor to save Em's legs on the stairs. It was a square, unfamiliar room, almost as bare and clean as the whitewashed hospital ward, and lacking any of its small compensations: the bed-to-bed gossip and scandal; the young nurses bending over him, cheeking him as they flicked to and fro; the flowers, the little treats on special occasions; the sense of importance, almost over-balancing the fear that sprang in him like a cold flame when they pulled the screen round his bed and came crowding about him, Doctor and starched Sister and scuttling probationer, with their rolls of bandages and shining silver instruments....

Here, nobody seemed to care. He was not important any

more. Old Doctor Waller came and shot out his lips at him and told him he was lucky to be alive. Mrs. George came and stood in the doorway and asked if there was anything he wanted, and he always said no, because he wanted only to be on his feet again. Em came in and out with the slops he loathed, and the bitter, dark-brown medicine, and the soapy flannel he smeared over his face night and morning. The District Nurse came popping along on her baby motorcycle twice a week to give him a blanket bath. She was neither young nor provocative. She washed him as if he were a kitchen floor. pulled the bedclothes uncomfortably tight, complained of her feet, her back, the bad roads and the worse weather, and went popping away again to her next case.

Iris had not been near him.

He had heard her laughing out in the yard with that tinker chap. He had heard her calling the cats, singing lustily as she beat the mats against the house wall, playing some game with the child. He had heard her feet on the stairs, in the passage; he had called to her but she had not answered. . . .

The need to see Iris grew and fretted in him.

Why didn't she come? Did she think he was done for, not worth worrying about? He'd show her! He wasn't done for yet, not by a long chalk. Happen he was older than yon chap, but he'd got summat yon chap hadn't got nor never would have. He'd got brass. A whole biscuit tin full of it, up in Em's bedroom. It was his as much as hers, wasn't it? Scratching and scraping for years she'd been, the owd buzzard, taking his earnings off him and hiding them away in her rotten tin—and him without the price of a pipe of baccy often as not. . . .
He brooded over it until his temperature soared.

And still Iris did not come.

It was a conspiracy he guessed, and set himself to outwit it.

"I want another look at last Sunday's paper," he told his wife. "Don't you bother—the girl'll bring it next time she's passing."

"Much obliged to you for thinking o' my legs," she replied dryly. "I'll bring it mysen—next time I'm passing."

Gethin came into his room one morning. He brought with him the wind and the sun, the smell of grass and horses and tobacco, the smell of life.

"I'm off down to Huffley. Anything you want, is there?"

Bailey glowered, hating him for his youth and freedom; for his white teeth and flat stomach and his long, strong legs.

"Nay, there's nowt."

"No baccy? Nothing you fancy to eat?"

"I'm wantin' nowt."

Gethin nodded, glancing round the bare little room with a grin of distaste.

"Clean they keep you, isn't it? Tired you must be of staring at the ceiling. Some baccy would help."

"I can't get at me brass." He wasn't going to admit that he hadn't any.

"I will get you some baccy. Pay me later you can."

"All right, then."

"Anything else?"

Bailey's head moved restlessly. He didn't want to ask favours of this chap, but seemingly there was nobody else, so he must swallow his pride.

"Aye, there's one thing. . . . Upstairs, in t'Missus's bedroom, there's a biscuit tin standin' on a table by t'bed. You might bring it down. I've a fancy for a biscuit now an' again, and they won't let me have none." Gethin smiled briefly. "Don't let nobody see," Bailey added hoarsely. A sudden excitement had made his throat dry. His hands trembled on the tightly smoothed coverlet.

"All busy they are."

He heard Gethin's soft tread on the stairs, the stealthy creak of an upper door. He swallowed several times with difficulty. He suddenly felt frightened. Em would go upstairs and find the biscuit tin gone and the fun would start. She would track it down in no time at all, and then what? . . . In his usual health he would have enjoyed her rage, her helplessness; but he was a sick man, tied to this blasted bed, too weak to put foot to ground.

He glanced angrily round the bare, tidy room. Where could he put the money? There was nowhere you could hide a flea! In his pillowcase? Under the mattress? That nurse woman would soon pounce on it. . . .

Nay, it wouldn't do. He'd been a fool to think of it. Best thing would be to take a couple of biscuits out and send the chap back with it right away.

Before long he'd be on his own feet, and then he could deal with the brass and with Em and with Iris, and the whole bag-shoot. . . .

Gethin came into the bedroom carrying the tin. "Best to take what you want and I'll put it back. We don't want no bother with the women," he said, grinning.

Bailey's trembling hands closed round the tin. Now he had got it he felt sick, his temples started to throb.

The kitchen door opened and Em's footsteps sounded in the passage. Quick as thought Gethin took the tin and slid it soundlessly under the bed. "When I get back," he whispered.

He met the old woman in the passage, stood politely aside for her to pass.

"You startin' today or tomorrer?" she said sharply—yet not so sharply as she would have spoken a few weeks back: tinker trash he might be, but she could not deny he was a worker; he never had to be told twice.

"Just off," he said with that smile of his.

She peered into the bedroom, her sharp old eyes alert for any signs of disorder or insubordination.

"What did yon chap want in 'ere?"

"Came to see if there were owt I wanted from Huffley," Bailey answered, schooling his voice to mildness.

"What could you want?"

"That's what I told 'im."

She came nearer, smoothed the immaculate bedcover, fingered the few ornaments on the chest of drawers, peered out of the window. . . . The District Nurse had come and gone. It was not time for his medicine. There was nothing to stay for. And yet she stayed.

She fought against the fear that nagged at her night and day—the fear that he was finished, done for.

A lazy tyke he had always been. A work-dodger. Too fond of the girls, too fond of his glass. She had to keep after him all the time. But he had been strong and lusty; goodtempered on the whole, with the wry sort of humour she understood, that could make her chuckle inwardly. And there had been a good ten years' work in him.

The hand of death had touched him, however lightly; still hovered near, giving him a certain cachet in her eyes.

Not for worlds would she have admitted, even to herself, that she was touched by the sight of him lying there in the bed, still and straight and helpless. . . .

She smoothed her hands one over the other on the curve of her stomach and gazed down at his face, altered and refined by illness, unfamiliar with its stubbly growth of beard, the washed-out look of the eyes, the yellow tinge of skin stretched tightly over the cheek bones.

"Do you want Gethin should shave you?"

He seized with avidity on this happy chance.

"Aye, I do. Soon as he's back send 'im in. I shall be glad to get shut on this beard."

She nodded, and after a further moment of indecision turned and left the room, shutting the door after her.

Would she now go to the bedroom? He lay rigid, hardly daring to breathe until he was satisfied that she had returned to the kitchen.

She would not be coming back for at least an hour. He had time to open the biscuit tin, count the money and get the tin back under the bed. Gethin could take it back upstairs when he came to shave him.

Rolling on his side he groped a hand under the bed, but touched nothing. Laboriously he shifted nearer the edge and tried again. This time his fingers touched the tin only to push it further under. Damn these women and their polish! . . .

Groaning quietly, he sat up in the bed pushing the rigid covers back. His legs were astonishingly stick-like and white.

Gingerly he swung them to the ground and, after a moment of panic and dizziness, pulled himself upright.

In spite of the oil stove in the corner, the room felt cold. He stood holding tightly to the chest of drawers, fighting the dizziness, the weakness, doubting his ability to get down on his knees. But after a few moments, slowly, painfully and with many groans and swift gasps for breath, he managed it. Reaching his hand under the bed, he grasped the biscuit tin and pulled it out.

It had been bad enough getting down but it was infinitely worse getting up. Three times he tried, only to sink back on his bony, shaking knees. He was not cold any longer. He was hot, terribly hot. Sweat started on his forehead, ran down the harsh, bearded furrows of his face. His hands were clammy with it. He felt it trickle in his armpits and the small of his back. Pain throbbed in his head, at the back of his neck.

But at last he was back on the bed again, arms and legs a-shake, head buzzing like a top. And then there was all the business of getting the bedclothes smooth: that had to be done, or Em would know at once he'd been up to something.

By the time this was accomplished he was so exhausted he no longer cared whether Em came in or not. Almost he would have welcomed her. She was an owd buzzard and for years had been a thorn in his flesh. But he knew where he was with Em. Nag and scold and complain as she might; take his brass and hide it as she certainly had, he knew he could count on Em to do her duty by him. They'd been together a good many years now, he and Em. She had been like a chain round his neck. But you could get used to chains. Suddenly freed, you might almost miss the weight of them, the rattle of the links, the sense of being anchored. . . .

Something of this sort threaded dimly through his mind as he lay there battling with his weakness, trying to believe that the pain was no sharper than it had been, that his heart would soon stop this jerking up and down. So that when he heard the slam of the kitchen door, the *slip-slip* of feet coming inexorably nearer, he did no more than lay his hand on the biscuit tin and hunch his shoulders with a feeble defiance.

He lay there, waiting for the door to open, waiting to be found out.

For a long time nothing happened. Someone was outside the door: small, shuffling movements and sounds of uneven breathing made him sure of it. And presently the handle wobbled; wobbled again; turned and clicked as the door swung slowly inwards.

The child stood in the doorway. His eyes were wide and wary; his fingers gripped the door's edge so that they showed white against the wood.

The tiny figure stood motionless, tense, poised for flight. He had been forbidden to enter this room. Having evaded all vigilance, surmounted all difficulties, he had entered it. But now he was frightened.

The old man in the bed was so still, his breathing so queer and loud. The smell of the room was strange, repellent. Yet his curiosity was even greater than his fear, so that he must stand there watching, sniffing, listening. . . .

Bailey swallowed, gripped at the sheets and swore in a soft, continuous stream.

The child blinked rapidly but did not move.

"Get the hell out," Bailey whispered.

The child advanced two steps into the room. Keeping an alert watch on the long, thin figure outlined beneath the bed-clothes, he still managed to take in the whole of the room. The whitewashed walls, with the picture of men eating at a long table; the red and blue rug on the polished floor; the chest of drawers with the medicine bottle, the mug, the faded photograph of a woman in funny clothes; the chair with a cane seat that sagged into a hole; the biscuit tin with roses painted on the lid. . . . He took in every single detail, rejected them all and backed again towards freedom.

"Hey—don't go!"

First this old man told him to go, then to stay.

Clem disliked contradictory orders. Balanced on wary tip-toes he swung slowly from side to side, frowning his confusion.

"You like biscuits—hey?"

Clem shook his head. He liked biscuits very much, but he wasn't going to tell this old man so. He didn't like the old man, or his room, and he didn't mean to stay.

"Ginger biscuits, hey? An' them ones with pink sugar inside? . . ." Bailey fumbled at the lid. If he could get the lid off and give the kid some biscuits, happen he'd push the tin back under the bed for him and save him all that bother. He wished most fervently he had never asked Gethin for the tin. It had been a false move. Time enough to deal with all that when he was on his feet.

"I'll give ye three if ye'll be a good lad an' put tin under t'bed for me after."

He swore helplessly as the child backed further from the room. He was going. Soon he'd be gone, leaving the door wide open and the tin lying on the bed for all to see. . . . "Hey!" he croaked. "Here, lad!"

And then another voice called, "Clem—where are you?" And it was Iris' voice—and those were Iris' footsteps coming up the passage.

And there at last, after all those weeks, was Iris herself.

His eyes gorged on her. The pale, full cheeks powdered with freckles; the white V of her neck under the straining blouse; the swelling line of thigh and the heavy legs. . . . He knew the way she breathed, the way she leaned against the wall, arms folded across her breast, hands tucked under her armpits. He knew the smell of her; that strong animal smell heavily overlaid by the scent she was so fond of.

She was neither pretty nor clean nor kind, but he was not concerned with that. It was her youth he craved; the strong, heavy warmth of her, the overflowing vitality. He lusted after them, and yet he hated her for possessing them, for making him feel so old and feeble and done for. . . .

"Now then," he snarled. "So you've deigned to come an' see me at last!"

Her small, pale eyes regarded him indifferently.

"I come to fetch Clem. He's not allowed in 'ere. *She* says so." She smacked the child's head lightly and affectionately. "Beat it," she advised. "*She's* calling you, down in t'orchard."

Clem flew at her, his face screwed up in laughter, kicking her shins sturdily, pinching the soft curves of her thighs, biting at her apron. "Bitch!" he shrilled. "Bitch!"

The girl laughed good-humouredly. She had taught him the word herself.

She ran him down the passage, slammed the kitchen door on him and returned, wiping her hands on her coarse apron.

"Whaddyer know! ... Couldn't hardly say a word when he came—or wouldn't, anyroad. He's a deep 'un, yon! See 'im with Mrs. George, an' butter wouldn't melt in 'is mouth. She hasn't got a clue!"

Bailey whined, "You never come to see me, down in t'hospital."

"Why should I?" She lolled against the wall in the attitude he knew so well. "It's a long way, that."

"No further than going to t'pictures. You mek nowt o' that!"

"I can see Gary Cooper at t'pictures," she jeered. "You can't kid yersen you're Gary Cooper—not if you've looked in t'glass lately!"

Bailey's hands clawed at the sheet, buck teeth splayed out between dry lips.

"I were good enough for yer while yon chap come ovver t'moor in 'is cart."

Her laughter turned to a heavy scowl.

"So what?"

"You've never come nigh me since I've bin back. Never opened t'door to see how I were doing. Never answered when I've called out."

"I've summat better to do," she said contemptuously.

"Wi' yon Gethin?"

She stared cruelly at him.

"Happen."

Anger surged through him, bringing a fictitious strength.

He raised himself in the bed, pointing a tremulous finger at the door.

"Shut it!"

Iris shut the door and leaned against it, marking his unshaven cheeks, the yellow muscles jerking in the thin neck, the voluminous folds of his old-fashioned nightshirt. "You don't 'alf look a sight!" she grinned.

"Don't look at me then," he croaked. "Look at this tin. There's summat in this tin as'll please you better. Tek a look at what's in this tin, an' you'll think a bit less o' yon tinker chap."

"Biscuits!" she scoffed. "I'm not fast for a biscuit, time I want one."

"That's what you think! I tell you there's more than biscuits in this tin. There's brass enough in 'ere to tek yer mind off Gethin for good. . . . There's brass enough to mck you remember the owd days when there was on'y me. You won't be so offhanded, my girl, when you see what's in this tin, underneath all them biscuits!"

"I don't believe it," she said. But doubt flickered in her eyes, and Bailey saw it.

"Call me a liar, would you? Right! Then tin can will stop shut!" He folded his hands on the covers and lowered his head, regarding her stealthily.

If Em came in now, the game was up.

On the other hand, once Iris knew about the money it could not be left in the tin, so the game was up anyhow. . . .

He felt hollow with apprehension, his body a mere shell stretched tightly over a seething mass of fear and rage and bewilderment.

She was coming nearer. She was standing over him, her thick red lips parted over strong, uneven teeth.

"Let's 'ave a look. Go on, Jos, oppen t'tin. Seeing's believing."

His hands closed round the tin; they trembled so that the nails rattled against it. The white walls of the room closed in round the bed, retreated mistily, closed in again. . . . The

figure of the girl loomed over him, suddenly enormous, menacing; dominating the small, chill room with a nightmare
quality.

"You got to give 'im up," he quavered. "I'm not showing
you while you promise to give 'im up. . . ."

She came nearer. She was bending over him, all the vitality
of her lusty young body reaching out to him. . . .

He was frightened. To have her near, to be able to touch
her, draw strength from her hot youth—this was what he had
craved. And now he was frightened. . . .

She did not bring him strength. She drew from him the
last, feeble remnants of his own strength, so that he must fall
back against the pillows, staring up at her in dread and defeat.

"Open the tin, Jos."

"Nay."

"Open it!"

"Nay, I'll not. . . ."

He could not. He knew it, and so did she. With a contemptuous noise of the lips she snatched the tin from him, flicked
off the lid and threw the contents on to the white counterpane. . . .

"You owd liar," she said quietly.

He stared at the biscuits, pushing them about with shaking
fingers, muttering and whimpering.

"They was 'ere. . . . They was 'ere all right. Pound notes
all bundled together, an' silver—aye, an' a bit o' gold, an'
all! . . . They was in this tin, I tell ye, underneath them biscuits. . . . Somebody's took 'em out. Somebody's pinched 'em.
They was 'ere, but they bin pinched. . . ."

"You're a rotten owd liar!"

Her hard young hand struck him across the face. She
laughed shortly, stumped out of the room, slamming the door
behind her.

He turned his face against the pillow, shutting his eyes.

It had not been a hard blow; it had not given him pain.
The humiliation was worse than any pain. . . .

This was the end. He knew that. He was old and sick and

done for. Never again would Iris let him hold her for dark, secret moments in the barn, or out on the moor when clouds scuttled across the moon and shadows leapt under the trees and the heather whispered. Never again would her eyes flicker at him across the kitchen, promising, inviting. . . .

It was the end. It was finished. . . .

Tears welled under his closed eyelids and sank into the pillow.

Now there was nothing left but Em.

When Gethin came into the room Bailey was lying so still he wondered if he were dead. But the narrow mound under the white counterpane stirred faintly from sleep.

"That you, Em?"

"Good job for you it isn't," Gethin grinned. He scooped the biscuits into the tin, deftly smoothed the bedclothes, turned the pillows and propped the old man up against them. He took the tin upstairs and came back again. "Here is your baccy." He threw the silver package on to the bed and blew on his hands. "Cold as charity outside it is. Lucky you are to be lying here in the warm, and nothing to do but smoke your old pipe."

"I'll pay you when I get at me brass."

"No hurry."

'You've pinched it,' Bailey thought suddenly. 'It's you that's pinched yon money.' He tried to feel angry, and failed. There was nothing he could do about it. He was old and done for.

"Where's Em?"

"Gone into Backshaws, so the girl says. It is too far for her. Perhaps I should go and fetch her in the cart."

Bailey nodded.

"Aye, do that. She ought to have sent yon girl."

Gethin made a noise with his lips: the same scornful noise that Iris had made to Bailey.

"No good for anything she is—only the one thing." He winked at Bailey. The wink flicked Iris into her unimportant

niche in the scheme of things; linked the two men in male
superiority, worldly-wise and tolerant, so that Bailey found
himself winking back; leaguing himself with this tinker chap
who was his enemy.

To cover his confusion he fumbled at the tobacco wrapping.
"Go fetch Em," he said gruffly.

Smiling and imperturbable, Gethin went out of the room.

Iris was leaning against the stove, stirring something in a
saucepan. As Gethin walked through the kitchen her eyes
followed him greedily.

"Where you off to now?"

"To fetch Mrs. Bailey back."

"Good grief!" she exclaimed in real astonishment. "Let the
owd buzzard walk!"

"Too far it is for old legs in this cold."

"Well, I don't know! Mighty considerate all of a sudden,
aren't we? Just when we've got place to oursens for once, an'
all!" She pushed the saucepan aside and came towards him,
her little eyes blinking invitation. "Come on, Geth. You don't
want to bother with the owd woman when you've got me. . . .
Come an' set down by t'fire, while we've got chance. Everybody's out." She caught hold of him, thrusting up an expectant
face. "Don't you want to kiss me?"

His eyes were cold as Tarn water. Gripping her thick,
freckled wrists he held her from him. His glance flicked over
the straggling hair, the bursting blouse, the downtrodden
shoes.

"Your face is dirty."

"I've bin working," she said indignantly. "Let go me wrists,
you're hurting! Don't look at me as if I was summat the cat
brought home!"

He laughed derisively.

"Cats likes their food clean."

He went out, whistling. She heard him cross the yard, call-

ing to the horses. A moment later the trap went rattling out
of the yard, followed by a shrill protest from the brown pony,
left behind in the stable.

She stared in the tiny mirror over the dresser, wiped her
face on her coarse apron. Muttering to herself, she began
clattering crockery on to a tray. Gethin bewildered her. She
never knew how to deal with him, his mood changed so
quickly. Sometimes he treated her like dirt. Even when he
was responsive—and her blood stirred, remembering those
too-rare moments—she was never sure if he liked her or not.

The saucepan spluttered on the stove and she stirred it
angrily. Work, work, work; it never ended. It wouldn't have
hurt Her to give a hand instead of playing around in the
orchard with the kid.... What Gethin saw in Her she couldn't
imagine. She was nowt to crack on, even when she made the
best of herself. Yet his eyes followed her everywhere, with
that look in them.... It was the money, of course. He wanted
the money and the good house and the land. That's all there
was to it. But it was enough. What chance had anyone else
got!

Money, money. Everybody had money but herself, she
thought resentfully. Even owd Jos had got some tucked away
—or so he said. Maybe he was lying, or going daft; but there
was just the chance he had spoken the truth for once.... It
would be Mrs. Bailey's brass, of course, not his. And she
wouldn't put it past the owd buzzard to have had it in that
biscuit tin all this time, right under everyone's nose. Just
where nobody in their senses would dream of looking for it.
Clever, really.... Iris grinned, acknowledging the cleverness
of Mrs. Bailey. Cunning owd devil.... How often Jos had
complained of the way she rattled the tin at night, munching
and crunching in his ear. They'd laughed about it many a
time. But how the old girl must have laughed, too....

Jos didn't care about biscuits but she herself was very partial
to them. Mrs. Bailey must have known Iris would help herself, so she had taken the brass out and put it somewhere
else. If there *was* any brass. . . .

She stared into the fire, stirring intermittently at the saucepan.

If there *was* any brass it was somewhere in this house. The old girl would never trust a bank. It must be somewhere in this house: a chimney, happen, or a loose board in the floor, or between the leaves of a book. She'd read a story once about a chap finding some boodle in a box made to look just like a book. . . .

Her little eyes gleamed in the firelight.

What was hidden could be found. She was a match for Mrs. Bailey any day of the week. And findings was keepings as they said.

If only she could lay her hands on some brass there'd be nowt to keep her in this god-forsaken place. She could go where she'd a mind, get herself some slap-up clothes, have the time of her life.

Gethin would sit up and take notice, too. . . . Ah, she'd get Gethin all right, once she had some money and some new clothes. They'd go away, she and Gethin and the kid in the cart together, and she'd be shut of Lost Hill for ever. . . .

She began to sing loudly, plunging about the kitchen in a sudden surge of excitement; setting the table with a clatter; blowing the bellows lustily before the sitting room fire; pumping water into a pail until it overflowed. The canary caught her excitement, hopping about his gilded bars, trilling and fluting madly. She flung the dishcloth at him, grinning as the cage swung crazily, filled with the fluster of feathers.

The more she thought about it, the more sure she became that Bailey had told the truth. There *had* been money under the biscuits in the tin! And now the money was somewhere else in the house, waiting for her to find it.

And find it she would. . . . She'd start today, as soon as ever dinner was over and she got five minutes to herself. She'd go over every inch of this house—aye, an' garden and barns an' all, if necessary. If there was brass to be found, she would find it.

Meals in the kitchen had become silent, difficult interludes in the routine of the day.

Knowing himself unwelcome, Gethin ate quickly, departing about his business as soon as hunger was satisfied. Mrs. Bailey kept her eyes on her plate, and Iris, though her eyes were everywhere, her foot stretched under the table to communicate with Gethin's foot, knew better than to talk when Mrs. Bailey wished for silence.

But today, no frown, no sharp command could keep her silent. She laughed and chattered incessantly, impervious to snub, openly defiant of rebuke. When the dining room bell rang, she remained sprawled in her chair, eating stolidly.

"Let her wait. Why should I get indigestion, jumping up an' down all through me dinner?"

"Go fetch them plates out," Mrs. Bailey snapped. She rose to dish up the pudding but Iris continued to eat. She winked at Gethin behind the old woman's back.

"Fetch them," he said briefly.

She stared at him resentfully.

"Fetch 'em yersen."

Without another word he took the tray and went out of the kitchen.

"Are you out of yer mind?" Mrs. Bailey shrilled. "Do you want to lose yer place?"

The girl pushed her plate away, pursing thick lips.

"Who does he think *he* is, anyroad! He's not mester here—not yet."

Mrs. Bailey's mouth went up under her nose. Her hands trembled as she lifted the pudding. That was a shrewd thrust Iris had dealt her.

Things were coming to a pretty pass, and she was not sure how to deal with them. She seemed to have lost her grip. . . . The hard work, the many little kindnesses Gethin had done, had slowly lightened her deep distrust of him. Now it came flooding back, stronger than ever.

"You're a bad girl," she quavered. "I've a mind to get you packed off. She'll do it if I tell her."

"You tell her!" Iris jeered. "See what it's like having all to do yersen. Go on, tell her. I couldn't care less."

Gethin returned with the laden tray.

"Clem is to have stewed fruit instead of pudding. And the top off the milk. I will fetch it."

Clem came running to the kitchen door. Iris pulled a face at him and he mimicked it, chuckling.

Jenny's voice called, "Clem!"

He danced up and down on his toes.

"I want pudding," he announced.

"Go back," Gethin told him.

"You come to Iris, ducky. Iris'll give you some pudden."

The child stuck out his stomach, swinging from side to side on his toes, his light, bright eyes weighing up the pro's and con's of the situation.

"Come on, luv, have some of Iris' pudden."

Gethin returned with the bowl of stewed apples and a jug of cream.

"Go sit down in your place."

Clem backed away down the passage and Iris snorted contemptuously.

"Why should he eat in yonder an' you out here? I can't understand you, an' that's a fact!"

"A lot you don't understand."

He took the tray into the room. Clem was sitting at the table, good as gold, smiling at Jenny. He hailed his fruit and cream with every token of delight.

"Why are you doing Iris' work, Gethin?" Jenny said.

He set the fruit before her, the pudding, the sauce-boat, the hot plates; fetched the silver bowl of sugar from the sideboard.

"I just thought I would."

Jenny fidgeted with the tablespoons. She said uncomfortably, "There's no need for you to eat in the kitchen, Gethin, if you'd rather be here with Clem . . . and me."

"There's kind," he murmured. She glanced up quickly to see if he were laughing at her, but his face was grave. He stooped to tie Clem's feeder more securely. "Proper little nob he looks with his silver pusher, isn't it?"

"Oh, Gethin! . . ." She jerked her chair back and rose from the table. "I simply don't understand you."

"A lot you don't understand."

"You can take this back, I don't want any," she said impatiently.

He picked up the tray and walked to the door, his face impassive.

"Eat you," he said, and went out.

'Tod,' she thought. 'Oh, Tod. . . .'

But she sat down again and tried to eat.

✳✳✳✳✳✳✳✳✳✳✳✳✳✳✳✳✳✳✳✳✳✳✳✳✳✳

CHAPTER TWELVE

IT was a good walk to the village, but Jenny had never known
it seem so short. It was over before she had formulated any
sort of plan.

'What shall I say when I see him?' she thought. 'What *is*
there to say! . . . Help me to get rid of Gethin? Help me to
be happy? Help me to run my own life? . . .' Her errand
seemed so childish, so fantastic, that she almost turned back.

But something urged her on; some inward compulsion more
imperative than all her doubts and fears. 'Tod,' she thought.
And she remembered how the sturdy little name had seemed
like a warm rock on which to sit in the sun. 'That's what I
need,' she thought forlornly. 'A rock where I can sit in the sun
and be warm and safe.'

Heads turned curiously as she passed through the village
street. One or two people greeted her with a reserved, "Now
then," but not many were abroad. The torpor of early afternoon lay over the little houses. Two women gossiped at a
door, arms rolled in their aprons. At her approach they bolted
into the house and she saw the curtains move cautiously. The
landlady of The Bell, carrying a pail across the road, ostenta-
tiously bent to stroke the fat ginger cat who accompanied
her.

'I don't care,' she thought; and found herself caring quite
a lot. It would be nice to be liked; to be accepted by these
dour, north-country folk as one of themselves.

At the turn of the road she halted, looking down on Shaws, undecided.

A long, black car stood in the driveway. Not Tod's car. Obviously Tod had a visitor. She must wait awhile until he was alone.

It was a long time since she had seen Shaws. She had forgotten how absolutely right the house looked; how mellow and serene; how confidently it rested in the gracious folds of the land. It had none of the stark aggression of Lost Hill. It welcomed you as a house should. Even on this grey, chill January afternoon its smoke beckoned a greeting, its open door smiled invitation. An answering smile touched her lips. How lovely to come home to a house like this. Lucky Tod. . . .

Cows were moving in slow procession across the yard, milling about the doorway of the milking shed. Their contented voices floated on the still air. The voice of the cowman issued commands. She heard the impact of his hand on a hard red rump, the shrill sound of his whistling, the clang of a pail. The cows dribbled in orderly file through the doorway of the barn.

Two women came out of the house. One entered the car, the engine roared and the gleaming body began to maneuver a turn. The other stood for a moment with folded arms, then went in again. The house door banged loudly.

The car negotiated the gates, began to climb the hill. It was an enormous, arrogant, Juggernaut affair and the lane was narrow. Jenny flattened herself against a rock to let it go by. She thought that the woman who drove it matched the car, with her groomed, golden head rising proudly from the dark fur of her coat. Her eyes flicked Jenny with indifference. Then the indifference changed to a scornful recognition as she swept past.

'How nice she looked,' Jenny thought.

She glanced down at the stained and shabby raincoat she was wearing: a man's coat, much too large for her, but so easy to slip on, and impervious to weather. Her shoes were heavy and sensible, muddy from the orchard field. There was a three-cornered tear on the left leg of her slacks. Her hands were red with cold. She explored the deep pockets for gloves. She found some leather ones, but they were still damp from a previous soaking. She blew on her hands and thrust them back deep into the pockets. 'I must get some clothes,' she thought. 'Why don't I have a fur coat like that? A car, too. Why don't I?. . . There's been so much to think about. . . .'

When she rang the door bell a dog barked shrilly somewhere at the back of the house and footsteps clattered inside, but nobody came to the door.

She rang again.

A man came round a corner of the house and she saw that it was Mr. Sanderson, whom she knew well by sight. He had always seemed more friendly than most, lifting his whip with a smile as he drove past her in the lanes, shouting a comment on the weather, offering her a lift. He came towards her now, touching his cap.

"Afternoon, Mrs. Rowland. Was it Mester Shaw you was wanting?"

"Yes. . . . yes, I wanted to speak to him. Isn't he in?"

"He's none here." His voice was dry and abrupt. "He's gone away."

"Gone away! . . . Oh." She stared at him helplessly, hunching her thin shoulders under the shabby coat. "Will he be away very long?"

"Nay, I know nowt about it," he said loudly, with an aggrieved expression. "I've got no more idea than them cows wheer he is. He just says to me, 'I'm going away,' he says—just like that. 'I don't know how long I shall be gone. Hold the fort, Sanderson,' he says. And off he goes in t'car. No address, mind you! Five days back, that was, and no word from him, no word at all."

"I see." Jenny stood staring at him, filled with an extraordinary sense of loss and frustration. "Well. . . . thank you, Mr. Sanderson."

"I'm right sorry, Mrs. Rowland. You've had a long walk for nowt."

"It doesn't matter. It wasn't anything important . . . really. It doesn't matter at all." She gave him a wan smile and began to walk away.

"I can give you a lift if you can stop a few minutes," Sanderson called. 'Poor little beggar,' he thought, 'she looks right done up.' He walked after her, touched by something helpless and forlorn that he sensed in her. "See, now, you come into the Lodge for a warm, and my sister'll be glad to give you a cup of tea. I shan't be above a half-hour. Mrs. Scobie—the housekeeper here—she's for off. She's packin' her box now. I'm tekkin' her down to catch the 4.8. It never rains but it pours, as they say! . . . But there'll be plenty of room. You come an' get a nice hot cup of tea inside you, an' wait by t'fire."

He led her into the Lodge where Miss Ellen was busy damping down the clean linen for ironing. The fresh, sweet smell of it filled the kitchen. The kettle was already on the boil.

Miss Ellen glanced sharply at Jenny but asked no questions. Under a hard, rather waspish exterior she hid an unbounded love and admiration for her brother. If he wanted that Rowland girl to have a cup of tea, she could have one and welcome, whatever the village might say about her and her tinker chap. Miss Ellen had her own opinion of the village gossips.

"Draw up to t'fire," she said, pouring milk into thick white cups. "It's a raw day for walking. You look right starved, luv."

Sanderson drank noisily.

"Yon Scobie's for off," he informed his sister. "She's in a rare tantrum. I'm tekkin' her down for the 4.8."

"Nay! . . ." Miss Ellen set her cup down sharply. "What brought that on?"

"Ask me another. Been workin' up to it for days. Don't like bein' alone in t'house, happen. . . . Without it was summat as Miss Scales said to upset her."

"I saw her car go past. Above an hour she's bin there!"

"Aye. They was havin' a bit of a set-to, as far as I could hear. Mrs. Scobie's for off, anyroad."

"An' no loss!"

Brother and sister stared at each other over the rims of

their cups; and Jenny, crouching near the fire, sat between them wondering what it was all about. Who was this Miss Scales, with her gold head rising so arrogantly from the dark, expensive-looking furs, who could come sweeping down to Shaws and send Tod's housekeeper flying? . . . She was conscious of a sudden sharp resentment.

"Is that any relation of Councillor Scales?" she asked diffidently.

"Daughter. The youngest." Miss Ellen had no intention of being drawn on the subject of Tod and his affairs. When Tod brought a wife home to Shaws she would have all Miss Ellen's loyalty, whether it was Alfred Scales's girl or another. Even if, as her brother sometimes hinted, it should be this thin, childish, unhappy-looking creature George Rowland had brought from London and left widowed in yon bleak house up on the moor. . . . Though you could hardly believe it when you set her against a bonny, bouncing lass like Susan Scales. . . . Still, men were queer creatures, thought Ellen, sipping her hot tea and watching Jenny out of the corner of her eye. And how like a man to go mailicking off the lord knew where, an' leave 'em all flying at each others' throats on t'doorstep, as you might say. . . .

"I'll go and bring the trap round." Sanderson went heavily out of the kitchen.

Miss Ellen held out her hand for Jenny's cup. "There's plenty more where that came from."

"You're very kind." Jenny's eyes glanced round the homely room with its winking brass, white-scrubbed wood and pleasant windows. "This is an awfully nice cottage, isn't it?"

"Might be worse. It's not as old as the house, of course, but it's pretty old at that, and in first-class condition. Shaws has allus looked after their property, you see. If owt wants doing it gets done straight off, not left while it's too far gone. Of course, we're more sheltered here, that's one thing. I reckon you'll know all about weather up at Lost Hill. A lonely, god-forsaken place, I allus say, an' a right name for it, an' all."

"It's not really the name of the house. It's named after that

hill that runs up from the orchard on to the moor. I asked
Old Missus about it once, and she said a battle was supposed
to have been fought and lost there hundreds of years ago. I
tried to find out more about it, but it wasn't in any of the
books."

"Aye, well, what's in a name?" Miss Ellen said prosaically.
She shook a snow-white towel with a crack like a gun shot
and began to fold it for mangling. "Yon's the trap gone to pick
up Her Ladyship's baggage. I shan't be sorry to see t'back of
that one!" She went to the door and Jenny put down her cup
and followed her.

Outside the door of the big house the trap waited, coach-
work and harness gleaming. The sturdy cob blew loudly and
its breath was visible on the dank air. It pawed the gravel
and whinnied as Sanderson came out carrying a brown tin
trunk which he stowed away in the back. He returned and
came out again with two suitcases. The cob muzzled his cheek
as he passed it.

Mrs. Scobie appeared carrying a coat and a paper parcel.
A small dog with floppy ears frisked and barked at her heels.
As she climbed into the trap it tried to follow her but she
kicked its head sharply and it ran back into the porch, squeal-
ing.

"Nay!" muttered Miss Ellen. She glanced at Jenny. The
girl's face was full of shrinking distaste, her shoulders hunched
defensively. She looked, Miss Ellen thought, as if she had felt
that blow on her own head.

"I think I'll walk, after all," Jenny said quickly. "Please tell
him." She went into the kitchen again, crouching down by
the fire until the sound of wheels had died away.

Miss Ellen came in carrying the dog which she set down
on the hearthrug with a rough caress. "Poor owd Wendy,"
she said. "You're a daft creature, but there was no call to tek
her spite out on you." The dog looked from one face to the
other, its mournful eyes imploring sympathy. "She were only
kind to you while it suited her purpose. Here, drink this up."
She set a saucer of milky tea on the rug and the dog drank

eagerly and then rolled on its side, sighing in the warm comfort.

"I must go," Jenny said, pulling her scarf closer about her throat.

"It's a long walk. You have done better to go in t'trap."

"I couldn't. . . ." She shivered suddenly. "Why is there so much cruelty in the world?" she said passionately. "Everywhere you go there is nothing but cruelty!"

She looked just like Wendy, Miss Ellen thought. The same bewilderment, the same shrinking appeal. She sniffed and rubbed her hard hands up and down her apron to hide the sudden impulse she had to put out her hand and pat her. A grown woman, married these seven years, widowed, and already carrying on, or so they said, with some tinker chap she'd picked up. . . . And you wanted to comfort her, like you'd comforted the dog. Nay. . . .

"There's kindness if you look for it," she said gruffly. "It teks all sorts to mek a world. You don't want to watch out for only the one sort."

When Sanderson came in for a late tea he was in one of his rare tempers. He stamped and blew, as was his custom when put out, clattered his knife and fork and banged the cup into its saucer so that Miss Ellen winced and protested sharply.

"Have done, do! Don't tek your tantrums out on t'pots, they're hard enough to come by."

"Pots be damned!" he growled. "I've had a bellyful today. I'm fed up. . . . I can't think what's come over Tod, shying off like this without a word."

"You've managed without him a good long while."

"Either he's Mester or he's not—let him mek up his mind." He pushed the plate across the table and Miss Ellen gave him a generous second helping of savoury stew. She refilled his cup with the strong tea he loved to drink with his meat.

"You got her off all right?"

"Aye. Thank the Lord for that mercy, anyroad."

"Have any trouble with her?"

"Oh, we had a bit of a weep on t'platform," he replied in deep disgust. "She started on about being a lonely woman with no soul to care whether she lived or died. Said she'd half a mind to chuck hersen in front of the train."

"And did she?"

Her brother laughed shortly.

"Last I saw of her, she were havin' a set-to wi' t'chap in the opposite corner about draught from t'window."

"You'd no call to wait while the train came. She were never civil to you."

"I waited to mek sure she didn't change her mind an' come mailicking back," he said dourly. "We shall have to get somebody else. I've half a mind to ask Cassie."

"Nay, Cassie's past it. Let Tod get somebody for himself. If worst comes to t'worst I'll look after him mesen. What he wants is a wife." She sipped her tea thoughtfully. "I'd give a good bit to know what Miss Scales said to upset her. Didn't you catch owt?"

"They was goin' at it like a couple o' wild cats. I'll tell you one thing I did hear. . . ." He drank slowly, maddeningly.

"Well—let's have it!"

"Yon Scobie called Miss Scales an interferin' little bitch."

"Never!" Miss Ellen's eyes popped.

"She did an' all. 'You're an interferin' little bitch!' she says. You could have heard her up at Heartbreak. 'You're not Missus here yet,' she says. 'This is my kitchen, an' I'll thank you to get out of it, an' the quicker the better.'"

"Well, I don't know!"

Brother and sister gazed at each other with a solemn enjoyment.

Sanderson said presently: "Do you reckon Susan Scales an' Tod has fixed things up between 'em?"

"What would he go away for if they had? She never even knew he'd gone, did she?"

"Seemingly not." His chair shrieked back over the tiles and he began to push tobacco into his pipe with a broad thumb.

"She's a masterful young madam, but she's got looks and health and common sense—to say nowt of brass. She'd mek Tod a good wife."

Miss Ellen gazed rather bleakly into the fire. She could not but agree with her brother. Yet, perversely, her thoughts dwelt not on the healthy, wealthy and suitable Susan Scales, but on the thin, shabby, wistful figure of the girl from Lost Hill. . . . You wanted to comfort her, like you'd comforted Wendy.

"What do you know about marriage," she said harshly. "Or me, either, for that matter. A crusty owd bachelor an' a sour owd maid. . . . There's more to marriage than health an' wealth; and as far as I can see, sense has got nowt to do wi' it." And she began to clatter the plates together.

There were others who wondered at the sudden disappearance of Tod.

His bank manager was annoyed because he failed to keep an appointment. A neighbouring farmer who wanted to buy two prize Ayrshires and a dealer who had found him just the tractor he had been looking for were both turned away without a reasonable explanation. The Vicar of St. Mark's, Huffam, who had already paid two fruitless visits to the house, went away from his third call with the sad conviction that Tod was not the man his father had been: certainly not the type to whom the office of churchwarden would make the slightest appeal.

Moving cautiously about the mist-shrouded moors and making free with Tod's rabbits, Gethin also pondered his sudden disappearance.

He and he alone knew where Tod had gone. *"You realise that I can check up on all this?"* That's what Shaw had said and that, of course, was what he was doing now.

And when he had checked up—what then?

Either Shaw was the kid's father or he was not. Gethin had no idea of the truth: you never could believe a word Angharad said. . . . As far as Gethin could see there was nothing in it for Tod either way. If the kid was his he'd want it kept dark. If it wasn't, nothing was altered. That a man in Tod's position should even consider openly claiming the child never once entered his head.

In the bleak dawns when the moor was sheeted in mist, he moved noiselessly from dip to coppice, along invisible tracks and under the shelter of stone walls. Upwind he crouched, patient and motionless, finger on trigger and sack beside him, waiting, and thinking his own thoughts. There was always a rabbit for Mrs. Bailey's pot. The rest fetched a fair price in the back streets of Huffley, and no questions asked.

It was not the money. Whether the sack were full or empty it was what he loved to do, this patient stalking, crouching, waiting. It was his life. It was the only way he ever wanted to live.

He could marry the girl—that much she had made clear. He could be master of the big house, the fields, the orchards and livestock. Sometimes he toyed with the idea that he would do it. He got a kick out of the thought. His mouth would open in silent laughter as he imagined the fat woman in the pub clasping her fat ginger cat to her bosom at his entry; scowling, yet not daring to refuse his orders because he was the master of Lost Hill. He thought of the Baileys' resentment and the sly complacency of Iris. He thought of Jenny; remembered with a quick stir of pleasure those few moments when he had held her in his arms. She had shrunk from his touch, she had been terrified of him. But she was not cold. Her mouth had trembled under his kiss and her body had moulded itself to his body in blind obedience. Her hands had beat against his chest. "Let me go; Please let me go!" . . . She did not love him; would never love him. But she was not cold. . . .

Loping homewards to his tent in the orchard field he would see the square mass of the house dark against the stars or looming faintly through the mist.

He would have to live in that house, sleep in that bed with

the brass rails and the white honeycomb quilt, with the roof pressing down on his head; eat in that dark living room with the polished furniture, the silver. He would have to take off his muddy boots and wear slippers and sit by the fire watching the slow hands of the clock, nagged at his immobility, while his fingers itched for the gun and the thought of the dark outside, so rich with secret life, so sharp with familiar scent, significant with sound. . . .

He thought of the child, too. Young Clem.

He was fond of the little beggar. He had brought him up from a baby; washed and fed and clothed him; worked for him; begged and lied and occasionally stolen for him. Had the need arisen he supposed he would have died for him. They were two of a sort: comrades, despite disparity of age.

He thought of all that Jenny would do for Clem: the fine clothes, the good, regular food, the book learning. He remembered all she would keep from him: the freedom, the sharp sting and joy of living, the knowledge and meaning of life that never were found in books, in security, in the thrusting down of roots. . . .

His thoughts went round and round making no recognisable pattern; dark as the Tarn water, restless as the dawn wind groping among the heather. Now and then a light shone on his thoughts, sharp and evanescent as moonlight leaping between clouds; and then he would see himself driving away over the moor. Sometimes he would see Clem beside him, and then Jenny's unhappiness was like a load he must bear always. Sometimes he would see himself driving àlone; and then the load changed to a hollowness within his own breast: a hollowness he resented, that astonished and puzzled him. 'I should never have come to this place,' he thought. 'Nothing I have got out of it.'

And yet that was not wholly true. His feelings for Jenny were hard to define. It was not in him to love where he was not loved; yet because he could have loved her he could not now feel indifference. His whole being softened at thought of her: her helplessness, her childish pride and defiance; the

swift response of her body; the promise of beauty awaiting
fulfilment; the arrogance and the humility. . . . Jenny, the
helpless creature, the sweet, silly, frightened creature. . . .

To Tod himself the thing became more and more fantastic
as day succeeded day.

What was he doing, he thought with exasperation, driving
along these frightful, endless Welsh roads between the menacing mountains; up and down the grey streets of town after
grey town where rain fell endlessly and the only light seemed
to come from wet, shining roofs and cloud-reflecting puddles?
What was he doing, plodding up and down grimy alleyways
and back streets dominated by the harsh shapes of towering
slag-heaps; knocking on doors that refused to open, on doors
that opened furtively, on doors that opened wide enough to
revolt him by what they revealed? Slatternly woman after
slatternly woman he talked to, pleaded with, his foot wedged
into the malodorous doorways. He drank unwanted pints with
shifty-eyed men. His money chinked into filthy, avaricious
palms. Singsong voices directed him here, sent him back
there, referred him to this person and that. He interviewed
disapproving parsons, shopkeepers who sniggered knowingly
and noncommittal officials. He bribed his way into the en-
campments of tinkers and gypsies only to encounter blank
stares and evasive replies.

It was like a nightmare. Like the needle in the haystack.
Worse; for if he succeeded in finding the needle, however he
used it, it must surely prick him to the heart. . . .

At last, defeated and sick of the whole thing, he turned for
home; longing for the wide, wind-swept spaces of the moor;
for flat, familiar voices and the feel and smell of home. He
wanted to be rid of these encompassing hills, webbed about
with the dolours of February and loud with the sound of
running water.

Water, water everywhere. It dripped desolately from leaf-
less branches. It rushed down between the grey, outcropping
rocks of the hillsides, sheeting the hollows of the execrable

roads. It gabbled along gutters and rattled against his wind-screen as if the whole world wept for him and his follies.

It was the merest chance that took him back to his starting point, the village in which his convalescence had been passed.

He had intended taking a more direct route, but for some time he had been conscious that all was not well with the car. Tod was no mechanic. He knew that when his engine developed a knocking sound his only course was to get to a garage in the least possible time.

The village was only a mile, if he turned right at the next crossroads, and there was a garage there.

He didn't want to go back. He never wanted to see the place again. But common sense prevailed. He knew he might go miles along this road without finding help.

He turned right at the cross roads, and a few minutes later thankfully abandoned the vehicle to a sour little Welshman with a cast in one eye and a pessimistic outlook on life in general.

"How soon will you be able to fix her?" Tod asked. "I want to push on."

"Not tonight. Closing time it is." The man wiped his hands on a waste rag and spat nonchalantly.

"Couldn't you stretch a point? There's not much amiss with her, is there?"

"How do I know when I haven't looked?"

"Well, hadn't you better look?" Tod said irritably. "It's rather important for me to get home."

"Important for me to get home, too. Choir practice it is tonight, and only the one pair of hands I have."

"Well. . . . Do you know of anywhere I could stay the night?"

"No, I don't," the man sang exultantly. "Mrs. Jones the Bread has a room, but it's let just now."

Tod took his suitcase from the boot and began to plod along the rutted lane in the sad twilight. The rain poured down. He was weary and stiff with sitting behind the wheel and his leg was giving him a good deal of pain. Nevertheless hope had risen at that name.

Mrs. Jones the Bread. . . . It was just on the cards she might remember him, and if she remembered him she would not turn him away on a night like this: of that he felt assured. He had been something of a favourite—if such a grim little body could be said to have favourites.

She had been very decent to all the boys from the Convalescent Camp. In the little parlour behind the shop there had always been a fire, hot tea out of a pot, real butter on homemade scones. She had not tried to mother them, and for that they had been grateful. She had not wanted to discuss their war experiences, their wounds and subsequent operations. She had fed them, warmed them and left them blessedly alone—and there had been no embarrassing nonsense about not wanting payment from our brave lads. She had charged one shilling a head for her teas, whether you ate one scone or made a beast of yourself with the whole plateful. You left the shilling beside your plate.

Once, old Skinner had made the mistake of leaving some coppers as well. They had been returned to him on his next visit. "Not a waitress I am," she had said with an expressionless face. After that, a collecting box for a Missionary Society had always stood on the table. It had filled rapidly, been emptied, filled again a dozen times. Old Skinner had cracked one of his heavy gags about it. "Those heathen of yours have got all the red flannel petticoats they can use, Mrs. Jones. We're starting on the step-ins now." Not a smile had touched her thin lips. "No blasphemy, please, Captain Skinner," was all she said. Poor old Skinner, he couldn't put a foot right with her. . . .

But she had liked Tod. He had sensed it. She hadn't approved of him, but she had liked him.

There was a light in the shop. There she stood behind the counter, weighing something in a blue bag for a small boy. She looked exactly as she had always looked: neat, colourless, dry. The flat, yellow cheeks, the broad pink parting were high-lighted in the gas-flare.

As the shop bell sounded she glanced up. For an instant her hands halted, were suspended in midair. She blinked twice and said, "Well!" and a smile briefly touched her lips. She went on serving her small customer, gave change, waited until the door banged noisily behind him. Then she said, "Well!" again and led him through to the firelit parlour; and there were tea and buttered scones, just like the old days.

Somehow Tod found himself telling her the whole story; and a shabby sort of business it sounded in that quiet little room under the quiet, unemotional gaze of Mrs. Jones the Bread.

"A pity it is you did not come to me at the start," she said when he had finished. "I could have told you."

"You?" He floundered, ashamed. "You knew about Angharad—and me?"

Her face was closed, expressionless.

"Everybody knew her. A bad lot she was, and came from a bad stock."

"And you—you're quite certain about the time?"

"Quite. You can ask Miss Evans the District Nurse. She was with her when the child was born."

"But she had gone away from here," Tod persisted. "I've been following her trail for ten days. One of the chaps at the farm along the road told me he thought she went to Cardiff. At Cardiff I found an old hag who sent me chasing on to Llandudno, and from there I was sent to Newport. I've covered pretty well the whole of Wales in these ten days!"

"Yes, she went away. But she came back, just for a time, and the child was born here. Miss Evans the Nurse, she can tell you. November it was. You can ask her."

Tod fumbled with his cigarette case, irritated to discover that his hands were shaking.

"Well. . . . that seems to be that." He stood up to go. "Is the Missionary box still operating?" He managed a stiff smile.

She took the box from the mantelpiece and he pushed a note through the slot.

"The bedroom is let," said Mrs. Jones the Bread. "I will make you a bed on the floor here, just for the night."

"I should be grateful for that, anyhow."

"Only for that?" Her hands folded themselves at her waist and her eyebrows lifted ironically. "Anybody would think you were sorry the child was not yours."

Was he sorry? Moving restlessly on his improvised bed he pondered the affair. The dying fire collapsed with a small crash and a last flame shot up, illuminating the ceiling, the mantelpiece with the Missionary box, the end of the wooden settle with its velvet cushion. His leg ached abominably. He felt tired and dispirited and sleep was impossible. Sleep had never been further from him. . . .

Jenny would marry Gethin now. She would have Clem and so, he supposed, she would be happy.

So that was that. . . .

He would go back tomorrow. Go home to Shaws and start again: make a real start this time. Sanderson should have no complaints.

He would marry Susan Scales. He would sit on the Bench, be a Councillor, a churchwarden. . . . It was all mapped out for him.

He thought of Jenny; the darkness of her straight, fine hair. ("*I plaited my hair for you.*") The thinness of her childish shoulders under the red dress. The lost look in her eyes. He saw her striding across the moor, gawky and coltish in her green slacks and George's old raincoat, a scarf flapping in the wind. . . . He thought of her life as she had briefly related it: the aunt who had done her duty; the impersonal kindness of the Convent Sisters; the solitary, dreamlike quality of her life in the Soho shop; the seven years of living with George Rowland, and all that must have meant. And now this child. . . .

'No wonder she doesn't know what she wants from life,' he thought. 'She doesn't know what life has to give. She knows nothing—nothing at all.'

His leg gave a wicked twinge and he shifted it gingerly, remembering suddenly how it had ached that evening they had sat together in the living room of Lost Hill, eating Mrs. Bailey's Christmas cake—the evening she had told him of her intention to marry Gethin. He remembered how he had wanted to pull her into his arms and say: 'Marry me. I'll give you children of your own. I'll teach you to love living for its own sake.'

Why hadn't he done that? What a fool! . . . Sitting there within touching distance of her; lighting his damn-fool cigarettes and trying to pretend that nothing mattered but Shaws. . . . Daft, pretentious, story-book stuff. . . .

Well, it was too late now. He had no claim on the child, and the child had been his only hope. She would go her own way, and he could not help her.

By a desperate effort he banished the thin, troubled face from his thoughts and dragged towards him the face of Susan, with its laughing mouth, pearls in the pink-tipped ears, wave of burnished hair above a bland forehead. . . .

But the mouth laughed too often, too widely, the pearls were too big, the wave too obviously manufactured.

Susan's face worried him. It would not keep still. The mouth twisted itself into hideous grimaces, the teeth snapped like an animal's and widened into indecorous mirth with outthrust tongue. He had no control over it at all. . . .

Sleep fell upon him suddenly and without warning and brought him little refreshment. So that, when the boots of Mrs. Jones's lodger woke him in the grey dawn, he was unaware of having slept.

CHAPTER THIRTEEN

IRIS stood at the scullery sink washing up the dinner dishes. She stood squarely above the steaming bowl, feet planted wide apart, sleeves rolled high up fat, freckled arms, their whiteness ending abruptly at sodden, scarlet wrists. She sniffed methodically, and each time she sniffed she pushed a straggle of ginger hair from her eyes with greasy fingers.

The house was very quiet. The two cats slept on the kitchen rug, paws folded decorously beneath them. The canary drowsed on his perch, feathers fluffed out. Apart from them the only living creatures in the house were herself and old Jos—and for all she knew *he* might be lying dead there in his room along the passage.

The house was quiet as the grave, she thought; and a prickle of superstitious fear ran up the backs of her arms and exploded lightly in her skull.

She dried the plates and stacked them in their places; rattled the silver into its baize-lined basket; slopped the greasy dishcloth over the draining board. She went into the kitchen and stood for a moment listening to the silence; feeling it close round her like a hand squeezing, until her breath began to come faster and her scalp tingled.

It was not often the house was as quiet as this.

One of Mrs. Bailey's few remaining teeth had been paining her for days. Her cheek had swelled up and sleep had forsaken her. There had been nothing for it but a visit to the dentist and Gethin had driven her down to Huffley as soon as dinner was over.

At the last moment Jenny had decided to go with them. Clem needed new shoes, she said.

It was only an excuse, Iris thought, shooting out her thick red lips and making an ugly noise. Just an excuse to be with Gethin. Lord knew what they'd be up to when they'd got rid of the old girl. . . .

Still, it was what she had wanted: a long afternoon to herself in which to search for the money.

For days she had been prying and probing. In any odd moment when she had been alone in a room she had gone poking behind furniture that had not been moved for months, pulling out dust-encrusted books, thrusting her fingers into vases, between the starched folds of linen yellowing with age and behind the heavy frames of pictures. Her arms had explored chimneys seldom if ever used. She had lain grunting on her stomach to peer under massive sideboards and cabinets and had climbed precariously to the tops of wardrobes.

She had found nothing. Nothing but dust, soot, balls of fluff caked with damp, such as would have made Owd Missus turn in her grave.

More and more the certainty grew in her that the brass was somewhere in the old girl's bedroom.

Since Bailey's illness she had been forced to share the bedroom. Lying there in the stuffy darkness, listening to the old woman munching at her biscuits, the girl had grinned contemptuously. The owd buzzard had been frightened she'd go down to Jos' room! As if anyone in their right minds would bother with a yellow, doddering owd fool like Jos when a chap like Gethin was around!

But though she had shared the room by night there had been small excuse to enter it during the daytime. The old woman swept and dusted it and made the bed herself. Iris' possessions were still in her own room. If she went upstairs she was always conscious of Mrs. Bailey listening at the kitchen door to find out which room she went into. . . .

But now, today, the room was hers to enter, to search from floor to ceiling. The brass must be in the room somewhere:

there was nowhere else it *could* be. If it wasn't in that room, then there wasn't any brass at all, that she would swear. And if there was no brass, then there would be no Gethin, either....

She stood in the silent kitchen, rubbing her elbows in the palms of her hands, blinking at the thoughts going round and round in her head.

It was born in her suddenly that this was the last day she would spend at Lost Hill.

If she found the brass she would take it and go quickly. Not home, for they would come and get her there: no, she was too clever to go home. Yet not too far away, for she must not lose touch with Gethin.... Maybe she could leave a note in his tent and hide up somewhere until he could join her, and they would go away together in the cart....

And if there was no brass, then there was no point in stopping, anyroad; for Gethin would either marry *Her,* or he would go away, leaving Iris in this god-forsaken dump—and either way the thought was intolerable. There would not even be old Jos to lark about with, for Jos was finished; as good as dead.

The whole house was dead and she hated being alone in it. She had waited for this chance, and now the chance had come she hated it and was afraid.

A clock chimed and she started, glancing over her shoulder; but she left the fire and pushed reluctant feet along the passage to the foot of the stairs.

Lying in his bed Bailey heard the feet go by, and he was frightened, too. He was all alone in the house with Iris: they had all gone away and left him alone with her....

He felt again the impact of her young, rough hand across his cheek; saw again the greed in the small eyes; heard again that contemptuous noise from those wide red lips in which he had once delighted.

He cowered beneath the bedclothes, listening. Her footsteps went past his bedroom door, along the passage to the foot of the stairs; began heavily to climb.

What was she up to?

He raised himself on one elbow, his head strained forward so that the cords of his neck stood out, rigid and mountainous.

Where was she going up those stairs? To her own room, or to his and Em's?

He counted the clumps of her heavy feet. Seventeen, eighteen. . . . So now she was up the first lot. The clumps became muffled thuds: there was carpet on that landing. And then, fainter but still distinct, the clumps started on the linoleumed treads of the stairs up to the attics.

Her own room, or his and Em's—which? He swallowed dryly, straining to listen, failing to hear.

He lay down again, weak with the effort and the fear.

He knew. He did not need to find out what she was up to: he knew. She was after the brass. The house was empty. They'd all gone out and left her alone, to do as she'd a mind. . . .

At first he had thought yon tinker chap had pinched it, but he had changed his mind about that. It was Em, of course. She'd never have left it in the biscuit tin—not while Iris slept in her room. Em had hidden the brass somewhere else; and now Iris was going to find it, and there was nothing he could do about it: nothing at all. . . .

It wasn't for himself that he minded. He had wanted the brass for Iris; now he no longer wanted Iris the brass meant nothing to him. He was finished and he knew it. He might go on living a long time, but he was finished. Money could buy him nothing he could possibly desire beyond a packet of tobacco, a newspaper, a few odds and ends of creature comforts, and for these there would be plenty and to spare. Owd Missus had seen to that. Even Mester George had remembered to leave them a bit. There'd be enough to pay for a couple of rooms down in Huffley and a few sticks of furniture. And Em would look after him.

He saw himself sitting at a window above a busy street, watching life ebb and flow like a river below him. He would sit there like a lord with his pipe and his paper, and there would be such a lot to see. Women shopping and gossiping;

girls tripping past with their bright clothes and bright glances
and their long, neat legs; children whipping tops along the
pavement and dogs fighting; folks he knew and strangers he
would come to recognise; horses spanking by and cars of
all kinds dodging and hooting. There would be hawkers pushing barrows and policemen moving them on; weddings and
funerals; accidents, with whistles blowing and white ambu-
lances tearing along the street; fights on the corner of the
square on market days; spicy bits of scandal perceived by
him, all unknown to the participants. . . .

Em would bring him his dinner and he would tell her all
he had seen, and happen they'd have a bit of a laugh together.
And then she would go about her work while he continued
to sit comfortably by the window, watching, and waiting for
his tea.

On winter afternoons he would watch the street lights come
popping out of the dusk and shopkeepers putting up their
shutters. On summer evenings he would see chaps and their
girls drifting by embraced, bound for the solitudes beyond
Hawks Hill. If it was warm, happen he'd open the window a
crack and whistle to the girls; watch their swift upward
glances and their escorts' scowls. A thin cackle rose to his
lips at the thought. . . .

But a sudden crash from upstairs sent him whimpering and
cowering under the bedclothes again.

What was she up to!

He wished she would find the brass and go: go right away,
where he'd never set eyes on her again. . . . He hated her:
the sound of her clumsy feet about the house; her great laugh
shouting across the yard; the amorous snatches of songs she
sang as she passed door or window of his room. They were
meant to mock his infirmity, and he knew it.

She played cruel, pointless jokes on him, pouring salt over
his pudding, adding vinegar to his hot milk so that it curdled.
Em always carried his trays in and she never noticed anything
wrong because her eyes weren't what they used to be; and
he was afraid to complain. . . . Her rough young hand had

struck him in the face, and she had laughed and made that noise with her lips.

He was afraid of her. If she didn't find the brass she might come down into his room in a great rage. She might hit him again. She might pull the clothes off him, open the window and let in the damp February wind and leave him to die. She might heat the poker red-hot and do him a mischief, or set the house afire. There was no telling what she might get up to in a rage....

He was frightened. Daylight was fading and there was no candle in his room, and the house was silent as the grave. They'd all gone out and left him alone with her—that was a fine way to treat a poor old man, helpless and bedridden....

He began quietly and painfully to cry.

He was afraid. He wanted Em....

Her sleeve caught the vase and it crashed to the floor, startling a small shriek out of her.

Instinctively she stood still, poised for flight.

Then she remembered. There was nobody but herself in the house—except old Jos, and he didn't count any more.

She pushed at the broken pieces with her foot. How wild the owd buzzard would be! It didn't matter, though. Any minute now she'd find the brass, and then you wouldn't see her for dust. It must be in this room somewhere—it *must!*

The room was in wild disorder. Bedclothes lay on the floor, pillows and mattress were ripped and a drift of dust and feathers lay over everything. The contents of drawers were spilled over the floor and bed and chairs and a trunk and several cases were pulled from beneath the bed.

But the crash had unnerved her.

She stared around uneasily. There was only one shelf left to search. One shelf with a pile of cardboard boxes on it. It wouldn't take long. But she was scared to stay in the darkening room.

The house was silent as the grave. Yet just below the surface of the silence stirred sound and movement, an uncanny sense of being watched. The scurry of a mouse; the creak of an unoccupied chair; the tapping of ivy-fingers against the pane. You trod on a board and something rapped in the skirting. You opened a cupboard door and a picture tittered against a wall. You moved a trunk and a slither of soot said *hush!* behind the paper fan in the grate. . . .

She was scared. Yet only one shelf remained unexplored: one shelf with cardboard boxes piled on it.

The brass must be in one of those boxes—it *must!*

She climbed on a chair and lifted the boxes down and stood for a moment, undecided. Then she carried the boxes carefully along the passage and down the two flights of stairs. The treads cracked like gunshots behind her and her breath came quick and shallow.

It was dark in the kitchen, too, for daylight was overcast by rain clouds. She poked the fire to a great blaze, and the two cats rose with arched backs, yawning pinkly, turned round several times and lay down again with small, comfortable cries. The canary cheeped softly. A flurry of rain beat against the window and a clock chimed a warning.

They'd be back soon. She must be gone before they got back. She must find the brass and be gone. . . .

Three shoe boxes, a chocolate box with violets on the lid, and two flat boxes of brown cardboard. They were all tied up with string.

She stared at the boxes and her mouth went dry, her legs trembled weakly. For suddenly she doubted that the money was here. Mrs. Bailey would never leave the money lying in the house while she was out. Never! She would take it with her. It would be in that old black handbag she had gripped on her knees, or in a pocket of her voluminous black skirts, or tied round her neck. She must have been daft to think Mrs. Bailey would leave it in the house. . . .

So all her trouble had been for nothing. She had burned her boats behind her—and all for nothing!

She could not stay at Lost Hill now, with all that mess and

destruction upstairs. She would have to go, and soon. She would have to go out into the dark rain and walk all the way across the moor to Huffley—and what her mother would do to her she did not care to guess. She would have to go without her week's wages, without her trunk or any of her clothes beyond the few necessities she had already packed in a small case. Her mother would half kill her. . . .

She began to blubber softly. She did not want to leave Lost Hill where it was warm and safe, where there was all the food she could eat. She did not want to leave Gethin.

Yet her fingers fumbled at the knots: she might as well look in the boxes now she'd got them down, just in case. She was certain the brass wasn't there, but she might as well look. . . .

The shoe boxes contained old letters and pictures post-cards, laces, scraps of dress materials and yards of narrow ribbon wound on a bobbin. In the chocolate box a few cheap trinkets lay on a bed of cottonwool. One of the brown, flat boxes was empty save for the faded photograph of a young man in the garb of forty years ago. A well set-up young fellow with a bold eye, and a flower in his buttonhole: a young Jos; a vital, devastating Jos that at another time would have moved Iris to mirth or admiration. But she did not recognise it. It was just the picture of a chap. She flicked the photograph aside and began picking and tearing at the knots of the last box, the last hope.

One by one she picked and tore the knots apart. The clock ticked loudly in the silence and her heart thumped as loudly as the clock. A sudden trickle of water spurted from the tap over the sink, and it was like a needle pricking her spine.

The last knot was undone and she lifted the lid. Fold after fold of blue tissue rustled loudly when she touched it, and the canary gave a few long-drawn chirps and shook himself on his perch.

Below the tissue paper white linen lay neatly folded. Iris saw tucks and lace and featherstitching, a ruching of satin ribbon, a row of tiny pearl buttons. A strong smell of orris root rose from the box; a smell that pricked flesh and memory into sudden, superstitious recoil.

The burying clothes. . . . The long white robe that hung on the washing line, its full folds bellying out in the wind so that it looked as if already a body filled it and hung there, swinging. . . . The lace-frilled cap with the broad satin ribbons to tie under the falling chin, the gaping mouth. . . .

The beastly burying clothes. . . .

Her probing fingers recoiled, stiffened like starfish above the box. Her feet stepped backwards and a cat squawked and fled across the room. Fear and disgust and disappointment seethed and rose in her and a cry whimpered from her thick red lips.

The old beast! The old horror! . . .

Seizing the box, she thrust it into the glowing heart of the stove, pushing and battering at it with the great iron poker until the edges blackened and singed and curled, and finally the whole mass burst into flames and the draught roared it into white-hot ashes.

Something tinkled through the bars into the ash pan: something that gleamed golden in the leaping light. But Iris neither saw nor heard. She was concerned only with finding her hat and coat and suitcase, with getting away from Lost Hill before the trap came back from Huffley. . . .

Presently the flames died down and the kitchen seemed darker than ever. The canary tucked his head under his wing. The cat came back to his place on the hearthrug and began to wash, and the rain chuckled sardonically along the gutters.

And old Bailey in his bare little room cowered beneath the bedclothes, wondering why her feet had pounded along the passage, why she had been blubbering, and why the house was suddenly so silent again. Wondering what she was up to now. . . .

✳✳✳✳✳✳✳✳✳✳✳✳✳✳✳✳✳✳✳✳✳✳✳✳✳

CHAPTER FOURTEEN

THE doctor stood in the doorway, slapping his gloves in the palm of his hand.

"How is she?" Jenny asked, glancing up from the soup she was stirring on the stove.

"Fairish." He came and stood by the fire. "I can't make her out. There's something I don't understand about this business. You say nothing was stolen?"

"As far as I know she didn't take a thing."

"Queer. . . ." His lips shot out.

"Of course the room is in a terrible mess."

"Aye, I've seen it."

"I haven't had time to clean up yet," she said defensively. "To tell you the truth, I don't know where to begin. All those feathers. . . ."

"Yon chap's seeing to it." The doctor began to stuff his pipe with tobacco, not looking at Jenny. He was in a hurry—but then, he was always in a hurry: he wasn't going without saying his say. "He's going to wrap it all up in a sheet and make a bonfire of it up in the field. It's all anyone can do."

"Gethin has been so good. I don't know what I should have done without him last night, when we got home. It was awful! All her things scattered over the floor and the bedding ripped to bits. . . . And Iris had evidently been burning something in the stove."

"What was it she burned?"

"I don't know. Mrs. Bailey won't talk about it. . . . She picked up a cardboard box lid that was lying on the rug and just stood holding it in her hands, staring first at the lid and then at the fire. Then she went upstairs. When she came down she went straight into Bailey's room and shut the door. After a while I took them some tea. Gethin had lit a fire and carried an easy chair in, and she was just sitting there by the bedside, staring into the fire. . . . I made up a bed for her in another room, but she wouldn't hear of it. Nothing would budge her. As far as I know she sat there all night. Gethin said we must leave her alone. He slept here in the kitchen, just to be near them. He has been so good. . . ."

"H'mmm." The doctor blew experimentally down the stem of his pipe. It spluttered and he poked at it with a wire.

"When I got up this morning he had all the fires going and the breakfast nearly ready. He's really marvelous—you've no idea!"

She was nervous, talking for the sake of talking, to stop him from saying that which he had to say. He knew it with pity, though he longed to shake her, shock her into acceptance of reality.

"She'll have to give up, that's what it comes to. This place is too much for her. Bailey will never work again, and now yon girl's taken herself off. . . . A couple of rooms down in Huffley, that's what they want. Somewhere on the main road where the old chap can look out of the window and the old girl can gossip in the fish queue. They can afford to rest —Old Missus provided for them I know. That little body at the baker's nearly opposite the Royal — she lost her husband recently and I wouldn't mind betting she'd take 'em if I put in a word."

"Yes, I wish you would do that."

She lifted a spoonful of the liquid and stared at it anxiously, trying to think of something else to say; but there seemed nothing.

The child ran in from the yard, laughing and important.

"Look what I got, Denny! Look!" He held two brown eggs in his grimy fingers. His blue jeans were streaked with filth, his hair stood on end.

When he saw the doctor he stood very still. Jenny could see the slight movement in his throat as he swallowed; and she was reminded of the lizard up by the Tarn that had stood watching her, struck into immobility by some chance movement of hers. Its throat had gone in and out, in and out; and suddenly it had vanished.

"Come and speak to the doctor," she said.

There was a small, light crash and an egg lay disrupted on the floor. A flicker of blue, and the boy was gone.

Mopping at the yellow slime: "He doesn't like strangers," she apologised.

He poked at his pipe, blew splutteringly. She rinsed out the cloth and went back to her soup.

"And what are you going to do then?" he continued presently, as if the small interruption had never occurred.

"Then? . . ."

He regarded her patiently, filling the pipe with the smooth, assured movements of habit.

"When the old folks leave. You can't stop in this great barn all alone."

"No. No, I suppose not."

"It wouldn't be right or fitting."

"I might get another housekeeper, another maid."

"Not so easy, these days. Times have changed. They don't make 'em like the Baileys any more."

"I shall think of something."

"Then you'd better think fast. If I can fix things up, they'll be out of here within the week."

"A week!" she repeated helplessly, standing with the spoon stuck out before her, frowning at the menacing, crowding hours.

"A lot can happen in a week. You can be dead and buried in a week. You can be t'other side of the world. . . . Or your life can be smashed to smithereens, beyond repair."

Jenny put the spoon back in the soup and turned slightly, so that her back was towards him.

Her hair, he thought, looked greatly improved by those big shining plaits; but the doctor in him deplored the sharpness of shoulder blades ridging the yellow jumper. She stooped, too, like an overgrown child. . . . He wished she would turn on him, tell him to mind his own business and go to the devil. If only she had the spirit for that, he'd take her at her word and be off on his rounds. Lord knew he'd got enough to do with people's bodies without poking his nose into their private affairs as well. But how could he just stand by and watch her hurl herself on the rocks a second time? . . .

"A week from now," he said, watching smoke circle greyly in the rafters, "I shall hope to get a postcard from Paris. 'Having a lovely time!'—eh?" His laugh was over hearty, false, and provoked no answering smile.

"One can't walk out of a place like this—leave everything—just in an hour or two."

"One can. Take a suitcase and what you stand up in. Buy yourself some pretty clothes in Paris—you could do with some, Lord knows!" he added with brutal emphasis.

She smoothed her creased and faded slacks.

"I've never thought much about clothes—not in relation to myself."

"Never too late to begin."

She turned her head, sent him an oblique glance, childlike, questioning.

And then that fellow had to begin whistling out in the yard. . . .

"You'll be a fool if you don't go to Paris," he said loudly.

"Why Paris especially?"

"Well—Timbuktu if you like! The further the better."

"What about Posy and the goats and chickens?"

"You've got neighbours," he reminded her.

"Tod's gone away," she said soberly.

So it was "Tod" was it? Well, that was something. And why the devil must he be away at just this time, confound him?

"Almost anyone would take them on, me dear, you know that well enough. You're just making difficulties."

"Am I?" Her huge dark eyes entreated him mournfully. "I don't mean to. I've got enough without making more."

"They're all your own making—every blessed one of 'em." His face reddened with exasperation. She stood stooped against the mantel, shoulders hunched, hands thrust in the pockets of her slacks, staring up at him like a spaniel that anticipates a thrashing.

"Don't be a fool, Jenny. You can't marry this fellow. Lord save us, haven't you had enough of marrying the wrong man? . . . Face up to it, lass. If you need an excuse to get rid of him, now's your chance. You're shutting the house up. You're going away indefinitely. The child's well and strong again. . . . Let them go on their way. Give the chap money if you like—though I don't advise it—and pack 'em both off. In a week you'll be thanking me."

"I want Clem," she said piteously: but underneath the words he sensed a stubbornness that defeated him, and he shook his head and went slowly out to his car. The two cats rose from the hearthrug and followed him.

Gethin was cleaning harness in the doorway of the barn. He gave the doctor a brief, flashing grin and went on with his work. The two cats ran across the yard greeting him loudly and began to weave themselves in and out of his legs. Old Posy, nodding over her stable door in a pale burst of sunlight, whinnied sleepily.

Jenny stood as he had left her, hunched against the mantel, her eyes watching the fire. The soup bubbled cosily in its pot; the good smell of it filled the kitchen.

Gethin began to whistle again. Clear as a missel thrush he whistled: some outlandish air, Welsh, perhaps, or Romany; sad and gay and magical; infinitely disturbing. She listened for a moment, then pushed herself upright and went on with the innumerable tasks that awaited her.

Clem came peeping round the door, screwing up his small clown's face to make her laugh.

"The doctor's gone," she said, and held out her arms. He sprang across the kitchen and she caught and lifted him, held him tightly, feeling the small, warm body mould itself to hers. He smelt of straw and soap and fresh, damp earth.

"Clem's a naughty boy," she told him.

"Broke an egg," he agreed brightly. "Bang! Wallop! It's a goner!"

"Not the egg. You mustn't run away from people. It's very rude."

He pulled his top lip down to an incredible length and rolled his eyes, knowing she was not angry.

"Nasty ol' man!"

"Nice old man, Clem. Kind old man. Make Clem better when he's ill."

"Denny make Clem better. Dear Denny." He stroked long, grimy fingers down her cheek and her heart melted with love. "Pitty Denny!"

"Say *Jenny*, Clem. Say *I love you, Jenny*—just like that. Like you talked to Tod that night you read about Mr. and Mrs. Rat and the baby. . . . Like you talk to Gethin sometimes."

"Yuv you, Denny." He wriggled to get down, but she held him hard against her.

"Say it again, Clem. Say it, darling."

"Yuv you, Denny." He kissed the point of her chin three times.

"Oh, darling! . . ." She put him down and he scampered out into the yard. "You should wear a coat," she called, but he would not heed. Snatching his coat from a peg, she followed him; held him, struggling and laughing, while she forced his arms into the sleeves, buttoned it high about his neck.

Gethin did not glance up from his work.

'How can I let him go!' she thought. 'What do they understand about it, any of them? . . .'

When Jenny came in with the soup Mrs. Bailey rose stiffly to her feet. Her hands clutched each other over her smooth, spotless apron. She made no movement to help as Jenny pulled up a small table, laid silver and the bowls of steaming soup on an embroidered cloth, mended the fire and swept the hearth.

"Thank'ee, Missus," she muttered, staring through the window. Swollen boughs of beech tossed in pale sunlight against a tattered blue sky.

"I hope there's enough salt in it," Jenny said, more nervous before this meek and accepting creature than she had ever been before the competent old shrew. She forced a laugh. "I'm not very good with salt. Either I put too much in or none at all."

"Thank'ee, Missus."

The old woman lifted her husband's bowl and began to feed the soup to him spoonful by careful spoonful. He had no need of being thus fed but he allowed her to do it. Her hands shook, spilling the liquid against his neck, but he only wiped it clean without a word. When the bowl was empty Mrs. Bailey started on her own soup.

The fire crackled and spluttered. The beech boughs tossed verdant buds against the sky. Gethin whistled in the yard and the child's high laughter threaded the light wind and the light, clear whistling.

Em sucked her soup slowly, noisily, without lifting her eyes. Jos lay and watched her. His coarse, strangely clean hands rested slackly on the folded sheet.

"It'll be champion down in Huffley," he said, speaking louder and more slowly than usual, as if uncertain of her hearing. "We s'll see all that's going on."

She nodded, supping away at her soup.

"There'll be women for you to have a jaw with, an' shops to look at. Happen you'll get to t'pictures a time or two." He remembered going to the pictures with Iris: how she had screamed with laughter at the funny bits, yelped over the shootings. Her hand had gripped his hand, hot and moist and young, young. . . . He rubbed the palms of his hands on the sheet. "We s'll see all t'weddings an' funerils an' processions— May Day an' Whit Monday an' all. An' if we fancy a bit o' fish an' chips to us suppers, shop's nobbut next door but one."

She nodded. Wiping round the empty bowl with a piece of bread, she placed the two bowls neatly together and lifted the table back against the wall. She sat down again, her eyes on the fire, her hands folded in her lap.

She did not want to talk. What had happened was so terrible that speech had almost forsaken her. Even her thoughts were thick and muddled and she was too shaken to sort them out.

" 'Tisn't as if we couldn't afford it," Jos persisted. "Owd Missus saw to that." He watched her narrowly but her expression was blank. She agreed with everything he said, gave away nothing. ". . . An' nobody to leave it to. So we might as well mek t'most on it, for we can't tek it wi' us. . . ."

He began to chafe at her silence. The faint ghost of his old impishness moved in him. "Ain't we goin' to get no pudden?" he asked. "I could do wi' summat sweet. What about one o' them biscuits o' yourn, Missus?"

After the slightest hesitation she left the room and returned carrying the biscuit tin. They each took an Oval Marie, mumbling the edges very slowly. Jos only ate a very little for he was not fond of biscuits, but Em ate two. He lay watching her nose and chin go up and down, up and down, and the firelight brightening the bib of her apron.

He wished most desperately that she would speak.

"Look after me, Em," he whimpered. "I ain't been all I might 'a been, happen, but that's all ovver an' done wi'. There's nobody else now, on'y you an' me."

She reached out a hand and rested it on his hand. It lay there passively, dry as a blown leaf; but it seemed to bring him comfort, and presently he fell into a light doze.

Aye, she would look after him, she thought. There was a good ten years' work in her yet.

A tear slid from under a sunken eyelid, jerked down the

furrows of her face and fell into the starched hollow of her lap. Other tears followed, but she scarcely felt them fall or knew why they fell. And presently she, too, slept.

When the van had gone, Jenny turned back into the house with a feeling almost of panic.

She had seen nothing of Gethin for a long time. As soon as breakfast was over he had disappeared, without any explanation, taking Clem with him. Dinner time was long since past and there had been no sign of them: though indeed, as she now realised, she had prepared no food, either for herself or them. There were always milk and bread, bacon, eggs and apples, she thought gratefully: nobody needed to starve in the country. She looked in the bread bin, just to make sure. Mrs. Bailey had baked less than a week ago. There were still three loaves, crusty and sweet under their white cloth. When those three loaves were finished, she would have to think again. . . .

The house was so silent. She walked in and out of the rooms, up and down the echoing staircases, feeling like a trespasser.

They had all gone. Old Missus, then George, and then Iris; and now the Baileys. The house had got rid of them all, and now there was only herself left—herself and Clem. Gethin did not count. Gethin would never belong to the house: he would never belong to anything or anybody.

She watched for them anxiously from all the upstairs windows; across the moor, over the orchard hill, along the meadows folding the back of the house; but there was no sign of man or child.

Beyond the orchard the cart's shafts tilted reassuringly against the green and the brown pony was safe in the stable: so he had not gone—he could not have gone taking Clem with him. . . .

She set herself to tidying up the house. These last days it had been sadly neglected. Ashes filled the cold grates and dust lay everywhere. Beds were unmade, the kitchen unswept, the scullery a clutter of unwashed pots and pans. The rooms were sullen, rejecting her, and she had no heart for their conquest.

She had given the Baileys all the furnishings needed for their two rooms above the baker's shop. The removal men had trampled mud into the passages, up the stairs. The house had been filled with the creaking protests of old wood long undisturbed; with laboured breathing and shouted commands strung with strange oaths, and the heavy thuds of descending feet.

Doctor Waller had sent an ambulance for Bailey and Mrs. Bailey had travelled along with him. If she had known any emotion at leaving the house where she had lived for so many years she had not shown it. She had gone steadily out clutching her black handbag in black cotton gloves, her nose well down over her chin.

"I hope you will be happy," Jenny had said; and on an impulse she had bent to kiss a leathery cheek.

"Thank'ee, Missus."

The nurse had helped her climb up, the door had slammed, and the white ambulance had gone purring away over the moor. . . .

Jenny made some tea and drank a cupful scalding hot. To eat was an impossibility until she knew what had happened to Clem.

She forced herself to wash up and sweep the kitchen floor. She put milk down for the cats, threw grain to the clamorous fowls. They ought to have a mash, she remembered. There was so much to remember, so much to cope with, so much to learn.

There was no fire in the sitting room and it struck cold as she opened the door. She stared doubtfully at the dreary pile of dead ashes.

In all her life she had never had to light a fire: even to Jenny that seemed incredible, but it was true. In her girlhood there had always been servants or electricity. Here, at Lost Hill, she had never been allowed to perform such tasks.

Shivering in the cold room, 'If Gethin stays,' she thought,

'I shall have to do it, I suppose. I shall have to learn. There will be so much to learn. . . .'

The drawing room was cold, too; cold and dark behind drawn, heavy curtains. She rattled the curtains back, and the spring sunlight pointed a pale finger across the dusty floor where the Christmas tree still stood, incongruous and pathetic. Its branches were brown and withered and a brown scatter of needles spread about the carpet. The coloured balls were dimmed by dust, the Fairy Queen hung lopsided and drunken from her topmost branch, and all the tinsel was tarnished.

Several times she had tried to dismantle the tree, but Clem had flown into a passion if she so much as touched it. She had been reluctant to deprive him of so great a treasure. Every day he had gone into the room to stare at the tree; sometimes sitting underneath it, gazing raptly up through the laden, colourful branches; sometimes pacing delicately round and round it, stepping on tiptoes and humming a wordless song to himself. Sometimes he had stood staring out of the window, turning every now and then with a sort of pounce, as if he suspected the tree of attempting to steal away from him.

She was half frightened by the intensity of his feeling for the tree. If was as if she had made him a promise she knew it was not in her power to fulfil; opened the gate into a forbidden country. . . .

She tried to dismiss the thought as morbid, flicking at the dust-dimmed coloured balls so that a faint tinkle of sound ran about the silence.

Should she dismantle the tree now, while Clem was out? . . . But there was so much to be done: the tree could wait a little longer.

She shut the door of the room behind her and went back to the kitchen.

They were sitting at the table.

Gethin was drinking beer. Bread and cheese were on the plate before him. Clem sat silently behind an untouched bowl of bread and milk. Neither of them glanced up as she entered.

"I didn't hear you come in," she stammered. "Where have you been all the morning?"

"Out," he said indifferently. He set down the empty glass and began to eat wolfishly.

She said more sharply: "You should have told me you were going. I have been worried."

"In all the time I have worked for you, never have I had a day off. Never an hour." He spoke as he ate, his mouth stuffed with food. He got up and refilled his glass.

Clem sat motionless before the bowl of bread and milk. He did not so much as raise his eyelids.

"Why don't you eat your bread and milk, Clem?" she asked. "Is it too hot?" She felt the bowl and it was cool enough. "Aren't you hungry, darling? Shall Jenny help you?" She offered a spoonful of the bread and milk, but the little boy sat with lowered eyes and thin, clenched lips. "Come on, darling: just one spoonful—to please Jenny!"

She put the spoon back in the bowl and stood up.

"What have you done to him?" she said angrily. "He is exhausted. He is past eating."

Gethin glanced across the table.

"Eat you," he said briefly.

The child obediently lifted the spoon and tried to eat, but the food choked him and he gave up the attempt.

Jenny caught him up in her arms and carried him to his bed. As soon as she laid him down he sighed deeply and shut his eyes. She kissed him gently, watched him for awhile and then went quietly out of the room.

The kitchen was empty. She went into the yard, into stables and barn, but Gethin was not there. The brown pony was not there, either.

She began to run down through the orchard to the field where his tent stood. Her heart hammered painfully, her throat was dry with a sick knowledge.

"Gethin!" she called. "Gethin!"

He was harnessing the pony to the cart. He whistled as he worked and did not look up.

"Gethin—what are you doing?" Her voice was brittle and she pressed her hand to her side.

"I am going away."

"Going away . . . *now?*"

"No need of me any longer. Time it is I went." He tightened a strap and stood up, smacked the pony's rough flank affectionately. He went into the tent and came out carrying a bundle which he stowed away in the cart.

Jenny tried to speak but her throat was constricted. She watched helplessly as he went to and fro, loading the cart with his belongings. The pony stamped and blew, as if eager for the road again.

The silence stretched between them, taut, like elastic; and presently it snapped.

"I am not taking the boy," he said. "He knows. I have told him."

The hammering stopped so suddenly that she felt almost sick. Her hands trembled. She clenched them together, pressing the nails into her flesh.

"Oh, Gethin. . . ."

There was nothing she could say. "Thank you" would be absurd, promises redundant, to offer money an unthinkable insult.

Suddenly he came to her, laid his hand along her thin cheeks, tilting her face upwards. His hands were warm, the thumbs smoothed her cheek bones with a gentle pressure.

"I could take you with me. We could go away together in the cart, all three of us, and maybe I could teach you how to live. You have never given me a proper chance, fair play."

She blinked back a shame of tears and shook her head, feeling the roughness of his palms against her face.

"You want me to go away and leave the child? . . . That will make you happy, Jenny *bach?*"

"I will be good to him. I love him so much, Gethin," she whispered.

"All this talk about love. . . ." He laughed briefly and

released her. "Love marches with life a little way—if you are lucky—but living is what matters."

He left her and went on with his loading of the cart. He began to whistle one of his odd, disturbing tunes. He seemed to have forgotten her.

"You will need food, she said uncertainly. "I will get some ready."

"And my wages," he threw over his shoulder. "Two months it is since you paid me."

"Oh, Gethin, why didn't you remind me!" She could have shouted with relief. He could think of money at such a time. . . . She had been wasting her sympathy.

She ran back to the house. She filled a box with bread and bacon and eggs, tins of soup and milk and fruit taken haphazard from the pantry shelves, bottles of beer, a jar of the pickled onions he loved, a pile of apples. She staggered out to the yard with the loaded box and placed it on the cobbles. She thrust a handful of notes into a purse and laid it on top of the box.

Blankets? Clothes? He had enough for his needs, but she laid a couple of warm rugs beside the box, a thick knitted waistcoat of George's that had somehow been overlooked. Probably he would sell them down in Huffley, but that was his affair. At the last moment she remembered soap. . . .

She went indoors and shut the door, leaning against it for support. Her legs felt weak, her body light and empty.

'Now there is only me,' she thought, 'and Clem.'

She would take him away. Tomorrow—the day after at the latest—she would take him away from here.

She would go first to Huffley, see George's solicitor. He would arrange everything, sell up the house and all that was in it: she wanted nothing from the house.

Maybe she would have to stay in Huffley a day or two. There would be things to sign, she supposed vaguely, arrangements to be made with the bank. . . . The solicitor would tell her. That's what solicitors were for. They saw to everything and you paid them for doing it. And that's what money was for.

She was suddenly glad of the money. Such a lot of it, too. Until this moment it had meant nothing to her, but now—what could she not do for Clem!

Her weakness passed and she went into the kitchen.

The fire was out but it did not matter now.

She bent to stroke the cats.

"You will have to go to Mrs. Bailey," she said aloud. "You, too," she told the vigilant canary. She covered the cage with a green cloth. He cheeped a protest at this early retirement; the cage vibrated with his displeasure.

She remembered thankfully that the goats were dry. No harm would come to them if she turned them loose for a few days. Someone would be glad of them. The fowls, too. George's solicitor would see to it all. . . .

She stared round the lifeless kitchen and drew a deep, quivering breath; feeling as a swimmer must feel when, after long battle with the current, he reaches at last the benison of shallows.

At first Jenny would not accept the bed's emptiness, the room's emptiness. Reason rejected the tossed blankets, the shadowy, untenanted cupboards and corners.

"Clem," she called softly. Then louder, more urgently: Clem!"

There was no answer, no sound at all.

Either he had awakened early or, more likely, had merely feigned sleep until she had gone from the room.

She ran along the passage calling his name; down the stairs, out into the yard, the barn, the stables and all the sheds and outhouses. He was in none of these places and there was no sign of his ever having been there.

Sunlight was gone and the yard was chill and shadowed. A raucous line of rooks swung along the sky and the beech buds shivered in sudden gusts of wind. The long-drawn *craw-*

awk of a sleepy fowl sounded from the barn and old Posy
stamped in her stable.

The Christmas tree. . . .

That was the first place she should have gone to, of course.
That's where he would be.

She went indoors, calling his name as she went.

The drawing room door was shut as she had left it. She
pushed it open slowly, almost reluctantly, afraid of what she
might find; utterly appalled by what she did find.

The Christmas tree had been stripped of light and colour.
Small, savage hands had wrenched off the bright balls of silver
and blue, scarlet and green and gold. Small, savage feet had
trampled them into a million glittering fragments. What he
could not reach he had battered down with a stick: it lay there
on the carpet, one of George's sticks. The tinsel streamers had
been torn from the branches, the Fairy Queen had fallen from
her precarious throne and lay with her wings torn off, face
downwards amongst the ruin.

The tree stood stark and bare, its withered arms stretched
in resignation above the gaudy wreckage that strewed the
carpet.

Jenny stood as if turned to stone.

This, then, was the measure of his fear and anger at Gethin's
going. The measure of his love for her. . . .

He was there, behind the tree, crouched in an angle of the
wall. His bright stare watched her through the stark branches;
wary, motionless; like a small, wild creature, trapped and
desperate.

"Clem," she pleaded. "Oh, Clem. . . ."

She took a step towards him. His glance flickered to right
and left and he saw that he was trapped. He rose from his
heels, warding her off with clenched fists.

"I hate you," he said, more clearly than she had ever heard
him speak: oh, much too clearly now!

"No, Clem, no."

"I hate you." His voice rose in a thin scream. "Bitch! Bitch!
I hate you! . . ."

The coloured glitter splintered and crunched beneath her feet. She lifted him in her arms. He kicked and fought like a wild thing, but she was too strong for him.

And suddenly all resistance went out of him: the small body slumped against her breast, limp and curiously heavy.

"Gessin!" he cried. "Oh, Gessin! . . ." The desolation in his voice was a knife turning slowly in her heart. It was more than she could bear.

'What am I doing to him?' she thought. 'Oh, God, what am I doing to him?'

He had despoiled the Christmas tree—killed the thing he loved—because she would not let him go with Gethin.

But already he had gone with Gethin—she faced the truth with a bitter courage. What she held in her arms was flesh she could command, a mind she might mould, helplessness that would, in time, turn to her for support. The essential Clem—that bright spirit—was no longer with her. . . .

If you were not free you were better dead. Gethin had said that. And he had said: "All this talk about love! It is living that matters."

She pressed her lips to the pale, tufty head.

"Live, then," she said with gentleness.

She carried him to the kitchen, washed the tears and grime from his face and wrapped him warmly. She made a bundle of the clothes she had bought for him and all his toys, and put them with the box of food in the yard.

The little boy watched her from behind the coats hung in the passage; a small, white-faced creature, bewildered and mistrustful.

She held out her hand to him. "Come along, Clem."

He hung back in the shadows, not knowing what next might be in store for him.

She took his hand and led him out into the gusty twilight. A thin sound of whistling came on the wind.

"You are going with Gethin," she said. "Go down to the orchard field and tell him you are ready. Tell him Jenny says everything is ready."

He stood for a moment, then took a cautious step forward; then another and another; pausing between each step, watching her intently with sidelong glance.

And suddenly he began to run. His arms lifted to shoulder level, as if he unfolded wings.

He ran across the cobbles and down the path that led to the orchard field, and he never once looked back: oh, not even once. . . .

Lights were springing along the streets as Tod entered the town.

He stopped in the High Street to buy tobacco and a paper, stopped again for petrol.

"How's she doing?" said the garage hand.

"Not so good. Knocks a bit."

The young man lowered his head into the engine and emitted sounds of scorn and incredulity.

"Knocks?" he said. "I should reckon she would knock, an' all! Tek a look at this, will t'a? *And* this! . . . Who's bin mucking about with 'er?"

"Some character in darkest Wales. Don't try to explain it to me, there's a good chap. We'll go into that another time. I know I'm lucky to have made it."

"Lucky! . . . You're lucky not to be laying on a slab in some 'eathen village, that's what you're lucky not to be!" said the garage man indignantly. "Look at yer tyres, look at yer tyres! An' as for yon steerin' gear—don't look at it, or 'appen you'll get the vertigo! I've seen some cars in my time," said the garage man solemnly, "but nothing to compare with this. Nor never wish to!" He wiped his hands on waste and grinned. "How long can you give me—twenty minutes?"

"Fifteen."

Tod wandered along the street and bought a bunch of violets for Miss Ellen. Sniffing the frail, chill little faces he thought: 'Spring. It's spring already.' And he looked forward with eagerness to the unfolding year and all the work that awaited him.

He had a quick, solitary drink in the Royal, and as he came out into the lighted street again Gethin drove past him in the cart.

He drove with one hand: the other rested on the child who slept, rocked by the cart's movement, curled against his thigh. Tod turned to watch them.

Whether the man saw him or not he could not tell. He was staring straight ahead between the ears of the rough brown pony and his whistling never faltered. Soon the cart branched off from the main road and the pony broke into a trot, making for the south. . . .

Tod collected his car and drove in the opposite direction. He drove thoughtfully, soberly, not daring to hope. . . .

The cart had been piled high beneath its tarpaulin cover. The child had been warmly dressed, a rug thrown over him against the evening chill. . . . He might be on some business for Jenny; yet who would take a young child on business at such an hour?

The crowded streets, the huddle of houses, the jewelled terraces of Huffam Hill. And at last out on to the open moor, with the old smells, the old sounds, the familiar sense of home reaching out to him, drawing him across the moor.

In the town, the street lights had dragged night down upon the houses, but up here on the moor there was still a little light. The sky above the Tarn was green and in a roadside pool a pale star floated.

A farm cart came trundling along the track and Tod drew in to let it pass. The driver lifted a finger in acknowledgement. "Now then," he said politely. The great fringed feet of the horse plodded past, its brown flanks gleamed like satin. 'Nothing wrong with *your* tyres, my beauty,' Tod thought. 'Or with your steering gear.' He sniffed up the good horse-smell appreciatively.

A hare started up from under his wheels. It raced before him along the track and then cut into the heather.

'I won't go in,' he thought. 'I won't see her—not until I know for certain he has gone.'

But the car seemed to turn in at the gates of its own accord. He climbed out slowly and crossed the cobbles to the open door.

She was kneeling on the hearthrug in the kitchen, battling inexpertly with a black, stubborn fire. A thin curl of smoke rose waveringly from a mass of coal and sticks, and underneath the mass a few sparks glowed faintly. She bent her head and blew on the sparks and they flickered and crackled and died down again.

One of her plaits sprang loose and slid over her shoulder. She tossed it back impatiently, and saw Tod standing in the doorway.

For a long moment they stared at each other, unspeaking. Then Jenny said: "I can't make it burn." A black smudge lay on her cheek bone, another on her chin; but Tod only saw her trembling, inexperienced mouth.

"Yes you can," he said. "It only wants patience. It's going to be a grand fire before we've done with it." He came towards her. "Come on, we'll do it together."

THE END